Party Crashers

Book One

A J Hox

1

"Eyeliner?"
"Got it"
"Lip-gloss?"
"Of course"
"Ear pieces"
"Check" Vanessa grinned as she put her earpiece in.
"Then I guess we're ready." Alana smirked as she struggled to do up the straps on her heeled sandals.
"Can we please go to the party now? We're already an hour late." Clara complained, lounging on the couch delicately, making no move to get up. Alana slid down the banisters, landing precariously and announced they would leave immediately as soon as her popcorn was ready.
Clara raised a perfectly arched brow in surprise.
"You're joking."
"Yes I'm joking mother." She rolled her eyes, grabbing her trusty leather jacket off the hook and swinging open the door.
It was a short drive to the location of the house party, and from the outside, there was nothing more to the trio than teenage girls ready to party.
Clara scanned the house from the outside, blue eyes sparkling in anticipation as she gave a dashing smile to her companions and flipped her silky chestnut hair over her shoulders.
"Well at least the location isn't too bad." she commented, referring to the large London townhouse from which music was blaring. There were several people stood outside smoking and chatting loudly, plastic cups strewn at their feet. Clara picked a drink up as she entered and widened her eyes in innocence as Vanessa raised her brows questioningly.
"How many times Clara, we are not here to party, we've got

a job to do." She said under her breath to Clara as she looked at the intoxicated, unassuming crowd. Vanessa frowned, her dark, diligent eyes looking for their target.

The instructions from their agency were simple. Their target was Anton Vergas. Small time drug dealer with big time connections. What those connections were, however, were beyond their clearance level.

"Alana, did you have to wear the jacket tonight as well? It's not exactly cold inside."

Alana looked at Clara indignantly, hugging the jacket to her defensively.

"How am I supposed to kick ass, if I don't look like I can kick ass." She retorted.

Vanessa sighed and linked arms with Clara and Alana, putting a halt to their bickering as they sauntered through the house.

Young crowds filled every corner of the expansive house, drinks in hand. The heady perfume of intoxication was thick in the air, and the music blurred conversation into deep bass tunes. The girls mingled into the atmosphere effortlessly, but stayed alert. Alana noticed the first potential target; a short, pale man with uneven stubble and a sweat stained shirt slipping a small plastic packet to a group of young girls. The next was a goth-looking man with dark, greasy hair and an assortment of golden rings on his fingers.

"Vanessa, you're the honeypot. Two dealers to your left, grey shirt with upturned collar, and nose piercing with plaid trousers." The words came through fast and clear. Neither of them were their target, but if anyone could bring them to their target, it would be his minions.

Vanessa strolled over to where her goth target was standing, her hips swaying side to side. He looked her up and down in surprise, the smell of smoke surrounding him like a cloud as he licked his lips.

"Where can a girl get a drink around here." She batted her eyelashes at him as he leered at her.

He looked around shiftily, eyes darting between Vanessa and the party, hands reaching for his pockets.

"What kind of drink you want babe?"

Vanessa spotted Alana gagging just a few yards away from them. Instead she looked at the dealer and nudged him playfully.

"Something with a kick?"

"Oh very seductive." Clara's voice piped up in her earpiece and Vanessa surpressed a smile. Like magic, Vanessa's companion got her a drink, passing it to her. She faked a sip and continued chatting to him, his eyes lustful and hungry.

"Let's dance," he said, leering at her as she giggled, eyes out of focus, leading Vanessa to the makeshift dance floor where sweaty bodies were moving drowsily to the beat. Her earpiece beeped signaling her cue. He began slowly dancing with her, holding her pressed up against him. Not enough fake drugs in the world could get the look of disgust off her face. Music blared and when he turned to face her, leering as she smiled back drunkenly.

"Can we go out for some air?" she slurred and he bared his teeth predatorily.

Once they got upstairs and found an unoccupied room, Vanessa sent the signal as she slumped on the bed. The guy grinned drunkenly and approached Vanessa until he felt himself being dragged back by the collar, a knee digging into his back. He landed on the floor and felt blinding pain as Alana's knee smashed into his nose. Alana's arm wrapped around his neck, tightening every time he struggled.

"Call the others." Clara growled menacingly.

"Screw you." he spat and was rewarded by a punch from Alana. He yelled in pain but the thudding of music and the increasingly loud drunken chatter of the party guests muffled the noise.

"Now." Clara hissed.

Alana nodded her head towards his pocket and Vanessa pulled out his phone. He took the phone reluctantly with fumbling hands and dialled quickly, his hands shaking, blood dripping onto the phone from his nose.

"Hey, I need something, come to the bedroom, second floor, third room on the left. See you there, bring the others." his voice remained calm as his nose gushed blood.

"You didn't think to hold back a little?" Clara chuckled looking at the blood around dripping around the dealer as Vanessa secured a pair of handcuffs on him. When she was done, there were two short knocks on the door and the girls stood, ready.

The door opened and the rest of the dealers appeared including grey shirt and their person of interest, Anton Vergas.

"Who are you?" Vergas grunted.

"We're your worst nightmares." Alana quipped back, smirking at her flair for the dramatics.

Catching sight of the other dealer's bloody face, they broke into a fight. The men lunged for the girls confidently and blissfully unaware. Alana swung under a sloppy punch and kneed her attacker in the groin, bringing him to the floor. She roundhouse kicked him in the head, knocking him out.

Vanessa grabbed a chair and swung at the shorter of the two, knocking him off his balance but he moved forward, lunging towards Vanessa who was easily half his size.

Alana quickly glanced over at Vanessa worriedly, but there was no time to go to her as the other man ran towards her with a switchblade in hand. She grabbed his wrist, jerking it away from her and elbowed him sharply in the side of his head. As he stumbled back, he lashed out clumsily with his knife and Alana held her hand up to shield her face, feeling the blade stab into her palm with excruciating pain. She yelled out and kicked her attacker with all the force of her rage, sending him crashing into the wall, which knocked him out cold. She swore loudly, holding her bleeding hand.

"Are you hurt?" Vanessa cried out in worry.

"No no, just a flesh wound." Alana yelled through gritted teeth.

"Your hand? I thought you were dying or something." Clara laughed, whilst watching Vergas carefully.

"Well now I have to punch with my left hand." Alana muttered back.

Aware of her best friends being in deep confrontation, Clara circled Anton, hesitating to attack. He had learned from his comrades' mistake going in unprepared. The girls were not run-of-the-mill teenagers. Clara raised her arms in front of her face in a combat stance and waited for him to make his move. He kicked out but she dodged it swiftly, moving behind him and kicking him in the small of his back. Alana came up behind him and wrestled him with a battle cry as Clara tripped him up and Vanessa quickly handcuffed his hands behind his back.

"Regroup." Vanessa said, tucking her hair behind her ears.

They stepped back and looked at the out-of-breath, handcuffed criminals.

"Stay still and you won't get hurt." Alana ordered whilst Clara and Vanessa circled them.

"Vanessa ... please get your foot off Vergas' head... we need him for questioning." She added.

"Oops, sorry." Vanessa stood up.

"Vanessa, call Beck now to collect these three assholes." Clara said while bandaging Alana's injured hand against her will, expecting that Beck would already be on his way. As their mission handler, guardian and best friend, he seemed to have a knack for knowing when the girls needed him.

"You think we've still got time to party?" Alana grinned at Clara as they glanced over at a job well done.

"Pass me that slicer thing for the pizza please." Alana mumbled eyes glued to the television. Clara passed her the pizza slicer and Alana attempted to slice her extra large pepperoni pizza. After a few laboured moments she sighed, put the slicer down and ripped her pizza apart with her hands.

"Oh God. You are such a savage." Clara sighed.

Alana gave her an innocent look as she reached for another

hand-ripped slice of pizza.

"NO!" Clara slammed the slicer in front of Alana with a loud thud.

"Alana...?" Vanessa started hesitantly.

Alana grunted, mouth full of pizza and stringy cheese dangling from her chin.

"Why are we watching Nickelodeon?" Vanessa giggled. Alana looked at her blankly.

Alana's explanation as to why they were watching Nickelodeon was interrupted by their phones ringing simultaneously. It was Beck.

"Hey Beck, what's the gossip?" Alana chirped into the phone turning the TV volume down. Beck cleared his throat.

"Girls, we need you to come into the office today, it's about your next mission."

"Right, we'll be there in 20." Clara confirmed. The girls gave each other a confused look, wondering what could be so urgent.

It was a typical English summer. The sun was shining but it was not quite warm enough to forego light jackets and an umbrella for the potential shower. As Clara had said, they were outside the Agency in exactly twenty minutes. They looked up at the unassuming, grey building that was their second home. What only a few people knew was that beneath the façade of an ordinary office block was a clandestine facility specialising in the training of secret agents. The Agency had been around for years, working side by side with its better-known siblings, MI5, MI6, and GCHQ. The Agency was a last resort when missions required special help. Special help such as three extra-ordinary teenage girls.

All three of their parents had worked as agents for the Agency. Both Alana's parents had died on a mission when she was twelve, along with Clara's mother. Clara's father was always away on important business that the girls never quite understood, nor questioned. In their line of work there were some things one never questioned. Vanessa's parents were still alive but lived in a safe house in an unknown location; she never got to see them, except for their monthly correspondence.

The girls lived under the protection of Clara's aunt, also a member of the Agency in a luxury London apartment overlooking the River Thames. The Agency decided to train the girls when they first showed potential at the age of 13, and were deemed ready for missions at the ripe age of 16; ready to be exposed to the underbelly of unofficial secrets.

Vanessa pressed in the code and scanned her fingerprint and the girls walked inside, greeted by Beck. Beck was 23, tall, well-built and well suited for the life as a secret agent. He had sharp, attentive eyes that missed nothing, but a warm, easy smile that was in place as he saw the girls. He ruffled his short black hair with a tanned, tattooed arm.

"Great job yesterday, how's your hand Alana?" he tilted his head to look at Alana.

"I'll live Becky," She grinned.

"Although Vivi and I had to practically tie her down to bandage it." Clara added. Beck laughed and ruffled Alana's hair, a habit he'd picked up ever since he shot up to be a foot taller than the girls.

He led the way upstairs and they passed the designer interior in the main office. As they walked into the briefing room the screen and lights turned on automatically and the girls sat down on the comfy red leather sofa, settling into the familiar atmosphere. Beck took his place by the projection screen.

"So, we told you that Anton Vergas had news of a huge deal going on. Well after some persuasion..." Beck smirked at this, the girls knew he was one of the best 'questioners' the agency had, mentally pressuring every captive until every detail was in his hands.

"We found out what little he knew of the operation." He handed the girls a plastic bound files each and continued talking as the girls scanned their mission briefs.

"Two of the biggest criminal organisations in California are involved in a deal; we don't know what it is yet, that's your job to find out. But one thing for sure is that the DeRico crime family have never done a deal with the Triad before so this is something we're interested in, particularly with the pressure from our friends across the pond."

The girls looked surprised at this. The Chinese Triad with an American crime syndicate?

Alana, munching some crisps, which had magically appeared in her hands, perked up." But how are three seventeen year old girls going to find out what the deal is from the other side of the world?" she said with her mouth full.

"I'm eighteen" Vanessa interjected smugly. Alana threw a crisp at her.

"How can you eat now? You just had a full pizza." Clara prodded Alana and stole a crisp.

"Clara Blake and Alana Hilford. Please behave." Beck said sternly resisting the urge to roll his eyes.

"Oh, he full-named us." Alana whispered before promptly shutting up under Beck's warning look.

"You girls are going to move to Los Angeles for three months. You leave on Wednesday; you have three months to befriend these three boys. They are the youngest of the DeRico family. They're not official members of the group but they are as close as we can get."

Beck motioned to the screen, which showed three teenage boys.

"Two of them are brothers, one eighteen and one seventeen, eighteen next month. The other one is a close family friend but he is as close to the DeRicos as anyone can get, he too is eighteen."

Mason DeRico, the youngest brother, had dark, curly hair that framed his face like a halo. The grainy photos made details and colours difficult to determine. He was pictured next to his brother, Lucas, who was tall, also dark haired, with a strong jawline and serious eyes. Zachary Rufus, on the other hand, had short blonde hair, and a playful smirk.

The first thoughts that came into the girls mind were that the boys were particularly attractive.

"Oh hell yes, I wouldn't mind getting close to them" Clara muttered under her breath.

"Wait wait, who's coming with us to California and how are we supposed to get close to them?" Alana questioned him, lying down with her head on a cushion and her black combat boots resting on Clara's bag. Beck turned the page of her mission brief and pointed at the page.

"I shall be accompanying you to California where we will stay at a house the Agency has arranged for us; you shall also go to Beaumont high school as seniors." Beck added.

The girls immediately squealed happily at the thought of California beaches and sun.

"Finish reading your mission brief and meet me at HQ for your identification papers and documents. Oh and Clara call your aunt, Jenny to tell her this news." He turned for the door before giving the three girls a grin.

"Better get packing, girls."

2

The next three days went by in a blur. The girls packed up all the clothes they bought after their extensive shopping trips.
 Clara called Beck early to help them with their luggage.
 "Goodness girls, its three months not three years." he puffed; face red from lifting Clara's suitcases.
 Clara flicked his nose affectionately.
 "You're a darling Beck; now get Alana's and Vivi's from their rooms." She hopped into Beck's car. Beck looked around in shock at Clara's five suitcases and brought his phone out of his pocket to call for another car for the remainder of the luggage.
 "Thanks Becky." Alana kissed his cheek and Vanessa ruffled his hair.
 "Weren't we supposed to meet him at the office?" Vanessa whispered once they were in the car.
 "I couldn't carry my own suitcases could I?" Clara admired her perfectly manicured hand.
 Alana looked around and quickly moved to the driver's seat. When Beck returned and saw Alana and shook his head vehemently.
 "No way Hilford. Remember what happened to the Agency Jaguar? You only just got your license, move along."
 Anna huffed in exasperation. "No, you drive like a granny, plus we've been driving since we were 11. As for the Jag; I was only trying a few stunts." She grinned and Clara leaned forward between the two.
 "Beck you know she won't shut up until you let her drive; besides, she'll get us there in half the time." She kissed the top of Alana's head and they both gave Beck their puppy dog faces. Beck looked at Vanessa for support but he sighed, admitting defeat.

The girls arrived at their private Agency flight in around half the time it would have usually taken, Beck made a point of ensuring everyone had their seat belts on. The plane journey also took considerably less time since Clara took over from the pilot, complaining he was 'too slow'. By the time the plane landed the girls were exhausted.

"How are we going to get home Beck?" Clara grumbled, annoyed by the lack of sleep.

Beck grinned; "Well the agency thought you would need a vehicle to get around so... we got you three." he said with a wink and nodded behind the girls. There, gleaming in the dying light of the sun were two cars and a motorbike. There was a bright yellow mini-cooper for Clara. All trace of annoyance disappeared from her face as she grabbed the keys from Beck without looking back and ran excitedly into the awaiting car. For Vanessa walked up to her sensible, less conspicuous, black BMW. She squealed and hugged Beck.

"Remember these are temporary so please don't hurt them" he warned.

Alana stood with her mouth open as she saw her brand new midnight black Ducati motorbike.

"THANK YOU BECKY" she ran off and revved up the bike. Shortly after, she zoomed off.

"Wait! You forgot your helmet!" Vanessa called after her.

"Ooh it's a race she wants." Grinned Clara as she checked her reflection, put on her favourite sunglasses disregarding the fact that it was dark, speeding off after Alana. Vanessa laughed and ran her fingers through her hair, slightly stressed at their disregard for speeding laws.

"You want a ride?" Vanessa asked Beck. But he shook his head and jerked his thumb towards a Jeep parked a few spaces away.

"Got my own ride."

Vanessa and Beck arrived to the house to find the door unlocked, and a travel-fatigued Alana and Clara on the couch watching 'The Notebook'. Beck looked dazed as he looked between the door and the girls. "Th-this door had the best security system, how did you get in?"

Alana smirked as Clara swallowed her popcorn. "Lucky I got here in time or our little one here would've kicked down the door to get the best room, I just picked the lock. As for the best security system well... You need to upgrade." Clara shrugged and turned towards the television again grabbing the popcorn off Alana.

The house was spacious, with minimal décor and the standard belongings any family would have lying around to support their cover story. There were four large bedrooms, an outdoor pool, and a pool table that Beck had specifically requested.

Vanessa's room was painted a delicate shade of pastel pink with paintings of flowers. It had a walk-in wardrobe ready for her extensive collection of clothes. There were fresh flowers by her four poster bed with white billowing curtains.

Alana's room was cream and gold with a huge king-sized bed which she instantly did a roly-poly on. The balcony was one she shared with Clara and she immediately rushed into the neighbouring room.

Clara's room was a deep shade of purple and her large bed was draped with rich purple silk covers. The room had a large mirror as well as several smaller ones, which made Clara's eyes light up with joy.

"Can we live here forever please?" Clara sighed happily as she directed Beck with her bags to the closet.

"Come on, Alana wants us to watch this horror movie she says is scary." Beck started for the door but Clara didn't budge.

"No, no way. The movies she chooses are scarring. Nothing scares that kid." She crossed her arms over her chest indignantly. Beck sighed dramatically.

"She told me you'd be defiant, sorry Clara ... Captain's orders."

Beck picked Clara up and threw her over his back. Without protesting Clara let herself be carried. He dropped her gently on the sofa and the four of them began to watch their nightmares on screen. Alana began drifting off peacefully despite the blood shed on the TV.

"What are we doing tomorrow?" She murmured sleepily from Vanessa's shoulder. Clara looked at Vanessa and Beck for confirmation.

"The beach." She grinned. Alana smiled softly, eyes closed, and the three girls anticipated their first day of many on the Californian beach.

"What is taking Alana so long?" Clara fiddled with her hair and re-applied her lip-gloss. She had her silky straight hair in a high ponytail and a large floppy sun hat in her hand. Her large glasses were covering half her face. She wore a violet, strapless bikini under her purple beach dress. Her nails were painted a matching purple and they were tapping the table, frustrated.

"I tried waking her about five minutes ago, but she threw her alarm clock at my head." Beck said, rubbing his head.

"I got this; I'll wake her up..." Clara started towards the stairs but paused to grab a jug of iced orange juice and headed towards Alana's room.

"Ooh this isn't going to turn out good." Vanessa muttered as Beck handed her another pancake.

"Thanks Beck." she smiled

Vanessa was wearing a pastel pink and white polka dotted bikini with a short multicolored sun-dress on top. She had the beach bag slung over her shoulder and her short, dark hair in a neat braid. Beck was leaning against the counter in Baywatch-red trunks, sunglasses resting on his head.

As Beck and Vanessa were enjoying their pancakes in peace they heard a thud and a crash shortly followed by Alana and Clara casually walking down the stairs. Alana smiled at them enthusiastically.

"She karate kicked me before I got to spill a drop." Clara explained before checking her text messages on her phone.

"Well your phone ringing kind of gave me the heads up." Alana chirped as she stole a pancake from Beck.

"You're fat enough already Becky." She said as he mocked hurt and poked his toned abs.

"Me? Looks like you're the one piling on the pounds Alana." he mocked, dodging a flip-flop flying at his head.

Alana was wearing a white halter-neck bikini with a pair of faded denim shorts. She was make-up free and her hair was in natural messy curls having just woken up.

"When did you get that?!" Beck pointed Alana's silver belly button piercing in shock.

"Hey! Do you mind? It's a communication device, we all have one dumb-ass." The girls showed him their fake piercings which now vibrated as Alana flicked it on. Vanessa headed towards the door, rallying the others to set off for the beach.

The beach was crowded which was not a particular surprise for that point in the season.

"Enjoy your time at the beach girls, you have school next week." Beck set their things down on the sand. The breeze was warm and the sun energized the three girls. The sea was crystal clear and the waves crashed on the beach gently. The three girls marched on clearly aware of all eyes on them, the locals picking up the scent of tourists.

"It's like I died and went to Abercrombie and Fitch." Vanessa gushed gazing at the attractive array of tanned surfers and beach-goers.

"Where did Clara go?" Alana looked around until she spotted Clara leaning over the beach bar flirting with the handsome blonde bartender.

"Beck ... grab her, it's sunbathing time." Vanessa told Beck ignoring Alana's groan at 'sunbathing time'. He walked over to the bar, threw Clara over his shoulder and walked back to their spot.

"What the hell, Beck he was really hot and totally into me. And why do you always have to carry me?" The look of annoyance on her face was too comical for the girls to hold back their laughter. Alana flopped down onto the sand lazily. She heard the growl of an engine and her head snapped towards the sea.

"That girl smell can a jet-ski from a mile away." Said Clara setting herself down on the sand. In the sea there were three shiny black jet-ski's racing around. The boys on them looked around their age. Clara who lay down motioned to Beck for her iced tea. She moved the obstructive Alana aside with her foot, giving her access to the sun.

"Becky says he has a surprise for us."

That got Clara's attention. The three girls heard a 'heads up' as three small items flew at them. This was followed by a small scream from Alana.

"Ahh! You rented us jet-ski's?" She ran to the pier and immediately mounted one of the red jet-skis waiting for them.

"RACE?" Alana yelled over to them.

Clara scoffed as she flipped her hair back, valuing her life too much to race and Vanessa murmured in agreement.

"Fine, I guess I'll just race with the hot guys over there-" Alana started but was cut off by Clara.

"Fine I'll come!" She grinned enthusiastically.

As soon as they started riding, the other three jet-skis had disappeared. But the girls were having too much fun to notice. They loved the breeze rustling through their hair and the sea spray on their legs. Alana and Clara immediately started racing as Vanessa and Beck circled around playfully, both keeping an eye out for any injuries the other two were in danger of. In all their excitement they did not notice three boys watching them intently from the pier.

"I haven't seen them before, have you?" One asked the other.

"No, but there's something strange about them."

"Lucas, you say that about every newcomer." Mason rolled his eyes.

"Lucas suffers from acute paranoia." Zach rolled his eyes as he watched the boys watch the girls. Lucas gave him a stern look and Zach raised his arms innocently.

"Come on, let's go play volleyball." said Mason as the three of them headed back to the beach.

The girls docked the jet-skis and Clara looked over at Alana.

"What?! You weren't wearing a life jacket?" She shook her head in exasperation.

"It was holding me back."

Clara not-so-gently pushed Alana into the sea, starting an underwater wrestling contest.

They were all in the water playing around and Beck dived under and yanked Clara's foot dragging her under. She then proceeded to do the same to Alana but before Alana could do the same to Vanessa, Beck dived under and lifted her onto his shoulders. Vanessa squealed and the girls all laughed as she was lifted out of the water. They eventually made it back to the shore, exhausted from their activities.

Alana lowered her aviator glasses over her eyes and listened to music as Vanessa flicked through her magazine pointing out cute outfits every now and then to Clara who was busy texting. Beck had gone over to the beach bar to get a drink, but he seemed to be chatting up a striking red-haired woman. 10 minutes later the girls noticed he had moved on to a petite blonde and another round of mojitos. Alana sighed and Clara scoffed.

"It seems our little Beck is a player. " She nodded her head in approval.

Suddenly a bright blue volleyball flew through the air and hit Alana's thigh. She jumped up, her eyes stormy, as the culprit approached. An teenage boy with guilty, honey-brown eyes looked at her apologetically.

"Oh no, I'm so sorry, I really didn't mean to hit that hard, I'm so sorry, I'm Fred." He gushed out with all one breath and Alana's frown disappeared. She gave him a warm smile and Clara stood up, hands on hips.

"What's going on?" She asked eyeing Fred curiously.

"Oh, I was just telling Fred here that we would love to join his volleyball game." Alana looked at her pointedly and raised an eyebrow at Fred.

"Fine with me." He smiled; a dimple appeared in his right cheek. Clara and Vanessa joined them towards the volleyball court.

There were only two other girls, including one short brunette with red highlights in her short hair who bounced over to kiss Fred fully on the lips.

"I'm Millie." She grinned shaking the girls' hands enthusiastically.

"Nice to meet you, I'm Vanessa, and these are my cousins Alana and Clara." Vanessa smiled politely.

"Oh my God. I love your accents; they are so cute! Are you British?" her eyes lit up excitedly. The words tumbling out of her mouth so quickly it took a moment to decipher. Alana nodded and smiled; this new girl had clearly gotten on her good side. Clara told her about how they had just moved here and were going to become seniors at Beaumont when the semester began.

Millie squealed with excitement.

"You're going to be in our year! Most of the people here go to Beaumont too, come play!" She beckoned towards the volleyball game.

Her attitude was infectious and soon the girls were put on a team together. Clara and Vanessa felt their belly button device vibrate and they saw that Alana had raised the signal. Alana nodded towards the other team and Vanessa raised an eyebrow when she saw the reason she had brought them there.

There on the other side of the net was none other than Mason, Lucas and Zachary ready to play volleyball. Alana smirked and Clara's eyes lit up. Vanessa looked at the other two and nodded. It was time to play.

Beck watched from the bar as the girls played volleyball. He noticed the DeRico boys and the Rufus boy and chuckled softly to himself. They sure move fast, he thought as he watched Clara slam the ball and Vanessa high fived her after she scored a point. The three boys seemed to have the fear and respect of everyone at the game Beck noticed. Beck smiled as he got his drink from the bar and scrolled through his phone. The girl next to him gave him a sultry smile and he put his phone down to turn to face her.

The hard blue ball slammed into Vanessa's face and the girls heard a thud as she fell backwards, her right eye quickly reddening. The girls instantly snapped their heads towards Vanessa's short scream, and they rushed to her side. Vanessa had her eyes squeezed shut and her hand fluttered to her forehead. Instantly a crowd gathered around the fallen Vanessa. She could hear a lot of hushed voices and whispers. When her eyes fluttered open, she found herself gazing into a pair of dark blue eyes.

"Step away from her." She heard Alana growl, but the blue eyes leaning over her did not budge. When her vision cleared, she saw the rest of the face in front of her, her mouth parted in shock. It was Mason De Rico. Long lashes framed his worried, blue eyes. His curly hair was soft and shiny, and his mouth was slightly parted in concern.

"Are you alright?" His voice was softer than she'd imagined. He was so close that Vanessa could smell his soft citrussy scent. She was aware of his warm hand on her shoulder and she made an effort to stand.

Mason took her hand and steadied her as she stood uncertainly, her ears ringing from the impact of the ball with here head. She was at a loss for words as Alana pulled her gently towards her and Clara glared at Mason.

"I'm sorry." Mason mumbled, his cheeks colouring a rosy pink under the scrutiny of Alana and Clara. Lucas and Zachary who eyed up the newcomers apprehensively quickly joined Mason. Vanessa's eyes widened slightly. They did not expect their mission to start this quickly.

"Bro, why you apologising? She was in the way," Lucas said glowering at the girls and Mason.

"Well, his damn apology wasn't even good enough; if he wasn't such a crappy player then no one would've gotten hurt." Clara hissed at Lucas. He raised an eyebrow

Zachary stepped forward, a smirk on his face.

"You don't understand, Mason here, never apologises... to anyone, well, except his mother."

Zachary had short, sun kissed blonde hair which he ran his hand through as he talked, flexing his arm. He was lightly tanned, and his sea-green eyes taunted them playfully.

"I don't give a damn, he's going to apologise properly." Alana moved closer to Zachary threateningly glowering at him. He then moved even closer mockingly. She could feel the heat radiating off him and his eyes sparkled dangerously, reminding her that he was not just an arrogant boy, but also a dangerous criminal.

"Careful girl, you wouldn't want to piss us off." He said his voice light, with warning undertones.

"More like, you don't want to get on our bad side." Anna hissed; aware he was standing very close to her. He smelled of the sea, cool and refreshing. She took a step back.

"Your accent's cute." He drawled and Alana's anger swelled. One warning look from Clara made her turn around and walk away from the argument and back to Vanessa. Clara who had been sizing up Lucas stepped forward.

"No one hurts our friends and gets away with it " She said with an equally playful yet threatening tone.

Lucas whipped his head towards her, and their eyes met for a brief moment. He had dark brown hair, slightly tousled from the sea water the salty sea, and the same dark blue eyes as his brother, but his face was tougher, less angelic than Mason's.

His piercing blue eyes looked into Clara's light ones and the corner of his lips twitched.

"Well, be careful princess, you wouldn't want to chip a nail." Lucas smirked, his voice low and dangerously amused.

Clara opened her mouth to speak but turned to Alana, blue eyes wide.

"He has a point." She shrugged and Alana rolled her eyes.

Vanessa and Mason moved between them inconspicuously

trying to cool their friends down.

"Guys, can we please go now? I'm feeling much better." Vanessa said, her big brown eyes pleading. Lucas' gaze remained firmly on Clara.

The other two girls turned and left but not before giving the handsome criminals one last glare. Lucas shrugged and turned back to the game. Zachary laughed easily as the girls walked away.

"Assholes." Alana muttered under her breath.

"Stupidly attractive assholes." Clara added.

"Does punching them count as getting close to them?"

Clara put her arm around her laughing at her hot-tempered friend.

Beck ran over to them. Eyes looking between them, taking in Vanessa's puffy red eye, Alana's dark look and Clara's dazed expression.

Clara recapped the events. He laughed affectionately at the riled-up girls and pulled them in for a hug, knowing they were more irritated at the fact they had been caught unprepared for confrontation with

Vanessa then felt a pair of eyes burning holes in the back of her head and she turned to see Mason watching her carefully. She shuddered as she remembered the tingles from where his hand touched hers.

3

"Hey guys guess wha-" Vanessa was cut off by Alana's primal war cry. Both Beck and Alana were red and gasping for breath.

"Another sparring session?" She asked Clara, who was hacking an Instagram account to delete a bad photo of herself. Clara nodded and Vanessa watched as Beck lifted Alana effortlessly and they both collapsed in a heap laughing. Vanessa had momentarily forgotten the reason she came downstairs.

"Ooh guys! Millie sent me a text, she invited us this this beach bonfire party tonight."

Vanessa smiled and Clara and Alana started jumping up and down dancing.

"Calm down! It starts in an hour and a half so get ready!" Vanessa said and she heard a trample of footsteps as Alana and Clara rushed to their rooms.

The next half an hour was spent in the girls' wardrobes as they browsed through their vast collection of clothes, running between the rooms frantically shouting for eyelash curlers and perfume. Alana had chosen a white crotchet vest and casual denim shorts She wore mid-calf steel toed combat boots which Clara made her swap for brown leather cowboy boots. Her hair was light and curly, the front strands braided away from her face.

Clara was wearing a striped nautical cropped t-shirt paired with a gold necklace and white shorts and shiny gold sandals. Her long brown hair was straight and silky down her back, which she played with as she waited on the stairs for Vanessa to finish getting ready.

Vanessa twirled around in a blue summer dress, her hair in an intricate braid. She had on a pair of immaculate white sandals and her nails were painted baby pink.

"Ooh who are you dressing up for?" Teased Alana looking at Vanessa as she slid down the banister. Clara slapped her hand to stop her from rubbing her face and ruining her make-up.

"Could it be ...oh I don't know ... Mason?" Clara teased.

Vanessa blushed a deep shade of pink. Alana giggled, earning Clara's attention.

"You're one to talk Alana, you were the one forehead kissing with our dear Zach, he was close enough to smell your cooties." Clara poked her tongue out and Alana stopped laughing to ruffle Clara's hair. Clara then chased her around the house. She caught up with Alana and ruffled her hair back. "You're deceptively slow." said Clara, laughing at Alana.

"I stopped for a snack." Alana argued, mouth full of cookies.

The girls headed towards to door after an hour of preparation and half an hour of chasing, but Vanessa paused.

"Beck you're not coming?"

"Nope, got an early shift at the beach bar tomorrow." He said with a wink as he typed something into his laptop. The girls looked at each other in shock, waiting for him to elaborate.

"Yep, turns out it's the perfect place to eavesdrop, he motioned to the listening bugs on the table, ready to put in place.

"Oh, you're going to be working with Brad the hunky Bartender. Drop in a good word for me, will you?" Clara smiled dashingly.

The girls had infiltrated many parties, at clubs, houses, underground, hotels, even weddings. It was rare for them to go to a beach party back in London, let alone actually be invited, except for a mission they had in Cornwall over New Years Eve, but they had to flee pretty quickly after that. There was a blazing bonfire which people gathered around and gave the atmosphere a glow, half illuminating everyone around it. Chill summer music blared from the beach bar's speakers and Millie bounced up to the girls excitedly.

"Hey guys! Glad you could make it." She smiled as she dragged the girls over to her crowd.

Millie introduced them to everyone; Vanessa made a point to remember all the names, Clara was already exchanging numbers and Alana was too distracted by the hot dog stand to register the names. A classmate tapped Millie on the shoulder excitedly.

"The brothers have arrived; who do you think they're going to pick a fight with this time?"

Clara, Alana and Vanessa and the majority of girls whipped their heads towards Mason, Zachary and Lucas striding towards the party, greeting people on the way in. The three were so close that everyone referred to them as 'the brothers'. Mason was wearing dark jeans and a blue t-shirt shirt that brought out his eyes. He smiled a crooked smile as he whispered something too his brothers. Lucas wore a plain black T-shirt that clung to his muscles and dark jeans. Zachary wore a plain white t-shirt, and a leather jacket was slung over his shoulder as he ran his fingers through his hair laughing at what probably was his own joke.

They made eye contact with Alana, Clara and Vanessa but their attention soon diverted to a short, dark haired girl pushing past them. She sauntered over to Lucas and he put his arm around her waist as she kissed him. Another girl joined them, a petite blonde with long straight hair, who immediately started making out with Zachary. Mason looked around awkwardly and the girls could hear Vanessa breathe out a sigh of relief. She laughed at the girls' expressions.

"I thought you two didn't care?" She teased. Alana's face was blank and emotionless. She was in mission mode. Clara gave a short cynical laugh.

"Oh, I just remembered, I was supposed to meet Brad the hunky bartender around here."

She sauntered off in the direction of the hunky bartender they saw her flirting with the first day on the beach.

"Rule # 1 in Clara's Guide to land any boy: Boys want what other boys want." Alana stated watching Clara with a hint of admiration. Clara joined them again whilst Brad was getting them drinks.

The brothers walked past them, a mixture of curious and interested looks moving between them. Their female companions quickly noticed this exchange and they hung back only to barge into Alana and made her spill her drink on her shirt.

"Watch where you're going fat ass." said the blonde. Vanessa's mouth dropped open in shock. Being up close to the blonde, Alana could see her roots were a mousy brown and her long hair was extensions.

"You got a problem?" Alana said in a very dangerous low voice. Her eyes turned to a stony dark shade of brown.

"Stay away from our guys." interjected the brunette cattily

"No one invited you to join in, wannabe." Clara shot back, having walked over to investigate the drama.

The blonde stepped forward to look Alana in the eye. "You don't want to mess with us new girl." She hissed; her strong perfume was eye-watering.

"I suggest you back off before we damage that not-so-pretty face of yours." Alana warned, her face a blank, emotionless mask.

"We don't start fights. But we sure as hell finish them." Clara added. Alana started forward to scare them and the brunette took a step back and squealed, much to Alana's amusement. The blonde opened her mouth to speak but Alana beat her to it.

"One more word blondie…" She snarled as fear washed over the girl's eyes.

"Ooh, the bitch bites." Quipped the brunette quickly before they felt the boys come up behind them. Vanessa raised her eyebrows in shock at the girl's rudeness.

"Ladies, do we have an issue?" Lucas smirked. The brunette cuddled close to him and widened her blue eyes looking innocent.

"These girls just started us for no reason." her voice had turned sweet and babyish. Zachary raised an eyebrow at them, like a primary school teacher disciplining their students.

Alana crossed her arms over her chest defiantly, A cold smirk appeared, and the satisfied grin disappeared from the girls' faces.

Lucas spoke up. "Do you know who we are?" he said, his voice dangerous.

"Do we look like we care?" Clara said smiling sweetly twirling a strand of hair around her finger.

Mason nudged Lucas giving him a 'let it go' look. Lucas gave them one last glare and they walked off with their girlfriends. The blonde turned to flip them off and Alana took a step forward as they scurried off with their boyfriends.

Vanessa burst out laughing.

"The look… on her face." She said between giggles.

Clara let out a colourful laugh and grabbed a few drinks. Whilst Alana and Clara where in conversation they realised they had lost a member of their trio.

They looked around until they spotted Mason and Vanessa by the bonfire, seemingly enjoying themselves.

"Well, she's got a head start, our guys loathe our existence." Clara laughed. Alana jumped slightly, remembering she left her phone in her bike. She began to excuse herself but noticed Clara already preoccupied with Brad the Hunky Bartender.

Mason looked at Vanessa with his big blue eyes and couldn't help but smile. They had walked away from the aftermath of the catfight and went to get a drink by the bonfire. Mason was having a surprisingly good time and found himself talking freely and laughing easily. He had not spent much time with other girls with the stigma of being a dangerous guy- they were too afraid of hanging around him. He was, however, drawn to Vanessa's intelligent, questioning dark eyes and her soft voice. Vanessa saw the perfect opportunity to befriend Mason whilst the girls dealt with the unfriendly girls. She worried though, she got lost in his warm blue eyes too many times and had to keep reminding herself about the mission, the reason she was there in the first place.

He's a criminal, she told herself sternly. His arm brushed hers as they walked together, and she felt tingles at the contact.

"So why does everyone seem to be afraid of you?" She asked Mason innocently. He stiffened slightly.
"Well, you know, unusual family, most people are scared of me and the guys, they've got it in their heads that we're ... dangerous." He chuckled nervously and ran his hand through his curly hair.
Vanessa raised an eyebrow.
"So, you're telling me you're not a bad boy?" she smirked
He grinned and moved closer to her. "Is that something you like?" he said in a low voice.
She stayed silent for a long time, watching him carefully, but finally shook her head.
"No." she whispered, which he was only able to hear as they were standing so closely. He stepped even closer, their bodies touching, fitting together like two puzzle pieces. He held her gaze, her breath catching in her throat.
"I don't think that's entirely true."

"Hey gorgeous." Brad wrapped his arms around Clara's waist. His soft brown eyes were wide with adoration as he looked at her, enchanted. She smiled softly and he leaned in to give her a tentative kiss. Clara pulled back slightly but Brad leaned in again, for a longer steamier kiss. His hands moved from her waist inching further down until he felt a strong hand drag him back by his collar.

"Could you keep it PG-13 please? I didn't come here to watch you getting it on in public." Lucas' eyes were shooting daggers at Brad. Brad stumbled forward due to one too many drinks.

"Jealous I got here first DeRico?" He slurred and Lucas' fist slammed into his face. Clara squealed as Brad's nose gushed blood. Lucas stepped close to Brad and murmured something too low for Clara to hear. Brad immediately stumbled back and walked away quickly . Clara wanted to run after him, but she knew she had to deal with the guy who put her in this mess.

Lucas walked away from the crowd of eager high school students ready for a fight. Clara followed him, her temper rising.

"HEY." she shouted at him. He ignored her and kept walking.

"HEY IM TALKING TO YOU!" she shouted again, and he stopped. He turned around with a smirk on his face.

"What the hell was that?" she said heatedly.

Lucas shrugged. Clara was visibly furious. He looked her straight in the eye, a smile on his lips.

He noticed her fiery blue eyes, like she was looking straight through him. Her porcelain skin was flawless, like a princess. He smiled at that thought. The wind was blowing her long, straight hair into his face and he tried to focus on her and not the feel of it on his skin.

"See something you like?" Clara said scornfully as his smile disappeared.

"Nope." He said, popping the 'p'.

Clara turned to leave but he grabbed her arm and pulled her back. She was so close to him she could smell his aftershave. She didn't notice him leaning in until she felt his hot breath on her cheek. But then she heard a shrill voice.

The short brunette was walking hurriedly towards them. Lucas and Clara quickly jumped apart and Clara's cheeks turned pink. The brunette shot Clara a look of disdain. Clara turned to leave, and she turned towards Vanessa's approaching figure.

"What happened?" she asked when she saw Clara's expression.

Clara muttered something like 'Tell you later' until something caught her eye. It was a boy of around seventeen; tall, dark skinned, with short black hair. He looked like an ordinary teenager, but there was something different about him. He had been there on the beach, only not with the others. He had been there watching them. Clara also seemed to recall him being on their street the day they moved in.

He was watching them. His eyes were watchful and calculating and he managed to blend in perfectly, his grey hoodie providing a cover. Almost too well. He had been watching Clara, Vanessa and Alana during the whole night, lurking in the shadows. Clara and Vanessa looked at each other and moved slowly into a crowd as they flicked their belly button piercings, sending the signal.

As Alana approached her parked motorbike, she saw the shadow of another bike next to hers and the owner leaning on it. In the dim light she could not make out who it was but as she approached, she saw the short blonde hair and the leather jacket.

He really is quite handsome; she thought to herself and immediately shook the thought out of her head. He turned towards her and smirked.

"Nice ride." he nodded to her black Ducati. Her stony expression flicked back on like a switch and she looked at him with cold, hard eyes. She opened the storage compartment of her bike but Zachary stood beside her.

"Do you mind?" She said in a cool calm voice. He shook his head and grinned.

"I'm Zachary, friends call me Zach. I didn't catch your name?"

"I didn't throw it. Zachary." She turned to face him, reminding herself that her goal was to try to get close to him, rather than continue the way she was. He looked into her golden brown eyes and caught a whiff of her perfume. He breathed in the nutty almond scent with a tang of cherry. He found himself thinking of playing with her hair and looked away when she brushed her hair back, off her shoulders.

Did she hear that? He thought, and then dismissed the thought; she could not read his thoughts, although her piercing gaze made him feel like she was examining him under a microscope. Her tanned skin glowed softly in the light of the bonfire and he felt the heat coming off her body. She stiffened as though she remembered something and broke away from the intimate space.

"I- I have to go." Alana had gotten the vibration from her piercing. The girls needed her. He look mildly surprised, but grateful for the break in tension.

She started walking away but turned back to give Zach him a surprisingly warm smile.

"It's Alana." and she walked quickly away to where the girls were waiting for her.

"What's up?" She said looking at Clara and Vanessa.

Clara smiled knowingly. "It seems we have a tail in our midst." She motioned towards the boy they'd been watching as they advanced towards him.

As the boy walked away from the crowds and the bonfire he did not notice three figures shadowing him until it was too late.

"Did you get what you came for?" Vanessa asked sweetly. He turned to see her, hands on hips, raising an eyebrow questioningly.

"Now, tell us. Who sent you?" Alana said in a menacing low voice behind him. Clara stood at his side blocking his escape route. The three agents circled him but his face remained unusually cool and collected.

"Alana Hilford, Vanessa McCloud and Clara Blake. I was looking forward to making your acquaintance." He had a calm, level voice. Alana rolled her eyes, losing patience. She stood close to him intimidatingly and Clara stared at her nails, bored. "Spill or she will hurt you tough guy."

He sighed and reached for his pocket. The girls tensed and Alana jumped him, pinning him to the ground but he was strong.

"I was reaching for my card! Let me go!" he huffed as Clara took the card from his pocket for inspection.

"Bandy Marsoti, Agent number 33921 from the American branch of your Agency." He stood, brushing himself off as he handed the girls a blank, white card. Vanessa brought a pen from the inside pocket of her jacket and shone a light from the end of the pen onto it, revealing the Agency logo.

"Why are you shadowing us if you're on our side?" Vanessa questioned. He looked down at his shoes and let out a low chuckle.

"I was sent to be your backup, but it doesn't seem like you need it from what I saw." Clara smiled at this and Alana scoffed.

"You're right, we don't need backup." She said.

Bandy shook his head and smiled softly to himself.

"You don't understand, I'm your technical support. You need a hacker? You need technology? I'm your guy. As far as we know, the DeRico's systems are protected by the best firewalls. Their firewalls have firewalls. You need me. Whether you like it or not." he said looking relaxed as the girls looked at each other and nodded. Vanessa cleared her throat.

"You can come home with us, we can discuss this further, do you need a ride?" she offered politely.

Bandy smiled.

"No need, got my own ride, I'll meet you at yours in 20." He left without asking for an address. He did not need one.

Back at the house, the girls debriefed Beck on their run-in with Bandy. Beck had a distant expression on his face as if he was recalling something from memory. A few moments later the doorbell rang and the girls rushed to the door. Bandy stood there smiling sweetly, is expression switching to shock when Beck came to the door. Then Beck grinned and the two boys hugged tightly, slapping each other on the back affectionately

"It's been too long man." Bandy put his arm around Beck's shoulder and Beck grinned widely, laughing in disbelief.

"Wait, you guys know each other?" Clara asked. Beck nodded.

"We were childhood friends, we did our training together. I haven't seen you in years Bandy." He turned to his friend.
   The girls decided to leave the boys to catch up and Clara mouthed 'Emergency meeting' at the others.

After letting Alana gather snacks, they headed to Alana's room and lay on her furry white carpet.
   "So what's the goss?" She asked Clara, happily snacking on Oreos.

"Vivi pass me the pink nail varnish por favor?" Clara asked before glancing at Alana's wide smile, eager for gossip.

"Well we need a debrief from the party, and I'm not talking in terms of the mission, but guy-wise." Clara added smiling eagerly. Vanessa raised an eyebrow.

"Clara, the mission *is* guy-wise."

"Vivi's up first!!" Alana shouted as Vanessa blushed and handed Clara the nail polish as requested.

   "Nothing really happened..." She said looking down ashamed.

   "Alana, do we really have to tackle her to spill the beans?" Clara questioned her best friend jokingly.

   "I guess we may have to, Clara..." Alana replied and jumped onto the bed where Vanessa was situated.

"Okay okay, well, it's just we got talking and he's a really nice guy and he's very handsome and he's just-"

"Totally into you." Clara interrupted.

"Yeah but.." She continued.

"He's bad news, and our target." Alana finished for her.

"Yeah I mean they all are, you'll never guess happened with Lucas yesterday... I was making out with Brad right-" Clara started.

Alana scoffed.

Clara ignored her, giving her a look.

"But anyway Lucas just turned up and dragged him back by the collar while we were kissing, and Brad got a bit carried away and said something about how Lucas can't get me and Lucas just punched him in the face."

The two girls gasped simultaneously.

"He then whispered something in Brad's ear which made Brad practically run away."

"Do you have any idea what he said?" Alana asked eagerly.

Clara shook her head.

"That's why you were furious when I saw you." Vanessa confirmed.

The girls heard a knock on the door and saw Beck's head peek through the door curiously.

"Nope! Girls only" Clara said walking up to the door to shut Beck out.

The other two girls threw pillows at him as he popped his head around.

"Fine, whatever I'll just stay with my best bud Bandy then!" He huffed as he left Alana's room.

"So, anything progress between you and our blond bombshell Alana?" Clara asked as Vanessa reached for the popcorn.

"No, nothing happened." She said, almost too quickly.

"Mamma Mia's on!" Vanessa shouted when she turned on Alana's television. She jumped to her feet, bouncing on the bed. The other two joined her immediately, dancing off the drama of the night.

4

Vanessa woke up at 6:30am. She looked around blearily and concluded that she still had an hour and a half to get ready for school. She went
downstairs to see Beck and Bandy in the kitchen looking intently at the computer screen. Vanessa yawned as the boys said good morning.

"What's going on?" she asked sleepily.

Bandy did not look up from his laptop as he explained his progress in hacking the DeRico's phone-calls and computer system. Vanessa ruffled his hair and he grinned, but did not avert his gaze from the screen. She giggled and started making breakfast when Clara and Alana slid into the kitchen from the garden door, in their bikinis, dripping water onto the floor tiles. Clara's feet flew out from underneath her and she found herself falling, but grabbed Alana's arm just before she did, dragging her down. Alana glared at her from her new position on the ground. Beck picked Alana up from the floor easily.

"We just went for a morning swim." Alana grinned and they both hugged Vanessa. She cringed away from their wet hair and faces and opened her mouth to speak but they had already started off racing upstairs to get changed for school. Vanessa later joined them to see them still in their bikinis, lying on the bed. With a little persuasion and a lot of begging, they eventually marched downstairs to greet Vanessa for breakfast. Alana piled several Nutella smothered pancakes onto her plate as Clara made an effort to pull Alana's curls away from her chocolatey face, but Alana was too busy talking to notice, or put any effort into preserving herself. Vanessa leaned over the counter and sipped her tea, organising what gadgets she would take to school. She had opted for a light coral blouse and faded denim jeans. Her hair was brushed away from her face into a sophisticated ponytail and she fiddled with her long gold necklace as she examined the blueprints of the school. Eventually the girls finished breakfast and set off to leave.

It was already warm, despite it being the morning and Clara was pleased with her choice of a breezy white peasant blouse and a denim miniskirt. She pulled her large, cat-eye sunglasses over her eyes and gently threw her white tote-bag filled with spy goodies and school supplies into her car.

Alana pulled her leather jacket over her floral playsuit and lowered her metallic, aviator sunglasses, her messy curls braided back loosely for the ride. She was stopped at the door as she was leaving by Clara who demanded to know where her bag was. Alana dug her hands into her pockets and pulled out the insides, clearly showing Clara she had no need for a bag when her pockets would suffice, although they were all well aware that Alana's vast collection of gadgets and snacks were stashed away in her motorbike.

They heard a scuffle as Bandy scurried to the door with them, his laptop in his arm.

"We're only going to school you know..." Clara said, wondering why he was in such a rush.

"I couldn't leave you girls alone and defenceless could I? I enrolled when you guys did." He smiled a teethy smile getting into Clara's car with her.

Clara hopped into her perky yellow mini and checked her reflection in the rear-view mirror.

"You know, I don't understand why you're all driving separately." Bandy commented. Clara ignored him.

Vanessa checked her mirror and applied some light red lip-gloss, her dark, chocolaty eyes sparkling.

Alana mounted her bike and fastened her helmet over her head.

Clara honked her horn and blew a kiss at Beck and Vanessa and turned the music up to full volume, heading off for their first day of school. Students lingered in the car park with flashy cars gleaming in the sunlight. All heads turned when they heard the girls arriving. Clara's bright yellow car parked next to comparatively dull ones, roof down so they could all hear her playing Britney Spears' old tracks. Alana parked her bike in the motorcycle section and took her helmet off, shaking out her hair. Clara and Vanessa walked up to her, aware that all eyes were on the new girls.

The elderly, jolly receptionist welcomed the girls warmly. She spent a considerable about of time testing out her British accent on the girls, which they cringed at politely. After a while of friendly tips and hints, and a tour of the school then receptionist gave them their schedules and a rough map of the school. The corridors were light and airy and there were lines of polished red lockers decorating the walls. The school grounds where they imagined students spent their break times were vast and green.

"Bloody fantastic, we have Biology next." Clara said sarcastically while walking down the hallway.

"At least we're all together." Vanessa stated happily.

"Not me, I have English now, see you guys later." And with that Bandy disappeared.

"I hope we dissect frogs!" Alana added eagerly.

"Gross." Clara muttered before taking out her mirror to check her eyebrows.

Alana sighed as Vanessa checked out all the leaflets on one of the notice boards.

"Wow this school is so cool! I mean they have loads of events and extracurricular activities."

Alana gave the over-zealous Vanessa an amused smile, this school was their extra-curricular activity, she thought.

"Oh it's the Londoners!" They all turned around to see Millie, Fred and another tall boy walking behind them.

"Hey guys, how ya'll liking the school?" Fred said with a great, big smile on his face.

"Oh by the way this is Tom, he's cool." He said gesturing to the tall boy on his side. Tom stood uncertainly, shoulders hunched, but gave off a friendly, if taciturn, vibe.

The girls each said 'Hi' in turn, smiling at Tom.

"So, what class do you have now?" Millie asked enthusiastically. "Biology." Vanessa replied. "With Miss

Spence."

"Good luck with her, she's a tough one, better not be late! We'll see you at lunch. We usually sit on the grass by the fountain!" Millie added, eyes twinkling as she bounced away.

They exchanged farewells and the girls trudged off to Biology, aware they were already late.

Clara knocked softly and opened the door cautiously, Alana and Vanessa trailing behind her timidly.

"Hi, we're new here and our time table says we have Biology with you now." Clara said smiling charmingly.

Miss Spence eyed each one of the girls very carefully and finally spoke in a shrill, nasal voice. From their impression, it seemed Clara's charm managed to chip away some, but not all the ice.

"There are some empty seats at the back. But next time, don't be so late!"

The girls' next class was History; the history class was nearby their previous class so they had no problem finding it that time.

Half an hour in, Alana was still arguing with the teacher about the Sarajevo assassination of 1914. Vanessa doodled on her page, and Clara mingled with nearby students. Alana's discussion was interrupted by a knock on the door.

"Why are you so late?!" the teacher shouted as Zach, Lucas and Mason walked in, ignoring Alana's last point.

"Traffic." Lucas shrugged dismissively.

Zach added, "There was an accident on Alta Loma Road. Messy stuff."

"Just sit down please." The history teacher said, returning to the board, frown lines, presumably from years of teaching appearing in his forehead as he pushed his glasses closer to his eyes and turned back to Alana who was waiting mid-sentence to continue the discussion.

Zachary put his hand up to argue with the history teacher, watching Alana with an amused smirk.

"The assassination in Sarajevo did not cause the 1st World War, the main factor that caused this spark was of course the growth of militarism."

"Sir, if I may?" Alana raised her hand, continuing before her teacher got a chance to reply.

"That would be incorrect; the growth of militarism, alliances, imperialism and nationalism all equally played major roles in this!"

Their history teacher looked between them, enthralled by the discussion.

"Well, if I'm not mistaken darling, the tension between Europe from Germany building up their navy is what brought about these tensions."

Before Alana got to counteract his statement, she was interrupted by Clara.

"Oh for goodness sake you two, get a room."

Alana glowered as Zach grinned at her. The class snickered until they were hushed by the teacher to resume their lesson.

Lucas remained silent at the back of the class, staring at the boy in front of Clara who had turned around to talk to her.

The boy suddenly turned back to the front mid conversation and Clara looked behind her confused as to what spooked him. She made eye contact with Lucas and gave him a questioning look which he pointedly ignored.

The school day passed by quickly and soon the girls were in the changing room getting ready for gym class.

"You've decided to come to this school have you?" Alana looked up to see the girl Zach was with at the party, sneering down at her.

She stood up, squaring her shoulders.

"Your boyfriends aren't around to save you this time, so I'd be a bit nicer if I were you."

She retreated glaring at her from a safe distance.

The gym-teacher blew her whistle and the girls got into a semi-circle around her, joining their classmates waiting for instructions. The coach announced they would be playing soccer and separated the class into boys and girls, starting two matches. Alana volunteered as team captain and she gathered with the girls and the rest of the team assigning positions.

On the other team were Lucas' and Zach's girlfriends, they walked up to the girls drawing the attention of the whole class who were eager for another cat fight.

"I hope you're not sore losers, 'cause you are definitely not winning this." The brunette sneered at them. Vanessa looked at Clara and Alana, amused at the audacity of her comment.

"Darling, football is our national sport, so you're going down." Clara laughed and slinked off as they stared daggers at her. They had found out that the blonde, Zach's un-official girlfriend was called Natalia. Lana, the brunette, was Lucas'. From their research, which was listening to Millie gossip,

In the final 10 minutes of the game, Clara saw Lucas and Mason approach to watch.

The girls ran together in a row swiftly passing the ball to each other, Alana tackled the blonde whilst Vanessa marked the brunette, blocking her from the ball.

Clara now had the goal in clear sight; she dodged the huge girl running towards her and booted the ball into the goal. The coach blew the whistle and declared a goal for Alana's team.

Clara looked over to suddenly see Lucas jogging up to her. He touched her arm gently. She looked at him quizzically.

"Look, about what happened at the beach party... I'm sorry. Not the way to introduce yourself to the new girl." He said truthfully with his hand still on her arm.

"Yeah, well I just hope Brad's okay." Clara lied, turned around and walked off, flicking her long, brown hair over her shoulder.

A few seconds later she turned around again and from a distance shouted back at Lucas.

"I thought the DeRico's apologised to nobody except their mothers?"

He laughed as she sauntered over to Alana and Vanessa.

The girls changed and got back into their normal clothes just in time for the bell signaling the end of the day.

"Vivi, I think I forgot my study planner in Physics, can you come with me to get it please?" Clara pleaded.

"Yeah sure, let's go quick before Alana leaves, she's waiting for us outside I think." Vanessa replied.

Alana left the other two girls and walked to her bike. She noticed a new motorbike next to hers and her eyes widened when she saw the black vintage Harley Davidson. Her mouth parted in shock, she didn't notice the person next to it until she heard Zach's low laugh.

"Figures, this is the only time you show interest." He smirked and crossed his arms over his leather jacket. Alana gazed lustfully at the bike as Zach moved closer to her.

"You want a ride?" he said, close enough that his arm brushed hers. She shivered as her wisps of hair blew into his face.

Her eyes looked at him, with a hint of annoyance.
"With you? No thanks." She gave him a smirk, which he returned.
"Fine. No Harley." He turned to leave but Alana grabbed his arm. She noted it was firm but focused on trying not to get distracted.

"Fine. I'll come." She said, a smile playing on the corner of her lips. He grinned triumphantly and tossed her the spare helmet. He did it up for her and she felt his fingers brush her neck
whilst adjusting the clasp.

She mounted the Harley behind him and held her arms loosely around his waist, being careful not to touch him too much. He chuckled and took her arms and made sure they were wrapped firmly around him. She rolled her eyes as he kicked the bike into action.

The roar of the bike was louder than she was used to but she loved the speed and the thunderous growl. She could not hold back a carefree laugh, she felt Zachary laugh too as he sped up, causing her to hold onto him tighter.

"You having fun?" he shouted to her over the roar of the motor.

"Hell yes!" She shouted back and he sped up even more. Zachary would have gone faster but he was distracted by the feel of her clinging to him. He smirked to himself, his usual pick-up tactics working a treat.

He finally stopped at the beach. The sun was slowly setting and they needed a break from the roaring engine and lashing winds. Alana took off her helmet, her hair had come undone again and the soft breeze blew it out of her face. Zach looked at her, the sun set the golden brown curls on fire. He smiled at her as she breathed out, exhilarated from the ride, beaming with happiness.

He turned to her and she was aware that he was very close. His hands gently lifted her chin making her look into his deep green eyes. He was surprised she had not hit him yet and was shocked, and thrilled when she faced up to him as he moved in closer. His fingers brushed her neck and he paused when he felt a jagged line of a scar near her collarbone. She stiffened, and he looked at her curiously.

"What happened there?" He asked, a smile still on his lips. The fire disappeared from her eyes and her expression hardened. That scar was from a mission a few years back when the girls saved a group of people from a bank robbery.

She shifted so that his weight was no longer pressing her against the bike and she moved away from him, putting her helmet on.

"I think it's time I went home." She said coldly. His green eyes locked on hers, but she remained defiant, her nose turned up at him.

He shrugged and they rode back in silence, with Zach wondering what he had said to change her mood.

"Goodbye Alana." He said as she walked away. She gave him a small smile and he watched as she got on her Ducati and rode off into the sunset.

Vanessa and Clara just came out of the building, the parking lot was empty. No sign of Alana anywhere.

"She must have left already." Said Vanessa heading towards her car.

"We'll meet her at the house, she's so impatient!"

"Girls I've been looking everywhere for you!" Bandy said as he came out of the school building behind them.

"Where's Alana?" The urgency in his voice and the darkness in his eyes suggested something of importance.

"She's probably already gone home. Why? What's wrong?" Vanessa replied softly.

"Something's come up; I need to speak to you girls."

5

Alana came in and shut the door behind her. The house was silent unusually silent. She walked into the living room cautiously to find the girls, Beck and Bandy gathered round the table.

"What's going on?" She chirped trying to evade the last hour from her memory.

Beck motioned for her to sit down and she took the seat next to him.

"Okay so here's the thing, you know I've been working on getting into the DeRico's system but I've been compromised. Their system is better than I thought and I've been sussed out, they're one of the most highly organised criminal group." Bandy paused to let that sink in. Everyone's attention was on him.

"So... what does that mean?" Clara prompted, getting impatient.

"It means that the only way to get in their system now is directly from a DeRico computer." He looked all three girls in the eye and smiled nervously. Vanessa groaned and Clara slumped her head on the desk.

"You mean to say we have to infiltrate their place and hack them?" Alana said eyes gleaming. Bandy nodded, smiling. His smile disappeared at Beck's dark expression.

"How are they supposed to get into the DeRico's place without getting caught?"

Vanessa perked up. "Well ... it's Mase's, I mean uh, Mason's birthday party next week and we are all invited." She smiled hesitantly as Clara and Alana's eyebrows rose to the top of their foreheads.

"Mase?" Alana teased but Bandy jumped up excitedly.

"That's perfect! You need to distract the DeRico's, Alana, Beck and I will go upstairs and copy the software, we'll be out of there in a second." Bandy's eyes lit up excited.

"How many days until Mason's party?" Clara asked Vanessa.

"It's next Friday." She said not missing a beat. She sat down on the kitchen stool and twirled her hair around her fingers, avoiding the mischievous glances from the girls.

"I guess there's only one thing to do then." Clara smiled and turned to Alana.

"Shopping!" Alana grinned as she grabbed her bag.

The familiar setting of gleaming shops and the scent of new clothes was a familiar one to the girls and they felt themselves at home.

They spent two hours in and out of changing rooms until they could shop no more, and finally settled down for a smoothie. Whilst arguing over whether smoothies or milkshakes were better, they noticed a group of men standing not far from them.

"Hey, that's Lucas and Zach, but who are they with?" She frowned as she saw a group of Asian men talking to the boys. They seemed to be in a very heated argument. The girls itched to find out what they were talking about but they could not get close enough without being compromised. Then they spotted Mason walking precariously close to them, headed towards the group, without realising the girls were sitting only a few feet away from him. Vanessa quickly opened her purse and jumped up.

"Mason!" She called waving. Alana and Clara looked at her wide-eyed as Mason gave her his crooked smile. Vanessa walked over to him and talked, even touching his arm a few times whilst Clara and Alana looked on dumbfounded. She eventually sat down with a smug smile and Mason walked towards his brothers and the group of increasingly pissed-off men. Vanessa reached for her pink, leather purse and took out her headphones.

"What the hell was that?" hissed Clara shocked.

"You just blew our cover!" Alana added. Vanessa said nothing and held out her headphones for Alana to use. Alana listened carefully for a while and a wide smile spread across her face.

"She bugged him."

Clara laughed softly.

"You're brilliant you know that?" She smiled at Vanessa.

Alana was listening intently, mentally taking notes of what the group of criminals were saying. The group of men in confrontation with the boys were members of the Triad faction active in the area. Her eyes widened slightly at how menacing Zach's usually-joking voice sounded.

"How did they find out is what I want to know." said a gruff voice.

"We dealt with the informant, we just need you to deal with the informed." Said another.

"Why can't you do it?" Lucas grunted.

"Well... they were warned about us beforehand, they expect the Triad, not three teenagers." Another replied, his voice mocking, sneering at the three teenage boys they were entrusting with this duty.

"We'll do it." Zach relented.

They then parted and headed towards the car park. Alana panicked as the sound crackled.

"Oh god, they're leaving, quick, we need to follow them." She said and the girls quickly stood and walked discreetly towards the car park. They saw Zach and Mason get into Lucas' black Jaguar and Vanessa hurried to her car but Alana grabbed her by the wrist gently to stop her.

"They know our cars." She whispered turned so they were out of view.

"Well, we can't shadow them on foot, I'm not walking anywhere." Clara hissed, pointing at her heels.

"No one said we're going on foot." Alana smirked.

She turned to a dark blue sedan, took something out of her back pocket and bent over. Clara rolled her eyes and smiled and in a few seconds the engine came to life. Clara got behind the wheel, raising an eyebrow daring Alana to protest.

"You would get us pulled over in a second."

The girls followed the red dot showing up on Vanessa's tablet which showed the location of the bug, fitted with a GPS tracking device.

Lucas' car came into view and Clara kept one car between them. From the seats Clara and Alana could hear Vanessa quickly fumbling with something in the back seat. After following the boys to Beverly Hills their car slowed down and the boys walked towards a small house. It was an inconspicuous house, fitting in neatly with its well-kept, picket fenced neighbours. A car was already parked outside which meant that someone was home. The boys looked at each other and nodded in affirmation. They did not notice a dark blue sedan parked across the road and three pairs of eyes watching their every move intently.

"Okay this is for you." Vanessa threw something at Clara; she held it out in front of her. It was a woolly hat with two eye holes. She looked back at Vanessa and noticed she had changed into baggy sweats and a hoodie. She was wearing a makeshift mask too. She threw a hoodie over to Clara who got the message and copied Vanessa.

"Where did those come from? Why don't I have one?" said Alana, looking confused.

"There was a gym bag in the back." Vanessa shrugged.

"We need to stop them killing whoever knows about the deal, we need him for interrogation. Alana, you need to stay here for our getaway, or if we get in trouble, you need to get backup." Vanessa put her communications device in her ear.

"We'll keep in touch."

"You better hurry." Alana said and she handed Vanessa her favourite Swiss army knife.

"Just in case." The girls headed towards the house swiftly, using the night sky as a cover.

Alana's voice came through their earpieces.

"Okay, they're in the living room, Mason has a weapon, they're asking him who he's spoken to." she said. Vanessa and Clara sent her a beep in reply and they headed towards the living room where they heard low voices.

"I'm going to ask you one more time, who did you, tell?" Vanessa almost did not recognise Mason's voice.

The guy whimpered something in reply as Clara got a quick glimpse of the scene. A middle-aged man was kneeling on the floor his face bruised and bloody. Mason held a knife at his neck and Zach had his fingers wrapped around the collar of his shirt, keeping him facing Lucas. Lucas was pacing the room. Mason backhanded the man when he started to blubber and Vanessa let out a small whimper and Clara's blue eyes widened as Lucas stopped pacing. Mason and Zach snapped their heads to the door frame where Vanessa and Clara were. The girls quickly calculated the odds, two girls against three trained criminals. Clara shuffled slightly, the wooden floor beneath her creaking, which was all it took for the boys to spring into action. Clara round-housed Zach who was the closest to her but he blocked with his arm, pushing her backwards. She quickly and firmly punched his jaw before receiving a kick in the back from Lucas. Mason lunged to punch Clara, but she blocked his attack with her arm. Lucas then faced off Clara while Zach and Mason moved in on Vanessa.

Lucas sent out a kick and Clara blocked the worst of it yet she still thudded into a wall knocking down a vase as she did so. She picked up the vase and smashed it against Lucas' head making him fall to the ground.

Vanessa backed away slightly, bringing out Alana's knife. She managed to cut Mason's hand and punched his jaw as he recoiled from the knife. Zach lunged at Vanessa and lifted her easily, putting her in a choking hold on her neck and bending her body back over his shoulders. She kept out of reach of Mason but she could feel Zach breaking her back. She brought the knife down onto Zach's arm. He yelled and dropped her on her front. She felt her ribs smash hard onto the hard floor and let out a cry. In her ear piece she could hear Alana yelling.

Their code names were yelled into their ears through the communications devices. "Cherub, Siren, retreat. Abort mission!"

Vanessa got up and ran for the door but Mason was blocking her getaway. She looked at Clara who ran up the stairs dragging Vanessa with her. They got to a bedroom and locked the door.

Clara cursed, looking around frantically. The door thudded, they were using something to break it down. Clara looked around and noticed a balcony door. She kicked open the door not bothering with the lock and smiled thinking how Alana would be proud of her.

"Siren here, Tiger, bring the car below the balcony out back. NOW!" She demanded.

Vanessa looked at the floor from the balcony, calculating the chances of them making the jump without breaking something when they heard a gunshot echo through the night and froze. Even the thudding on the door paused. Clara took Vanessa's hand in hers, and with one last encouraging look, they hurled themselves off the balcony.

Clara winced as a pain shot through her foot as she landed sideways. They rolled and Vanessa's arm shifted and took the impact of the fall. Her wrist gave way and she yelled out in pain. They looked around, they were in the back garden and Alana was nowhere to be seen.

"Where the hell is she?" Clara screamed in frustration.

The girls heard an engine roar and the back-yard fence flew into pieces as the familiar stolen car smashed through.

"Get in." Alana shouted and Clara let out a sigh of relief. They got in and Alana sped away. Mason, Zachary and Lucas ran out to the back yard only to see the get-away car speed off, tires screeching. Zachary let out a low whistle and Mason spat out blood from where Vanessa had punched him. Lucas kicked a piece of fallen wood angrily.

"Damn it! He escaped." he spat. The man they were questioning had gone.

"Who the hell were they?" Said Zach as he held his arm where the small silver Swiss army knife had stabbed him.

"What was the gunshot?" Lucas asked. The two boys shrugged. By the time the police had arrived there was no trace of the boys, only a broken fence and a missing tenant.

Alana remained quiet during the whole ride looking pained. Clara had her eyes shut to deal with the pain in her foot and Vanessa just looked around at the darkness. Alana stopped the car at the mall where they retrieved Vanessa's car. She opened the boot and inside was the man the boys had been interrogating.

Clara let out a small gasp of shock and Alana nodded to Vanessa to get him into her car.

"How...how?" Vanessa started.

"Caught him as he was leaving the house. He had a gun in his car." She muttered tiredly. She opened the back-seat door and got inside without another word. Clara looked at Vanessa who was equally confused at Alana's behaviour, but they got into the car and drove home without a word.

Alana was the first out of the car and went straight inside as the other two dealt with their captive.

When they got inside Beck was waiting for them, his dark brows low over his eyes.

"Where's Alana?" Clara asked Beck, noticing his expression shift to weary.

"Beck. Where. Is. Alana." Vanessa said slowly, her voice hardening at Beck's reluctance to reply. She looked down at his hands, which were by his side, covered in dried blood.

"Girls ... Alana..." His voice cracked. "Alana was shot."

Clara's mouth dropped open and her perfect eyebrows knitted together in anger.

"What?! Where?! When?!" her voice was loud and shrill and Vanessa rushed inside immediately.

"She was lucky, it missed any vital arteries, but she's lost a lot of blood." Beck assured as the girls rushed inside. "She's passed out. The bullet wasn't inside her which was a blessing but she's in a lot of pain."

"She didn't even say anything, she just drove us and... and ..." Vanessa trailed off, her eyes watering as they saw Alana lying on the couch, face pale, wearing Beck's shirt- her blood-stained clothes discarded on the floor.

Clara sat beside her, listening to her and stroked her hot forehead.

Alana's eyes fluttered open and closed again and she groaned in pain. Bandy was icing Vanessa's swelling wrist and putting an ointment on her bruises, dubbed the 'miracle gel' by Agency spies who used it to recover quickly when undercover.

Beck took Clara's hand and brushed broken bits of glass out of her palm. She winced as he patted the ointment onto her sore face but she breathed out a sigh of relief that her face would go back to normal quickly. He moved his hand gingerly over her ankle and she let out a hiss as a flood of pain shot up her body. Beck raised and examined her ankle and let out a low whistle.

"We're going to have to pop this out you know." he said, tenderly massaging her swollen ankle. Clara nodded, clenching her jaw.

"Bandy, restrain her." Beck told Bandy who rushed over and planted his hands on Clara's shoulders firmly. She squeezed her eyes shut and Beck quickly twisted her ankle the other way sharply and a sharp crack echoed through the room. Clara let out the breath she was holding in and Beck gave her and Vivi some strong painkillers. Beck kissed the top of Clara's head and smiled.

"Come on, sleep is the best cure, you have school tomorrow." he said, the girls were expected to deal with injuries over the space of a few hours. Clara nodded and headed upstairs but Vanessa paused.

"What about Alana?"

Beck nodded and went over to Alana and lifted her carefully, she moaned slightly but she was too deep in sleep for the movement to hurt her much. Her body was limp in his arms and she was motionless. He headed up and laid her on her bed and turned to see Clara and Vanessa in their pyjamas holding their teddy bears. He let out a low chuckle as they snuggled into Alana's bed without a word, careful not to disturb her.

"Goodnight girls." he whispered and flicked off the light.

Alana woke up, staring up at her ceiling confused. She stretched out and immediately recoiled when she felt a sharp pain in her abdomen. She looked around at Clara and Vanessa's sleeping bodies wondering why they had ended up in her bed. Vanessa woke up at the sound of Alana stirring and she looked at Alana with wide, concerned eyes. After a moment of silence she squealed and hugged Alana gently. Clara mumbled in her sleep and woke up, ready to let out a torrent of insults for her awakeners but she then saw Alana and opened her mouth to yell for Beck.

"Come on, we have school." Vanessa mumbled. She looked at Alana's watch and blinked a few times.

"We have 10 minutes until school starts!" she said flustered.

"No. sleep. is. good." Alana mumbled into her pillow turning and closing her eyes. Clara tucked her in, assuring her she had a whole day of bed rest and comfort food ahead of her.

"I see you're back little one." Beck said as Clara and Vanessa rushed into their rooms to get dressed. Their bruises had improved considerably, and all traces of injury disappeared after some makeup. Beck changed Alana's bandages, putting more healing cream on her wound. It was an angry, jagged red wound but it was not infected, and would heal soon. She watched him, her eyes half-open and golden. He focused on the wound, tutting to himself as he gave her a reassuring smile. He handed her the remote and let her have full reign of Netflix.

They drove to school and arrived 20 minutes late for their first lesson, English with Miss McGreen. They signed in late and walked to their class. Walking down the deserted hallway they heard footsteps and they turned to see the brothers heading towards them. Vanessa sighed and Clara crossed her arms in annoyance. They were not the people they wanted to see at that moment.

"You're late."

6

"Well aren't you observant" Clara shot back at Zach, who grinned at her reaction. They continued walking, intending to walk past them but Lucas grabbed Clara's arm gently, but touched a bruise causing Clara to wince involuntarily. He immediately let go, confused as she stormed past him.

They headed inside without another word. The teacher questioned their tardiness but let the matter drop as she became more preoccupied with the couple making out in the back row. Whilst sitting through the lesson pretending to digest information they already knew, their eyes caught sight of Beck was standing outside waving frantically to get their attention. Clara looked at Vanessa and gestured to Beck with the slightest movement of her head, indicating that she should go to him.

Vanessa mumbled something to the teacher and was excused from the class. Clara noticed Mason watching Vanessa leaved and smiled to herself. It was not his fault he fancied her, Vanessa was beautiful, clever and charming, he was not the first and he would not be the last. Clara's concern, however, was that Vanessa was also falling for Mason's charms. She doodled on her paper as she thought about how complicated their lives would be with boyfriends. The dating, the tricky explanations. They enjoyed their work too much for that. Clara opened the textbook in front of her and resumed with the lesson, watching the back of Mason's head carefully, as if trying to guess his secrets.

Vanessa hurried over to Beck who was leaning on his car.

"What's going on?" she asked. Beck fiddled with his phone and a moment later her phone beeped. It was footage of the conversation with the man Alana had captured the night before. The man looked petrified and during the whole questioning he trembled, but said nothing. Beck's voice sounded persuasive, presumably playing good cop at this point, but the man was defiant. He opened his mouth, as if considering saying something.

"They're keeping it safe ... away from..." He broke off; it looked like he didn't plan on saying anything else. Beck turned the video off and Vanessa looked at him confused. There was a third party. A party other than the Triad faction in LA and the DeRicos who wanted involvement with whatever the two were working on. Vanessa walked back to class, her mind reeling with thoughts of what he could mean when she stopped at the sound of footsteps. She turned to see the girls that had made it their mission to take them down, who she discovered were called Lania and Natalia, along with another girl she had seen around school. The girl had silky auburn hair and almond shaped green eyes. She had a look of disdain on her face whenever she saw Vanessa around school, that was how she recognised her.

"I hear you and your herd are planning on going to Mason's party." snarled Lania. The three girls circled Vanessa and she give them a blank, almost tired expression.

"You heard right." Vanessa replied, not in the mood for their high-school games, and tried to move out of the way but evidently they were not finished with her.

"Keep away from Mason." said the one with the auburn hair. Vanessa thought back and remembered her name; Sophie. This was getting exhausting. Was there anyone that wasn't going to jump at their throats for getting close to the boys.

"And tell your friends that if they come to the party, we'll deal with them." Natalia added. She froze as she felt a presence behind her.

"Why don't you tell them yourself?" Clara said lightly. Clara watched them evaluate the change of their odds with mild amusement, waiting for them to figure out their next move. Lana eventually spoke, crossing her arms.

"I guess you'll see at the party." and with that the trio walked off, heels clicking on the floor. Vanessa shook her head in disapproval. Of all the despicable people they dealt with on missions, high-school bullies were the most detestable. Clara looked at Vanessa and shook her head.

"You'd think the ladies would look out for each other a little more."

After a few days of school had passed, Alana recovering from 'the flu' as the school believed, everyone at the house was too exhausted to do anything that required more movement than passing the remote control. Vanessa and Clara would come back to find Alana slumped on the sofa, having ignored the order to stay in bed, watching old episodes of Desperate Housewives. Her hair was pulled back in a messy bun and some colour had come back to her face. Clara checked her forehead with the back of her hand, but she had no fever. She was recovering. Vanessa brought her laptop down and was online shopping, one fluffy
slipper crossed over the other on the sofa, resting on Clara's legs.

"No way!" Clara burst out, laughing on the phone. Alana threw a cushion at her telling her to move the conversation elsewhere whilst important things happened on screen. Clara got up, barely paying attention to her surroundings.

"He did not! That's just too bad." She carried on walking around the house. Beck gave Vanessa a questioning look and Bandy came in the room and sighed.

"She's been on the phone for hours, first talking to Paul, then to Jake, Maria and now she's on the line with Leslie. Someone please shut her up; she keeps walking round the house distracting me!" He blurted out, collapsing onto the sofa next to Vanessa. Alana mumbled something about not even knowing there was a Paul, Jake, Marie and Leslie.

"Bandy why don't you just tell her?" Beck replied hesitantly.

Vanessa giggled knowing there was no way Clara would get off the phone before she was done.

Beck wasn't convinced and went up to Clara himself.

"Hey Clara?" He tapped her shoulder.

"Nuh-huh, I don't think so." She grabbed his hand and twisted it so Beck left, holding his hand in pain.

"Sorry Les, what was I saying?" She let go and walked away into the kitchen where her voice carried through, albeit faded.

Beck grumbled and sat down next to Alana, defeated. Clara eventually walked back into the living room still gabbling on the phone.

"Shhhh... I'm watching Desperate Housewives." Alana growled at Clara who paid no attention to her and carried on speaking. Alana pulled herself up with difficulty, launching herself off the couch and jumped on top of Clara, tackling her down onto the sofa. Clara tried to kick her off but Beck leaped in and held her wrists down. Vanessa quickly grabbed her phone out of her vice like grip. Beck and Alana immediately released Clara and braced themselves for the torrent of abuse from Clara.

"I'm hungry." Alana broke the comfortable, lazy silence, after everyone had calmed down. "Someone, get me something to eat."

Beck picked up the phone and called the local Chinese, reciting the girls' order from years of experience.

Only a few moments later the doorbell rang but no one made the effort to move. Alana stared at Clara with doe-like eyes, waiting for her to get up.

"You ordered this food." She mumbled before getting up to get the door.

"Anyway, why are they here so early, we only ordered five minutes ago."

Clara opened the door and jumped slightly as she saw someone other than the delivery man leaning on the wall outside.

"What are you doing here?" She questioned angrily.

"You forgot this at school, I wanted to bring it back for you." Lucas said as he handed Clara a small blue bag which contained all her makeup. The blue makeup bag she had purposefully left within Lucas' range of vision. She took a moment to watch him carefully, leaning against the doorway, hand in his pocket as he assessed Clara, waiting for a reaction.

Clara loosened up and smiled.

"Well thank you, it's very kind of you." Beck got up and walked over to Clara and Lucas.

"I'm Beck, I live with the girls, you must be Lucas." He smiled at the Lucas who looked at Clara, pleasantly surprised she had mentioned him.

"Come in, come in." He looked at Clara who gave him a quick angry look.

Lucas hesitated but turned around and motioned Zach and Mason who were in the car to come.

"The more the merrier." Clara said dryly and kicked Beck in the shin as she walked past.

The boys entered, Bandy and Vanessa let out a quick yelp of surprise and Alana stiffened up.

"That doesn't look like my Chinese." She commented, eyeing up the boys. They grinned at her boyishly.

"Well you can't stay. We have no food. I mean we wouldn't want our guests to be hungry. What terrible hospitality, why don't you just come another time?" Alana delivered uncomfortably.

Clara rolled her eyes at her friend's terrible excuse. The doorbell rang and Vanessa shouted. "Food's here!!"

Alana growled. Vanessa smiled apologetically at Alana.

"Quick word in the kitchen?" Clara smiled awkwardly and shuffled to the kitchen followed by Beck the girls entered the kitchen.

"What the hell Beck?" Alana said angrily.
"Think mission." Beck replied, eyes gleaming. "A- Perfect way to get close to them and B- I'll bug them all!"

"Be nice, get as much out of them as you can." he added. Alana snorted but they all went back to the boys smiling.

"Mason... a quick tour?" Vanessa quickly said to break the tension.

"Yeah sure." He responded with a huge smile as she led him to the garden.

"I'll take this one." Clara winked and grabbed Lucas by the hand taking him upstairs to her room.

Alana glanced at Zach, gave him an unenthusiastic smile, and made her way upstairs alone leaving him with Beck and Bandy.

Vanessa walked to the garden with Mason following her. The garden was impressive, it was a beautiful expanse of grass surrounded framed by trees, with a marble table in the middle. The grass smelt freshly cut. The trees were imposed their long, fruitful branches and dangling leaves over them. Vanessa sat down at the table and Mason joined her. He smiled at her, as her shoulder length hair flew around her as the breeze came. She faced the gust of wind to move her hair out of her face and giggled.
"So, tell me something about yourself." He said jokingly, smiling at her warmly in a way which made Vanessa's heart flutter.
"Hello, my name is Vanessa McCloud and my favourite colour is pink." She teased, earning a laugh.
"Well hello Vanessa." He replied, getting down on his knee and kissing her hand. She laughed, swatting him away. She walked to the old oak tree and propped herself up on the lowest branch.

Mason gazed at her longingly before standing up and joining her.

"Why here?" He questioned.

"You wanted to know something about me, well I come here to think. I just sit up in this tree and it helps clear my mind." She said looking at the sky.

He smiled up at her, not looking away when she met his expression with dark, intelligent eyes.

"What's making you smile so much?" She asked seriously.

"You." He said slowly bending down to meet her lips with his. Her lips parted and she placed her arms around his neck. The innocent kiss grew deeper as their bodies melted into each other. His hands gently caressed her hair. With every stroke she inched further into the kiss. Whilst her mind initially blanked, the sound of Mason threatening the man only a few days earlier made her pull apart. Focus Vanessa, this was not the plan.

"Come on." She said whispered shaking off the horrible thought. "Where?" He questioned.

"Up there!" She looked up smiling, with that she started climbing the tree, Mason followed her up.

They found themselves at the top of the tree, sitting on a branch gazing at the neighbourhood lights. They stayed up there, holding onto the branches, their hands brushing occasionally until eventually they descended.

Mason jumped down first and reached out to help Vanessa, who jumped into his open arms lightly, laughing sweetly as he swung her round.

Clara dragged Lucas up the stairs to her room. He sat on her bed as she put on some music.

"So, why did you really come here?" She asked as she walked to her desk fiddling with her makeup.

"To give you back your bag." He stood up and walked up behind her, so close she could almost feel him. He lifted his arm to touch her but before he had the chance she turned around and walked towards the big purple bed.

"Liar." She said laughing as she sat down on the bed and patted the space next to her so he would sit down too. Her blue eyes sparkled as she watched him contemplate his next move.

"I came to see you, clear the air." He said as he looked into her eyes. He could smell her vanilla scent and as she started to smile he gently brushed his hand across her cheek, tucking a bit of hair behind her ear.

"That's a bit forward of you." She teased, her tone hiding the somersault her heart did in her chest.

"How would you know?" He replied as she stood up and walked over to the balcony. She could not stay still for long, she was feeling jittery. She had to keep him on his feet but something about him was keeping her on her feet too.

He followed her and stood next to her admiring the view.

"I heard my ex-girlfriend has been giving you all a bit of trouble." He started, unexpectedly. Clara noted the way he had slipped in that he had broken up with Lania in the conversation.

"Oh, what made you finally come to your senses?" She joked and turned to face him.

He ignored her quip.

"So what's the deal with this Beck guy?" His question caught her off-guard.

"Wouldn't you like to know." She flirted.

"Do I have to beat him up too?" He asked jokingly and raised an eyebrow. He stepped closer.

"I'd like to see you try." It wasn't a lie, she thought as she pictured Beck and Lucas in hand-to-hand combat. He moved closer towards her, making her breath catch in her throat.

He jerked back when he was interrupted by Bandy walking in on them. They both jumped apart and smiled sheepishly at Bandy. Bandy's eyes widened and he turned on his heel immediately, walking straight into the door, but eventually finding his way out.

"I have to go." Lucas quickly reminded himself, touching Clara's shoulder, lingering on her soft skin, leaning in again but thinking better of it. He left without another word leaving Clara standing in shock. Clara slumped herself on the bed and gave a long, exasperated sigh.

"Not this one Clara" She whispered to herself.

"So, you guys good?" Zachary said nervously with a smirk on his face as Bandy and Beck watched him curiously. He started making awkward mouth noises and fiddled with the cushion on the couch.

"I'll go find Alana." He said, mostly to himself as he made his way upstairs. Alana had gone to the attic. The attic was dark except for the ray of moonlight that shone through a small slanted skylight. There were not many furnishings other than the disarray of books and cardboard boxes around. He opened the door and saw her. She had her back to him and had something silver in her hand.

She quickly flicked a wrist and a dart flew at a dartboard and hit the bullseye. Zach let out a low whistle and chuckled. Alana turned to him and scowled.

"You looked pleased to see me."

She took another dart and aimed it at Zach but he grabbed her fist before she got a shot in and the two rolled around sparring, Alana trying to cause some damage to his face and Zach trying to stop her. She fell limp, defeated, and still weak from her injuries. Zach chuckled, he had her wrists pinned to the attic floor and he was inches away from her face. He leaned in closer and she stiffened. He suddenly began tickling her neck with his nose and she shrieked with laughter begging him to stop.

"I'm begging you please, STOP!" She gasped out and he

stopped to look at her, a cheeky expression on his face.

"Did you say... you're begging me?" he said tauntingly.

"Nope. I don't know what you're talking about." She said and stuck her tongue out.

Zach leaned in again and tickled her until she was gasping for breath. He became aware that they were physically very close and her white tank top left a lot of skin bare. Her eyes were shining and her cheek dimpled with a smile. He moved closer but she instantly tensed, putting on a straight face and detaching herself from Zach's grip, clearing her throat. Zach watched her as she avoided his eyes, and the smile he was so encapsulated by had disappeared.

"Why do you do that?" Zach asked, exasperated.

"Do what?" she said blankly.

"I don't know, it's like the second we start having a good time you go back to being miserable and serious." he ran his fingers through his short hair frustratedly. Alana tried to get up and a pain shot through her body from the bullet wound and she couldn't help but let out a small wince. Zach looked at her, confused.

"What's wrong?" He said, concern in his eyes as she stood up slowly. She did not answer and looked him in the eye. He was surprised when she eventually took a step forward, her face more relaxed and open. She reached up and ran her fingers through his sun-kissed, blonde hair which had grown out a little more than his usual short cut. He tried to ignore the tingles he felt as her delicate fingers brushed his neck.

"Don't you think it's time for a haircut?" She asked her eyes warming up again. Zach looked surprised. It was true, he was in dire need of his short, fresh cut.

"How do you know I don't like it like this?" he said, now twirling a bit of Alana's hair in his hand. She laughed musically.

They were now standing and Zach moved closer and put his hands around her waist. To his surprise she did not move away.

"If I cut it, will you finally give in to our undeniable chemistry?" he asked teasingly raising an eyebrow. She looked at him with amused curiosity.

"Maybe just a kiss?" he pressed on further, encouraged by her good humour. She leaned in and he felt himself anticipating her kiss onto to feel a light kiss on his nose. Alana laughed again and turned away.

"Just get a haircut Zach."

Zach began to leave as well when his foot hit a metal box, hitting the latch, causing it to open. He froze as he picked up the gun inside the metal case. It was heavy, but not loaded. He examined it confused. It was a Walther P99 semi-automatic hand gun. He ran his hand over the barrel and noticed an engraving of a Tiger on the hilt. He put the gun back carefully, confused as to why the girls would have a gun in the house, and an engraved one at that. He heard Alana coming back and quietly closed the box, ruffled his hair and standing up. Alana came in and saw him standing, smiling nervously. Her eyes roamed around and stopped at the box. Damn, I hope he hasn't seen the guns, she thought, she smirked and crossed her arms.

"Your miscreants are leaving."

He nodded, not bothering to make a sarcastic remark. Alana punched him playfully and he let out a nervous chuckle, heading downstairs. By the time the boys left the girls were exhausted, each heading to sleep, minds occupied by thoughts of the day's visits.

7

The girls and Bandy were growing restless, eager to get into the action of a mission and do something, anything other than being taught what they already knew in the classroom. They had already been through this back home.

The girls each walked separately to their different classes. Vanessa skipped over to art joyfully- her favourite subject. Alana stopped by her locker to get her books before making her way to Maths. Maths, she thought, the only good thing about Maths is that he's in my class. For mission purposes only of course, she told herself. Maybe he would let something slip whilst writing down equations. She mentally kicked herself for even bringing him up and arrived at class. She sat down and noticed Zach was nowhere to be seen. His motorbike wasn't parked outside this morning either Alana made a mental note before Mrs Lopez walked in and began talking.

Clara ran to Geography as she was late for the third time this week. She quickly arrived and proceeded to the back of the classroom under the condescending glare of her teacher. They were all finally reunited in English class. They sat together and participated in the group activities Miss McGreen had arranged for the class, pitying the enthusiastic teacher with the unfortunate luck of an uncooperative class.

After having lunch with Millie's group, the girls walked down the corridors once more, weary and impatient for the unproductive day to end.

"Look what we have here..." They turned back at the familiar, grating voice seeing the two scorned girlfriends standing hands on hips.

"Oh my, I thought they didn't allow dogs at this school."

Natalie said and winked at Lania who smiled at her encouragingly.

"Come on girls, you're better than this." Clara rolled her eyes, tired of their antics.

"One would hope." She added under her breath.

"I'm sorry?" Natalie said at Clara's comment, tapping her heel onto the floor impatiently.

"Apology accepted." Clara smiled, walking away arm in arm with Vanessa and Alana.

The girls joined up in the parking lot after their last lesson only to be hit by the ghastly sight before them. Zach was leaning on Lucas' car publicly making out with Natalie. Next to them Lania was throwing herself at Lucas.

"Alana, I thought you were making progress with your target?" Clara questioned keeping her eyes locked onto Lucas. She had thought the same for herself. Alana dismissed the scene before them and continued walking with Clara. They looked over and noticed Vanessa not too far from the boys, chatting with Mason animatedly. They didn't need to be their girlfriends, just their confidants.

"You want a ride?" Alana looked at Clara who quickly agreed.

Clara said and hopped on the back of Alana's motorbike. She had come with Vanessa so there was no worry of leaving her car and allowed Vanessa more bonding time with her target.

When the girls came home they saw Beck alone watching TV. He had his equipment scattered around him and Alana jumped over the couch into the seat next to him.

"What did you get?" she said, referring to the bugs he had put on the boys. Beck brought his laptop to her and she played the feed. She listened closely whilst Clara made sandwiches. Alana signaled that she would like two and resumed listening. Beck had cut out the parts with no talking and the remaining audio was the boys talking about school and how hot Natalia had gotten now she was blonde. The girls rolled their eyes at the banal boy chat.

"I knew it wasn't real!" Clara muttered as Alana swatted her.

At one point she heard Zach's voice go low, and almost inaudible.

"Bro, you're overreacting, everyone has a gun nowadays." Lucas said brushing him off.

"No, you don't understand, how many girls have a personalised gun? It had a tiger engraving on it!"

Clara looked at Alana with disapproval at her careless weapon storage. Alana looked back guiltily and shrugged.

The conversation soon turned to normal everyday ordeals, and they stopped the audio.

"Come on, stop moping around, Bandy's coming with snacks, we're going to have a V-A-C-B-B sleepover!" Clara smiled and dragged Alana up by the arms to dance around.

"Okay, we'll do it in Vivi's room because she has the fuzziest cushions and is probably the cleanest. Regroup in 20." She added and the girls rushed upstairs.

When Bandy and Beck were ready, they came upstairs, loaded with food and saw the girls on the floor in a circle giggling. Beck shook his head, looking at the girls with a mix of disbelief and admiration. Sometimes it was hard for him to believe what they go through when they act like normal teenagers. The boys sat down and armed the girls with spoons and Beck opened up a tub of Ben and Jerry's dramatically.

"Okay so what are we doing first?" Alana moaned after consuming two thirds of the food and lying on the floor. She chucked Bandy's baseball cap to Vanessa, having passed it around for the best part of an hour, much to Bandy's annoyance. Clara then smiled and pulled out a game of Twister from under Vanessa's bed to receive groans from the surrounding food-coma victims. They played until they eventually decided to watch a movie, and relocated to the living room, armed with pillows and blankets.

"Hurry up, it's only a party!" Alana shouted at the closed bedroom doors and turned to quickly look at her reflection in the mirror. She was wearing ripped denim shorts and a white off the shoulder blouse. A thin gold necklace hung around her neck, she fiddled with it and turned it on - it was a communications device gifted to her from Clara. Her long hair tumbled down her back in light curls which had been sun-kissed with golden highlights and her tanned skin was glowed more than it did in rainy, grey London. She turned to see Vanessa coming down the stairs wearing a black shimmery shirt, shorts and ankle boots, hair pulled up in a sleek ponytail.
"Sorry I'm late." she said looking in the mirror and fiddling with her fringe.
"You look lovely. Irresistible." Alana winked. Vanessa beamed and headed to where Beck and Bandy were discussing video games in the kitchen. The boys were dressed in all-black clothing - they were not guests at the party they would be going to.
"I'm ready and it's not just a party." Clara announced and came down the stairs giving them all a lasting look at her outfit. She was wearing a short, black skirt which elongated her legs and an eye-catching gold halter-neck top.
Alana unlocked a drawer and began preparing herself for her mission. She slipped a pocket-knife up her sleeve, and some gadgets in her pocket as Bandy brought his hacking equipment. He gave Alana a nervous, giddy smile and she punched him lightly.
"You'll be fine, it's not so scary out in the field." She assured him and smiled at his wide, infectious grin. For the girls, this was another day on the job, but Bandy was facing a new, glamorous lifestyle away from the computer screens.
The DeRico's house was what would be expected of from a criminal family. The place was flooded with people- most of Beaumont High's students did not seem to care about the criminality of the host if a good party was involved. The girls

gave each other amused looks as they approached, seeing familiar faces in a completely different light. One of their Chemistry classmates was already throwing up and red and blue solo cups were littered around the grounds. The girls entered, ignoring the many curious looks from the people sober enough to realise they had walked in. They were still the 'new girls' and still earned a lot of attention around school. More than their role as covert agents desired. Vanessa spotted Mason as soon as she entered, flocked by a few girls giving the birthday boy undivided attention. As soon as he saw Vanessa he walked over to her, pulling her into a warm hug, his flock of admirers quickly searching for a new focus of admiration. Alana and Clara gave Vanessa a sneaky thumbs up and went to find drinks, preferably something that would not get them in the state most of their classmates were in.

"Okay, target spotted, I'll distract him whilst you and the boys scale the wall and get in from outside. Come back in 20 minutes and keep me updated." She said, spotting Lucas across the room. She flicked her earpiece on and headed straight to Lucas, flipping her hair over her shoulder, a flirtatious smile already playing on her lips.

Alana moved through the shadows with Beck and Bandy following closely behind. They moved silently to the side of the house where , the balcony was quite a few feet higher than expected but Alana pounced up like a cat, her fingers gripping where she could and lifting her slight frame over the balcony edge. She turned to help Bandy and Beck climb up. Bandy let out a sigh once he reached the balcony, nodding at Alana in admiration.

"We're lucky she's with the Agency otherwise she'd be in prison as a cat-burglar" Beck whispered jokingly. Alana gave him a stern look.

"Of course I wouldn't. I wouldn't get caught." She grinned wolfishly at Beck and raised an arm to break the glass of the locked door. Beck grabbed her arm just in time to give her a small leather wallet with lock-picking tools. Alana sighed dramatically, kneeling down to get to work on the door. A few seconds later the door clicked open and they walked in silently, checking if the room was empty. The coast was clear. As predicted, this was the study. A large, oak table was on the other side of the room with a computer, a small golden globe, and a telephone. Bandy rushed to the computer and Beck stood by the door, listening for approaching footsteps. Bandy's face was illuminated by the computers glow as his fingers moved across the keys with lightning speed, his eyes darting across all the corners of the computer. His mouth moved silently, as if muttering to himself. Alana looked over the balcony. They would not have much time left before someone headed around the house or to the room. She walked over to Bandy to see if she could help but he shooed her away, not breaking focus from the screen.

The party was becoming more populated by the minute and everyone was getting into the party buzz. Vanessa had indulged in a drink or two. Mason lifted her onto the kitchen counter and chuckled as she wobbled uncertainly on the counter. Think of the mission, she thought as he slowly leaned in closer. She kissed him but held back slightly. He kissed her again and this time she relented, melting into his arms. The loud music had drowned out and all she could think about was Mason. She ran her hands through his curly hair and brought them behind his neck and looked at him, smiling. A part of her worried that the smile was not only genuine, but involuntary.

"Tiger here, updates on downstairs Siren?" Alana's voice rang out in their earpieces.

"Vanessa's been making out with our little Mase and Lucas has gone to get us drinks, Siren out." Clara whispered as she saw Lucas heading towards her, handing her a drink. She took a sip of the sweet, heavily alcoholic punch and decided a sip was more than enough.

"You enjoying the party?" She said and
purposefully brushing his muscular arm. He grinned easily and put his arm around her shoulders.

"Let's just cut to the chase Clara ... will you dance with me?" He said nodding towards the makeshift dance-
floor where people had been dancing animatedly for hours.

She nodded but he then looked up like he remembered something.

"Damn it, I need to get something from the study, I'll be back in a second, wait here." he said and headed for the stairs. It took Clara around two seconds to realise what this meant.

"Wait, Lucas wait, stay here!" She called after him hurrying to catch up in her heels.

He turned but held up a finger to signal he'd be right back.

"Damn." Clara muttered and followed him up the stairs.

"Lucas I need to tell you something important." She huffed as she saw him on the landing reaching for the door. He turned the handle and Clara dropped to the floor and shouted out in mock pain. Lucas turned leaving the door open and helped Clara up.

"Are you alright?" he asked her. She looked behind him at the open door and saw Alana motioning frantically to stall him.

"Yeah, damned heels." Clara laughed nervously as he helped her up. He turned for the door again and Clara looked at Lucas panicked. Alana's eyes were wide and Clara did the only thing she could think of. Clara grabbed Lucas by the shirt and kissed him. He seemed momentarily shocked but kissed her back, pleasantly surprised. Her arms moved to the back of his neck, keeping him occupied. She stole a glance at the open door and saw that Alana and the boys had gone, but she did not break away from the kiss, she did not want to. The kiss grew deeper and she found herself to be disappointed when he broke away.

"Let me get my phone." He whispered into her neck, he retrieved his phone from the study, slipped it into his pocket and led Clara downstairs to re-join the party. She watched him with a smile plastered to her face, hiding the fear in her eyes.

Alana slipped back into the party unnoticed and began to mingle. She talked to a few of her friends from school and grabbed a drink. She took a sip but stopped before she got carried away. She looked around and spotted Mason and Vanessa in the corner snuggling and looking loved-up and Clara and Lucas both in deep flirtation. She realised she had made no head-way with her target. A boy called Jimmy from English class approached her smiling, opening his mouth to talk, but took a look behind her and turned the other direction. She was glad she did not have to talk to another obnoxious drunken teenager but she frowned, wondering why he had turned away so quickly. Her question answered itself as she felt someone approach behind her.

"Do you want to dance?"

She turned and looked straight into a familiar pair of green eyes. She opened her mouth to tell him to take a hike but stopped herself. It was a party after all.

"Yeah sure, what the heck." Alana shrugged and Zach grabbed her hand and led her to the centre of the dance floor. Alana put her arms around his neck and he brought his hands to her waist. They started moving to the music and he brought her closer until they were pressed up against each other. She could not help herself laughing as he grabbed her waist and dipped her in the middle of the dance floor. People started cheering them on as he twirled her. Alana turned back to face Zach who was chuckling at how people crowded.

"You want to go?" he asked and she nodded, he slipped his arm around her waist and led her out to the porch which was now unoccupied.

"You've got some moves you know" Zach smirked at Alana who let out a short laugh.

"You weren't so bad yourself partner."

He reached up played with a stray curl. He put his hand around the back of her neck to tilt her face up and she closed her eyes at the warmth of his hand. She opened her eyes and found him close to her face, she could smell his cologne, and feel his breathing, sending shivers down her spine and to her surprise she did not pull away.

"Zach! I got us drinks." Natalia's voice was edged with malice and urgency as she took in the scene of Alana and Zach standing close together.

"Damn." Zach muttered under his breath, still holding Alana's arm as Natalia sauntered over to him. Natalia passed him a drink, looking up at him eagerly. She leaned in to kiss him but Zach looked around instead, but Alana was nowhere to be found.

The weekend passed by quickly. The girls went out surfing and jet-skiing, taking in the last of the summer heat as the majority of their classmates recovered from hangovers. They had not seen the brothers since the party but had heard from an animated Millie that Zach and Natalia were no longer an item. Vanessa had the rare opportunity to call her parents, assuring them she was safe, and catching up- although without disclosing any mission details. They also caught up with Clara's aunt who was on a mission in Egypt. It seemed sometimes that everyone they knew were scattered around the world. Clara and Lucas were the school's gossip when the girls came into school on a Monday morning. Millie had called them the 'it' couple, although Clara hardly believed that was what they were. It was difficult to tell what Lucas was thinking but she was certain that was not it. The reconnaissance mission had not given them much hope since all Bandy found on the computer were a few emails- none of any interest. The girls had visited his apartment over the weekend and immediately started redecorating when they discovered Bandy lived amongst cardboard boxes and electronic wires.

"You're joking me, you moved in weeks ago." Alana had said, nudging a box with 'video games' scrawled on it. Bandy had shrugged, saying he practically lived with the girls at that point and decided he had no need to unpack.

The brothers had been absent for a few days now and the girls surmised that something was wrong. That was how they found themselves outside the school's reception at midnight waiting for Clara to pick the lock. It was a standard procedure, Alana keep guard, Clara deal with the entering and Vanessa prepared the tools needed. When they finally got in Clara stood by the door as Vanessa did a little rewiring on the phone. A faint hum could be heard as the device she had attached retrieved phone calls for the past week and the rustle of Alana looking through files. She finally pulled one out, opened it and burst out laughing only to be hushed by Clara and Vivi.

"Look at little Lucas!" Alana handed the file to Clara and Vanessa who frowned in shock.

"That's just a bad angle, plus it's not as if we looked great when we were 12." She shrugged and nudged Alana out of the way to find Zach's file. Alana scoffed.

"Please, we were born attractive." She winked. She slapped her hand away and drew out Zachary's file.

"N'aww who's boyfriend is an ugly duckling now?" Clara said as Alana snatched the file and burst out laughing at the picture of Zach, then stopped, a frown on her face.

"He's not my boyfriend."

"Is someone getting defensive?" Clara teased. Vanessa laughed and Alana and Clara whipped their heads towards her. She stopped laughing immediately and looked down at the phone.

"And what may you be laughing at dear friend?" Alana said slyly. As if from thin air Clara had Mason's file in her hand.

She sucked in air, gasping at the file. Clara showed Alana who reacted just as vehemently.

"What?" She said in a small voice.

"Yup, I would not want to kiss that face." Alana chortled.

"I wonder how he got rid of that mole." Clara commented.

"And he was bald!" Alana added only for Clara to slap her shoulder.

"Too far?" She said and Clara nodded exasperated.

Vanessa snatched the file but breathed out a sigh of relief when she found a baby-faced, smiling Mason, with a full head of hair and straight, grinning teeth.

"Very funny."

Once the phone calls were recorded they started to go outside back to Vanessa's car. Alana and Clara couldn't resist doing a typical spy roll on the floor. Once they were home they listened to the calls. The DeRico's parents had called in for the past three days saying the boys hadn't been well enough to come to school. There were no calls about Zach and the calls could not be traced on copies of recordings. They just had to wait for them to turn up again.

The girls lazed at home for the rest of the night playing cards in Vanessa's room whilst Bandy played pinball on his laptop. A breeze blew in through the window and the girls shuddered.

"Who left the window open? Loads of crap can come in now." Clara huffed angrily staring intently at her cards.

As if on cue a fuzzy bee flew in front of them and the girls erupted in piercing screams. Bandy instantly looked up confused and alert as the girls scrambled up. Vanessa ran for the nearest door, which was in fact her closet, Clara reached for stuff to throw at the bee which was gently swaying in the air, she reached for Bandy's laptop to throw but Bandy threw himself in front her screaming, protecting his laptop with his life. Alana reached under the bed for where she knew Vanessa kept her gun and began shooting hysterically still screaming. The bullets shattered Vanessa's vases but the offending bumblebee was still doing its rounds of the room. Beck had heard the commotion and rushed into the room with his gun ready.

"WHAT HAPPENED?! WHATS WRONG?!" He bellowed standing by Alana protectively looking around for the impending danger.

"WHAT'S WRONG? THERE WAS A DAMN BEE!" Clara screamed back.

His face froze in shock as he slowly lowered his gun, looking around at the destruction they had caused. Alana clicked the safety of the gun on and gently placed it under the bed again, guiltily.

"Of all the things you girls have dealt with, you scream like that for a bee?" He sighed and began to leave the room when he paused.

"Girls ... what have you done with Vanessa?" He said bored.

"Don't you take that condescending tone with me Becky." Alana started and leant towards the closet thumping on the door.

"The bee's gone, you may come out now." Clara said, now

adjusting her hair. Vanessa walked slowly, looking around once for the bumblebee, then straightening up, giving Beck a small smile.

When they went to school the next morning, the DeRico's car and Zach's bike were already parked in their usual places. The girls looked at each other surprised- they had almost given up on them returning. Vanessa parked her car next to Mason's who strolled over immediately to talk to her. Clara also noticed Lucas walking towards her, putting his arm around her shoulder. She tried not to look too surprised and turned her face towards him.

"Missed me already?" she teased and he let out a low chuckle, kissing her forehead. Clara's heard jumped at the unexpected show of affection as they walked to class together.

Meanwhile Alana drew her bike to the parking spot for bikes and she noticed Zach leaning on his bike.

"Zach?" She said, he face bearing a look of total confusion.

"No boots?" He replied smirking and looking at her strappy sandals and the sunglasses perched on the edge of her nose. She scowled and moved closer to him staring at his hair. She pushed them up to hold her hair back from her face.

"You cut it!" she laughed softly, reaching up to touch the short, cropped hair, making him look even more handsome. She bit her bottom lip, pulling her hand back.

"You did ask me to did you not?" his voice silky. He pulled her slightly closer, giving her a level gaze, and before she could stop him he leaned in, lips crashing onto hers. He felt her stiffen with surprised, then relax as she kissed him back, his lips moving softly against hers. Zach pulled her closer, his hand in her hair, stroking the curls gently. The whole parking lot had faded out-all Alana could think about was the feel of his lips on hers. Her eyes which had fluttered closed now shot open and she pulled away. Her eyes met his angrily. Zach looked at her and then felt her fist connect with his jaw. He drew back covering his jaw, his expression so comical Alana would have laughed if she was not so angry.

"What the hell?! You're insane!" He yelled, rubbing his jaw.

"Why the hell did you do that?" She shouted back. She grabbed her bag and walked away, not giving him a chance to reply, still thinking about the kiss. How could he just kiss her like that in the middle of the parking lot, with no warning, and so well, she thought, trying to shake it from her mind. When she reached Clara and Vanessa they stared at their angry little friend in shock until they both burst out laughing.

"Oh goodness, that was epic." Clara gushed laughing and waving over at Zach who now looked stormily at Alana's retreating figure.

The girls giggled and headed to class, already looking forward to what they day would hold for them after such an interesting start. The girls mainly passed notes to each other covertly- Alana insisted they wrote in code to maintain an air of secrecy.

Walking down the hallway after class, they ran into their hallway hauntings, Natalie and Lania.

"Saw you at the party girlies, weren't you ... cute." Lania hissed.

"You want to see cute, step closer." Alana warned Lania who had stepped closer to Clara threateningly. Lania smirked menacingly and looked Clara in the eyes.

"You're wasting my time , say what you want and say it fast." Clara said, bored.

"I thought I told you to stay away from our guys." Natalie quipped in and moved in front of Alana now. Alana looked at her amused.

"I saw you kiss him." She growled and Alana rolled her eyes.

"Kissing who? oh... him?" She motioned to Zach who was walking by. She grabbed him by his jacket and pulled him down to her, kissing him on the lips and letting him go, looking back at a furious Natalie.

"Girls, let's calm down..." he started but was interrupted.

Natalie raised her hand to slap Alana but Clara caught her wrist and twisted it behind her back. Lania moved closer reaching for Clara's hair and Alana's resolve cracked as she punched her. Lania staggered back, her nose gushing blood as she screamed profanities at Alana. A group of people had assembled now and Alana looked up at Zach guiltily.

"Believe it or not, I didn't want to do that." She said to a dumbfounded Zach, as Clara grabbed her by the arm and pushed through the crowds to get out of there.

They left school immediately and headed home where they recapped the events at home to Beck and Bandy who found the cat fight more than amusing. Clara went up to her room to go on Facebook and check the updates for upcoming parties. There were five, but she decided she and the girls would only attend about two of them which she deemed 'suitable for the mission'. Vanessa stayed downstairs to make cupcakes with Bandy as Alana went to her room to do a Zumba fitness video. Alana was humming to the music, dancing energetically and heard her balcony door slide open.

"Wrong room." She said over her shoulder, her eyes still glued to the TV.

"Thanks." A low voice chuckled and she continued with her fitness video.

Clara did not hear the balcony door slide open and was only alert when she felt a hand on her shoulder. She ripped off her headphones, grabbed her attackers hand and kneed him so he fell on the floor on his back. He groaned as he slammed into the floor. Clara looked at him wide eyed and her hands flew to her mouth.

"Lucas?!"

8

"Yeah, that's me." Lucas grunted lying flat on the floor.

"Oh gosh, I'm so, so sorry." Clara said quickly helping him up onto the bed.

"Where the hell did you learn that?" He demanded, sitting up on the bed and cocking his head to the side questioningly.

"My aunt gave me a few lessons on self-defence." She lied convincingly, shrugging her shoulders.

"Oh okay." He brushed off before getting up to meet Clara who was on her feet pacing up and down the room.

"So, word's going around that we're now an item." He said, grinning at her boyishly.

"Didn't they ever tell you not to listen to rumours?" She sat next to him, keeping a slight, playful distance.

"Certain rumours carry some truth you know."

The moment was shattered by a loud banging on the wall. Clara listened to the noise only to realise it was Alana, morse-coding through the wall. She stood still decoding the tapping patterns Alana was sending her.

Hey, forgot to tell you but Lucas is coming to your balcony.

Clara sighed and knocked back on the wall.

No kidding. Now leave me alone.

She tapped back briskly.

"HEY!" She heard Alana shout through the wall and rolled her eyes turning back to see Lucas sitting on the bed bewildered.

"Um, Alana's nailing some artwork..." She smiled innocently, joining him on the bed.

"Can I ask you a question?" She said and looked into his deep blue eyes. Lucas just smiled and nodded.

"How dull was your life before we moved to L.A?" Clara laughed and pushed him onto his back on the bed.

"Well it was rather dull but also stress-free."

"Hey, what's that supposed to mean?" She poked him playfully in the ribs.

"Well, I speak for Mason, Zach and myself when I say you girls are each frying up our brains." He laughed and leaned up to kiss her.

"Lucas, why have you and the guys been missing school so much?" She briskly broke off the kiss, thinking of the mission.

He stiffened and got up.

"In fact, why do you always miss school?" Clara pressed further.

"I don't see how that's any of your business." Lucas said coldly avoiding eye contact.

"It's an easy question." Clara stood up.

"Why should I tell you? It's not like you're my girlfriend or anything." They stared at each other angrily before he walked to the balcony exited the way he entered.

"Asshole." Clara muttered, grabbing a magazine and lying on her bed.

"Clara! Did you eat the Ben & Jerry's ice cream?!" Alana marched in a while later into Clara's room furiously.

"No of course not, it rots your teeth!" Clara snapped back quickly before Alana could attack her.

"Hmm...Okay." Alana replied, not convinced checking all of Clara's cupboards and drawers. "Oh, where's lover boy gone?" She perked her head up as she realised Lucas was nowhere to be seen.

"Yeah he left a half hour ago" Clara spat out and carried on reading her Vogue magazines.

"I take it your meeting didn't go according to plan." Alana softened and sat down next to her friend.

"Yeah no kidding." Clara replied and fell back onto the bed dragging Alana with her until they were both lying on the bed. Alana yelled out for Vanessa to join with snacks and soon the girls were huddled on Clara's bed.

"Okay, boy debrief, Clara you start." Vanessa said filing her nails. Clara blushed delicately.

"Well Brad is sweet-" She joked, only to be cut off by Alana throwing popcorn on her. Clara grinned.

"Oh you mean Lucas?! Yeah well, he has nice moments..." She paused gazing wistfully into the distance.

"But I don't want to get too close. Plus he turns into a moody bitch every time I mention something serious." She shrugged and stole a handful of popcorn from Alana who gave her a death stare.

"Well what about you and our dear Zachary?" she smirked at Alana's frown.

"Ignored him since he got his slimy frog lips on me. He's an ugly, self-absorbed narcissistic-"

"Oh please do NOT tell me you did not enjoy that kiss, and you so don't think he's ugly." Clara interrupted prodding Alana who blushed slightly and gave her a goofy smile.

"Fine, he's not a horrible kisser, he's just not my type." She said indignantly.

"Gorgeous, smart and charming is not your type." Clara rolled her eyes.

"Your go Vivi" Alana said rolling around on the floor.

Vanessa raised her hands to her now red cheeks and smiled a little.

"Mason's... great, but it's always about me, I can't get any information out of him either. We've been out for drinks a few times but still nothing."

The girls thought hard about their next strategy but Beck came in.

"Bandy's leaving, you might want to say bye." He said looking disheartened.

"Why? We'll see him tomorrow." Alana said from underneath her bed looking for Clara's secret stash of chocolate.

"Actually, he's being transferred, you probably won't see him again anytime soon." Beck said and the girls gasped and ran downstairs. Bandy was by the door with his arms cross around his laptop. Vanessa sniffled as she ran to hug Bandy.

"I'm sorry you have to leave." She muffled into his shoulder.

"Ah don't worry guys, you'll see me again soon, just hit me up after your mission. Just about two more months left." he smiled and Clara and Alana hugged him tightly.

"Hey I got you guys a little something each, open them when I'm gone." He smirked and winked passing each of them a parcel.

"Couldn't it have been a little bigger?" Clara said, shaking her parcel and Alana flicked her head.

"I was joking!" Clara whined and kissed Bandy on the cheek, hugging him tightly.

"Thank you." She smiled warmly and the girls all said their thank you's.

"I'll miss you girls. Goodbye." and with one teary last hug for the girls and a friendly man-hug to Beck, he left.

The girls were noticeably glum about Bandy's departure and decided to open the presents. There was a letter attached to each of them. One was a copy of some coding which Beck typed into his laptop. It turned out to be the DeRico's system. But Bandy had managed to highlight something. It was clear what he had highlighted, there was another way to get a piece of vital information. They had to tail Zach to his next meeting, evidently according to the phone calls. Zach had arranged to meet up with some others of the DeRico clan on Friday night.

"Hmm, if only we had someone to go out with him early Friday night so we could tail him after..." Vanessa said smiling deviously.

"Yeah, okay guys, we need to think hard about this." Alana said, her face focused on thinking.

"She means you moron." Clara said and Alana laughed dryly.

"Me? I'd end up strangling him."

"Nope, starting tomorrow will have a full attitude makeover. You will get a date on Friday if it's the last thing you do." Clara said firmly.

"Okay okay if it's for the mission, go for it." she held her hands up in surrender. The girls opened the next letter that

Bandy got them.

Hey my little party crashers.
I just want to say that the time I spent with you girls (and Beck) was one of the most fun missions ever. I really hope you do well and get more out of the mission than just a checked box.
I got you guys a little something I hope should be useful in the future. Please think of me every time you see a male model... or a laptop.
Just be careful, know who to trust and don't get in too deep.
I hope to see you soon, if you're ever in California again.
Lots of Love
Bandy xoxo

The girls smiled softly and Beck hugged them.
"Well we might as well look at the last one." Vanessa said and she opened the last envelope.
It had a stack of printed photos of the girls, Beck and Bandy. There were some from their first days at schools, messing around at home, photos of them during missions and at parties. The girls were surprised he had taken the photos. They opened Clara's package first. It was a small compatible makeup kit.
"Why would he get me just make-up?" Clara said confused, opening it up to admire the pretty shades of lip gloss and eye-shadows.
"Are you, or are you not a spy?" Alana said and laughed at Clara's expression.
She took the makeup kit and looked around, finding a small, discreet button. A little blue light illuminated the makeup kit. It came from the mirror and made some numbers appear into the cubes of lipgloss and eyeshadows. Alana pressed in Clara's year of birth and the makeup kit flattened out completely.
"Ohh it's your very own comms unit." Vanessa said admiringly.
"Wow, how did you know it was like that?" Clara asked Alana
"I saw something like it developing in the labs back at the

Agency." Alana shrugged.

Vanessa's gift was a small notepad that could record phone conversations from up to 200 metres away.

Alana's present was a small Victorinox Swiss army card. It had all the things a Swiss army knife would have but in a tiny compatible card that she could keep in her purse.

She immediately fawned over it pulling gleaming knife after knife out of it. The girls smiled, suddenly feeling weary after their long day so Beck brought them cushions and blankets and they snuggled up on the sofa to watch a marathon of 90's chick flicks.

"Freddie ... Prince ... Junior ... is ... hot..." Clara mumbled as she fell asleep as the others did, snuggled up on the couch with the flickering lights of the television lulling them to sleep.

'Alana's makeover, come NOW.' The message popped up on Vanessa's phone. She looked over her coffee mug at her phone and Mason let out a chuckle, noticing the message. They had been talking for hours over coffee, sitting outside in the sun.

"Good luck with Alana, she threw a glass of water at me when she lost monopoly. That glass hurt." He shuddered at the memory. Vanessa's phone buzzed again.

'Oh and bring Curly with you too, yes Mason, we know you're reading this.'

Vanessa laughed at Mason's shocked expression and she signalled for the bill.

"We're home!" Vanessa called out as she and Mason ran up the stairs to Clara's room where Alana was tied to a chair by a collection of Clara's belts.

"Hey, isn't this mine?" Mason said inspecting one of the belt around Alana's arms.

"Yeah you left it here a few days ago." Clara wiggled her eyebrows suggestively and Vanessa blushed at the implication.

"Ooh, that's why my pants felt loose after swimming." Mason chuckled and Clara slapped him round the head playfully. They had grown accustomed to having Mason around as an extension of their cosy little family.

"Right, Alana, I shall release you, if you promise not to harm any of us." Clara said and Alana reluctantly nodded.

"Okay , we'll start with make-up , then hair, clothes, then flirting. VANESSA GET MY KIT!" Clara said and Vanessa came back with three well-stocked make-up cases.

Clara babbled about how Alana should act, speak, eat, look, whilst Alana looked at the others desperate for help. Mason and Vanessa shrugged, amused at Alana's helplessness. Mason mentioned Alana did not have to put much effort in with Zach but Clara was having too much fun, and decided to keep that fact to herself.

"Fine, let us begin." Alana said and braced herself.

Alana, Clara and Vanessa all took Clara's perky yellow Cooper to school. Clara admired her work as Alana stepped out. The jacket and boots were replaced by a lace, white summer dress. Her wild curls had been tamed into gentle waves and everything about her exuded 'approachability' as Clara liked to call it. She smiled sweetly, her cheeks dimpled and approached Zach who was parking his bike. He turned at the sound of heels clicking on the ground and was astonished as he realised who was now leaning on his bike. He let out a low whistle.

"Seems the tiger's been tamed." His eyes roamed over her appreciatively, not noticing how she momentarily froze at the use of her codename.

"My eyes are up here." She replied harshly then remembered Clara's advice, and gave him a smile instead.

"How have you been Zach?" She batted her eyelashes.

Perhaps a bit too much, she thought when she noticed Zach holding back a laugh. Zachary smirked and leaned over so he was almost nose to nose with her.

"Alright, what do you want?" He said. She widened her eyes in innocent surprise.

"I really have no idea what you are talking about Zach, sweetie." She gave him a charming smile. Zach raised an eyebrow and Alana sighed.

"I need a date." She said and he burst out laughing.

"Don't you mean you WANT a date?"

"Yes Zach I REALLY want a date. So what do you say?" Alana grinned, brushing his arm. He watched her movements curiously, until she sighed and dropped her arm, smiling up at him expectantly.

"After what you did to my pretty face? You'll need to try a bit harder, I do like the look though, we can work with that." At that moment a petite blonde waltzed up to him and slipped her arm through his.

"Zachary, we have French" She practically hung onto him. Alana snorted Zach raised an eyebrow.

"Absolutely Bianca." he said, keeping his eyes locked onto Alana's.

"You mean Beth..." she glared at him.

"Of course I did." Zach replied and the Beth giggled, gazing up at him.

Alana muttered silently under her breath. Lucas, Mason, Clara and Vanessa joined them. Clara gave her a thumbs up.

"Very nice, very smooth." She joked. Alana sighed and headed to class. Lucas lingered back with Clara, giving her a shy smile.

"You're forgiven if you carry my books to classes." Clara eventually said and he grabbed her school stuff holding out his arm for her to hold onto. She obliged with a smile as he led her to class.

"Move." Alana said to the blonde in her seat.

"And why should I?" She replied back haughtily, turned towards Zach who watched the exchange amused. Alana raised her eyebrows at Zach who gave the girl a look and jerked his head. The girl hugged indignantly.

"You're such an asshole" Alana said, putting her bag down on the desk next to Zach.

"Did you want to sit next to me that bad?"

She sat down and began doodling on her page. Lucas leaned over to see what she was drawing.

"That's pretty good, what is it?" he said and Zach laughed.

"It's Zachary... dead." Alana replied and Zach stopped laughing. Clara scribbled a note and slipped it down Zach's collar.

He squirmed as it fell down his shirt.

"Couldn't you find another way?" he hissed and managed to get the scrunched up ball of paper out. She shrugged and applied her lipgloss.

'Are you going to ask her out or you wanna wait for someone else to?'

Zach looked back and shrugged. He motioned towards Alana and mimed being strangled. Clara snorted with laughter.

"Risk it." She whispered.

He shrugged and smirked cockily. He put his arm around Alana's bare shoulders. She looked slightly shocked but did not move away.

"Alana wou-"

"Nope."

"No? You didn't even le-"

"I am trying to study." she said and continued doodling.

Zach raised an eyebrow and leaned in to whisper in her ear.

"So how about that date? Friday? Cool, I'll pick you up at 7:30." He said before she had time to interrupt him again.

"Sure." She said, her attention on her paper. He looked taken aback.

"Sure?" he repeated incredulously. She turned to face him, her brown eyes gleaming she twirled a strand of hair in between her fingers and gave Zach a small dimpled smile.

"Sure." He smiled back. It wasn't his usual arrogant smirk, it was a genuine smile.

"Perfect, I'll find out why you needed this date."

"I'm trained not to talk."

"So where are you going again?" Vanessa said as she fastened a bug on the strap of Alana's dress.

"He didn't say, he just told me to dress up." She grumbled as Clara applied her make-up.

"Ow, that was my eye."

"It is called *eye*-liner."

"Why are we doing this all over again, I already got the date, we'll track him then BAM, we'll be done." Alana whined as Vanessa began braiding her hair.

"Personal reasons. Ok you're ready." Clara winked at Vanessa and she brought Alana to the mirror.

Her hair was in a long French braid, her make-up perfectly applied. She wore an emerald green dress with cross cross straps on her back. Under it were her combat clothes ready to appear after she ditched the dress to track Zachary. She widened her eyes at the sophisticated transformation in the hallway mirror. The doorbell rang and Alana went downstairs, a little too eagerly she noticed. She opened the door to see Zach standing there; wearing a black shirt and dark jeans. He gave Alana a once over and smirked at her, leaning in to give her a gentle kiss on the cheek. She rolled her eyes but could not help a smile, when suddenly Mason and Lucas popped out from either side of the door. Reflexively, she punched Mason in the stomach and he doubled over.

"Boo!" Lucas said happily not noticing his brother wheezing for breath.

"I brought entertainment for the girls." Zachary said, raising an eyebrow at Mason.

"Sure, that should be fun." Alana said monotonously, wondering how they were going to track one criminal if they were being 'entertained' by two others. The boys headed inside to surprise the girls and Zach and Alana left quietly to enjoy their date.

Zach and Alana arrived at a busy restaurant. It was one of the best and newest restaurants in LA and overlooked the Hollywood sign. The night air was cool and there was a queue of glamorously dressed people. Zach held out his arm as they dismounted the motorbike. Alana gave him a dimpled smile as he held out his arm and she looped hers through his. He led her past the queue and straight to the entrance where the security guard gave him a swift nod as he entered. The restaurant was dim, lit by a crystal chandelier hanging above the guests. The twinkle of wine glasses and faint murmur of secret conversations could be heard over the tinkling piano music from the bar. A tall, smartly dressed waitress led them to a table by a large window which gave them the best view.

"Can I get you anything to drink sir?" The waitress asked, her eyes wandering over Zach. He looked up and checked her name tag 'Rebecca'.

"No thank you Rebecca, my girlfriend and I will need a minute." And she sauntered off.

Alana turned to Zach, raising an eyebrow. "Girlfriend?!"

"I didn't happen to like how she was eyeing me up."

Alana rolled her eyes before he spoke again.

"Oh and I like annoying you too."

She folded her napkin over her legs delicately, trying to calm her nerves. She would have gladly taken a fist fight, or a high speed chase over this date. Alana took a sip of water, feeling herself blush under Zach's intense gaze.

The first half an hour was pleasant; they talked about the usual things in addition to the constant, playful teasing. Their hands were inches away from each other and Alana found herself blushing more than once, but something was off.

"You know, I'm enjoying this more than I should b-"

"Zach. Look at me and keep talking normally." Alana cut Zach off, her expression serious. He looked at her confused but did as he was told, eyes meeting hers in confusion.

Alana quickly fiddled with her phone and brushed her hair back with her hand, turning on her comms device.

"So.. what's wrong?" He said, his face stretched into a fake smile, eyes looking around without changing his overall demeanour. She looked up at him, her light brown eyes wide and worried. She pressed her lips together and quickly glanced around.

"Do you know anyone who would want to hurt you Zachary?" She put her hand over his and smiled flirtatiously so to outsiders they would look like a normal couple. Zach pondered over this for a moment and smiled cheekily.

"Yeah quite a few."

"Good to know. We've been followed, we've got to get out of here, and quickly, they're armed."

"They will kill us if they knew we were having a pool party without them." Mason said and shuddered at the mental image of Alana angry. Clara, Lucas, Mason and Vanessa were in the pool, it was night but the pool lights were on and they had been playing around for the best part of an hour. Clara was on Lucas' shoulders and was wrestling Vanessa who was on Mason's. Lucas dived under dragging Clara with him and she shrieked with laughter. She grabbed fistfuls of his hair and dragged him up so he was facing her. His arms were around her waist and he drew her to him and she drew in a breath at how close they were. With a moment of insanity she brought her hands to the back of his neck and kissed him passionately. Suddenly she jumped up and pushed Lucas down under the water shoving down hard on his shoulders. He jumped right back up and shook out his hair looking at her confused.

"And that's what you get for wetting my hair." Clara said and dived under the water to swim away.

Lucas shook his head in amazement and wolf whistled as Clara got out of the pool. Vanessa was in an inflatable pink ring that Mason was leaning on it as they talked. Clara walked towards her clothes and noticed she had a new message on her phone. It was from Alana, her forehead creased in confusion, surely her date couldn't be that bad, she thought and opened the message. It was blank. A blank message for the girls meant there was trouble. Clara panicked and she sat down as she set up her phone to check the latest GPS point of Alana's phone.

"Vanessa can you help me do my nails on my right hand? I'm right handed." Clara smiled sweetly and Vanessa immediately got the hint, Clara could paint her nails with her toes, she never needed any help.

"What's wrong?" she said seriously as she reached for the nail polish.

"Blank message from Alana." Clara said and wiggled her fingers at Lucas in a wave. Clara looked down at her phone and cursed.

"Damn! She turned off her phone. How are we supposed to find her now?! She's probably left the last location ages ago, and we've missed the beeps on our ear pieces." she fumed mentally cursing the earpieces' inability to work underwater. She'd bring that up with the Agency technicians the minute she got back.

"That girl attracts trouble all the time." Vanessa assured, they both knew that Alana and Zach together would be safe. They quickly grabbed their towels, drying off, getting ready to track them.

- - - -

"Meet me in the bathrooms." Alana whispered to Zach as she left her seat.

"Darling... it's only our first date." He joked as she slapped his head on her way past him. He waited a few moments and walked over to the bathrooms. He spotted two burly men and a short stocky woman in dark clothing nearby and assumed they must be who had followed them.

How had Alana noticed them when I failed to, he thought and swore under his breath as the stocky woman noticed him looking at them and walking away. They briskly walked towards Zach and he sped up until he reached Alana.

"They're coming." He said and they heard footsteps behind them and Zach grabbed Alana by the hand and brought her into a bathroom, he locked the door and put a finger to her lips signalling her to be quiet. She stared into his eyes and felt a flushed as she realised she was pressed up against his body. He stroked her cheek and smirked when they heard a bang against the door and they turned their heads towards the door.

"Zach- the window." Alana said as Zach flipped his head to a small window in the wall. It was small enough to fit Alana's tiny frame but it was too small to fit Zach through. He raised his leg and with powerful kick the glass was shattered. He motioned Alana to come but she made no move to leave.

"What about you?" She said and he shook his head.

"They want me, you go and I'll catch up." He smiled but Alana shook her head.

"It's only 2 against 3, they won't know what hit them." She said, determined, as the door crashed down.

Instantly she and Zachary launched into action. Zach went for the two men and Alana attacked the shorter woman. She was short but she was extremely strong. The women advanced on Alana, baring her teeth at the teenager. She blocked the worst of Alana's roundhouse and punched into her gut. Alana groaned in pain but managed to knee the woman in her stomach twice and shoved her off. Her attacker brought out a gun but before she could get a good grip Alana kicked her wrist and the gun flew out of her hand, skidding into the corner. The woman sent a kick to Alana's back but Alana dodged it, elbowing her in the chin. The woman lunged forward and grabbed a fistful of Alana's hair and brought her back to smash her head into the tiled wall. Alana felt a wetness as her nose began to bleed onto the tiles.

"Oh. You. Wanna. Fight. Dirty." Alana gasped as she struggled to stop her head smashing into the cold tiles again. She quickly turned so she was facing the woman, spat in her eye and head-butted her face. She could hear the sickening crunch of her attacker's nose breaking. She noticed the woman had a scar from her ear to her jaw. Alana removed her hand from the woman's grasp and punched her hard in the side of her head. The woman retaliated by kneeing her in the ribs and she winced at the pain.

"You better not have broken anything." Alana wheezed and shoved the woman off her.

She feigned a punch but kicked her instead, hitting her square in the chest, sending her crashing into a sink. She hit her head with a loud clang and dropped to the floor in an unconscious heap. Alana sighed, spitting out blood and ran over to Zach. The smallest of the two men was unconscious and he was struggling to get rid of the other man's gun. Alana rolled her eyes and snuck behind the larger man and elbowed a pressure point in his back. He was big that it did little damage but it distracted him enough to shift his position which allowed Zach to twist his arm and slam down on it. The attacker shouted out in pain as his arm broke and Zach pushed him into an empty stall. Alana nodded at Zach who was out of breath, she went round and collected the guns and went over to Zach who was dealing with one of them who had woken up. The larger man had his head in the toilet bowl, gurgling, with Zach's hand around his throat.

"Who sent you here." Zach said dangerously and Alana shivered involuntarily at how cold his voice was. He grunted in reply but it was clear he wouldn't speak.

"He won't talk, he never will." Alana said and Zachary caught the meaning of it. Instead of continuing the interrogation he ripped off the man's right arm sleeve to reveal a tattoo of a red viper curled around a knife. Alana bit her lip, she learnt about the Vipers about a year back, they were a dangerous criminal organisation but there was something else about them that she just couldn't remember at that moment. She wondered why they would be involved with Zach at all.

"Damn it." Zach cursed and turned to Alana. He definitely knew why they were after him, she thought.

"Wait, where did you learn to fight like that?" he looked around confused as if all the events suddenly dawned on him.

She repeated the well-rehearsed lie.

"Clara's aunt is a martial arts instructor, I've been learning since I was young." Zach still looked unconvinced.

"Well how did you notice them following us since the car?" he said and she shrugged.

"My dad always taught me to look out for things, plus you were concentrated on driving."

"Where are you parents now?" Zach asked and noticed a flash of emotion in her eyes.

"Dead." She said without missing a beat. He crossed the room in two quick strides and pulled her towards him in a hug. She rested her head on his shoulder and sighed into him, breathing in his intoxicating scent and he kissed the top of her head.

"You were great. Like, really incredible." She pulled away as he smirked at her.

"You weren't terrible yourself." She winked at him.

He looked around and let out an awkward laugh.

"Well... this isn't the best date ever is it?" He said and she laughed, reaching for his hand.

"On the contrary, it's just my type of date." She smiled and stood on her tiptoes to kiss his cheek.

His green eyes twinkled and he tugged her golden brown braid playfully.

"Who were they Zach?" Alana said, her voice was soft, enticing him to open up.

He sighed. "It's a long story." He left it at that.

"Let's take you home before they wake up." He said and drew out his phone, sent a text and headed towards the door.

They stepped out of the car when they arrived at Alana's house.

"Sorry about the sucky date Alana."

"Trust me, it's the only date I didn't die of boredom at." and he chuckled. When they reached the door he paused before softly kissing her cheek. She tensed slightly but gave him a small smile before opening the door. Mason and Lucas were already tumbling out of the door, still in their swimming trunks. The girls looked at Alana shocked but Alana nodded once. Everything was okay for now, she conveyed the message with her eyes.

"Hey, nice abs!" Alana said to Lucas and he smirked proudly. She stopped walking as realisation washed over her.

"Wait... YOU GUYS HAD A POOL PARTY WITHOUT

ME?!" She yelled glaring at Clara, Vanessa, Mason and Lucas accusingly.

Mason and Lucas glanced at each other quickly. They lunged for Alana, lifted her on their shoulders and ran towards the pool. They then jumped in with a screaming Alana. When she surfaced she burst into a torrent of threats and aggressive language. Zach covered Vanessa's ears, protecting her from the foul language.

As soon as the boys had left the house, Clara and Vanessa ran towards the garage for a decoy car to follow Zach, they would have to change cars later to keep him off their scent but they had it all arranged. Alana stayed behind, researching the Viper's role in the deal with Beck and resting after the unexpected energy required on her date. After Zach dropped off the boys he drove off to the suburbs of Los Angeles and stopped at a dark abandoned warehouse. Clara and Vanessa had ditched the car a while back in favour of stealthily running after his car, he drove slow to not attract attention which worked well for the girls. They stayed near the entrance of the warehouse, listening devices on to pick up sounds easier and they heard another pair of footsteps.

"You came Rufus." Said a snarling voice. Zachary laughed harshly taking on a completely new tone.

"Wouldn't miss it for the world. Now stop wasting time DeRico, what do you want?" He said coolly.

After the girls heard all they needed to, they called Alana.

"Hey, we got a deal Zachary knows about, may be useful, you wanna gate-crash? It's next week." Vanessa chirped once they were safely in another decoy car.

"Wouldn't miss it for the world." Alana said. Vanessa and Clara could hear Beck in the background telling the girls to be careful. They could hear Alana teasing Beck for being such a grandmother.

"Goodnight Beck, 'night Alana, we'll see you at home." Vanessa said and they hung up, eager to get home to sleep.

9

The doorbell rang and Alana slumped down the stairs.

"Who the hell would ring at this time? It's like 8 o' clock in the morning." Clara grumbled, still in her pyjamas. The girls were the only ones at home, Beck had already gone to work.

Alana snorted and went to open the door in a large plaid shirt. Clara's hair was immaculately straight and her purple silk pyjamas shimmered as she walked down the stairs. Vanessa also came in her pink fluffy pyjamas, hair twisted into a messy bun.

Alana opened the door to reveal Zachary, Lucas and Mason. Clara and Vanessa shrieked to run to their rooms and change into something decent whilst Alana crossed her arms and looked at them furiously.

"Would you care to explain why you woke me up?" She said, staring each of them in the eyes angrily.

"You might want to put some clothes on." Zach said, glancing at her bare legs, receiving a withering look in response.

"Surprise!" Mason shouts eagerly stepping forward to enter the house.

"Uh-uh, lover boy." Alana blocked his way.

"So Alana are you going to let us in?" Zach grinned.

Alana showed the boys in, Vanessa came down the stairs and greeted the boys with a hug having changed into a pink summer dress.

"We'll wait until Clara comes down to tell you the news." Zach grinned, plodding down onto the sofa.

"I'll go get her." Lucas realised that if it was Clara they were waiting for, it would be a while.

"So what do we owe this pleasure to?" Clara muttered, unamused by the early wake-up call.

Lucas smiled at her. "Well we thought to spend the day with you guys, maybe the beach or something, but this morning Zach had a sudden thought which turned into a kick-ass plan." He said looking between the girls excitedly.

"So, Zach thought that we should go to..." Mason carried on slowly.

"VEGAS! For the weekend." Zach shouted and the boys grinned eagerly, awaiting a response.

Clara and Alana looked at one another and high fived each other while Vanessa raised an eyebrow, considering their options.

"You have 10 minutes to pack your bags." Zach said and helped Alana up off her chair.

"Consider it done!" Alana ruffled Zach's hair and proceeded to go upstairs following Vanessa.

"Wait a second, did you say 10 minutes?" Clara stood in the kitchen in shock.

"I will be needing at least 1 hour and even that would be working up a miracle."

Alana ran downstairs and flung her bag at Zach, smiling and ready to go.

"In the boot boys, thank you." Clara kissed Lucas on the cheek and winked at Zach.

"Okay, so Mason and Vanessa are going in the other car, you two can either come with Clara and I or go with them. Your choice." Lucas positioned himself in Clara's yellow Mini Cooper and started.

"And before you ask, no, you cannot bring your motorbikes."

Zach and Alana sighed and hopped in the back of Clara's car, aware of the excruciatingly slow driving they would be experiencing if they went with Mason.

"My bets on 20." Zach watched Mason check his mirrors and

put his seatbelt on.

"Nah, I say half an hour, you're on." Lucas slapped Zach's hand, revved up the car and sped away.

They were soon at the hangar waiting to board the jet. Clara and Alana boarded the plane awaiting Vanessa and Mason, trying not to act too surprised at the private jet set-up. It hardly seemed a surprise from a crime family. They took their places on the plush, leather seats and ordered a couple of drinks whilst Zach and Lucas were anticipating Mason's return in order to claim their money. Mason and Vanessa arrived only 15 minutes later and Lucas handed Zach 10 dollars reluctantly. Only a few minutes on the plane and their conversation was accompanied by Alana's deep breathing as she slept, her head resting on Zach's shoulder.

"Right Zach, you have scored 50 points which means you are attracted to bad boys." Clara said and looked up from her magazine quiz laughing to see Vanessa and Mason confused.

"I wish I could say I was more surprised." Zach shrugged.

Alana woke up with a jolt at Zach's voice but fell back to sleep immediately, as the plane was setting off.

"Wow, this is fancy." Vanessa giggled, sliding into the gleaming black limousine waiting for them once their plane landed.

They arrived shortly at the dazzling Vegas 5 star hotel and were greeted by a short man with brown hair and a small, neat moustache at the lobby. He welcomed each of them, especially the relentless Alana and Clara who were dying to get to their rooms. Alana was in her normal bad mood after waking from a nap which did nothing to help Clara's restlessness.

"Zach you're slouching." Clara quipped.

"Take a hike, Mom."

The boys had booked out the penthouse suite with separate rooms for each of them. Vanessa, Alana and Clara's rooms were all next to each other and the boys' on the other side of the suite with a vast, luxury sitting room between them, decked out in stylish black couches, gleaming crystal chandeliers and dark grey marble floors. Vanessa glanced at the girls, raising an eyebrow at the girls appreciatively.

Alana and Clara entered the bathroom to simmer in the jacuzzi and were greeted by splashes of water, much to their surprise, from Vanessa and the boys. They held themselves together for a brief moment of time before running to the kitchen and filling up two jugs of ice cold water. They quickly returned with a thirst for vengeance only to find Vanessa in the tub with the boys.
"We're so sorry for this Vivi, but you asked for it by joining them." Clara grinned.
The chaos began as Clara and Alana poured the ice cold water on Zach, Lucas and Mason but some managed to splash onto Vanessa too. They retaliated with the water from the jacuzzi which was, to their disadvantage, warm and pleasant. They saw that this had no effect on them and soon got out. A water fight had started. Vanessa and the boys against Clara and Alana. Alana grabbed Clara's hand and dragged her to one of the other bathroom. They gathered glasses of water and started stacking them up. Lucas opened the door and the girls threw all their ammunition at him. Zach pounced in and Clara had no choice but to use the shower head. She grabbed it and instructed Alana to turn on the tap. The boys ran out and they followed after them leaving the tap on. Arriving into the kitchen Clara slid on the wet floor and dragged Alana down with her. They were soon both on the floor and unarmed, joined by Mason who glided to a heavy fall on the floor.
"Vanessa help me up!" He shouted. Vanessa entered the room but he dragged her down as she tried to help him up. Lucas and Zach entered with two water guns. "What where did you get those?" Clara shouted out from the floor.
"From Alana's bag!" Zach laughed menacingly.
"Alana? Why the hell did you bring water guns?!"
"Precisely for situations like this."

Zach, Lucas and Mason loitered at the entrance to the casino, waiting for the girls to arrive, the noise and bustle of the casino calling them. They wasted no time in changing their cash into chips. Smartly dressed, they caught the attention of many attractive girls, all in formal attire. Waitresses walked around serving glasses of champagne and light refreshments.

The casino itself appeared infinite. The carpet was a red with patterns on it mimicking the patterns on a deck of cards, with large crystal chandeliers gleaming overhead. The room was filled with many different tables, voices clamouring over the sound of money being lost.

Zach already noticed those who would lose it all tonight, putting their car keys on the table and slowly increasing the stakes until their house was up for grabs. But of course the boys knew better as they had been here many times before. Drunken women shrieking in the corner were to be heard as the security slowly made their way past the boys. Security. This place was packed with body guards, but that didn't matter this time because the boys already opted out on cheating in the presence of the girls.

"Oh boys, I sense that we are going to wreak havoc in this place." Lucas cracked his knuckles. Zach patted his back smiling as he, with his other hand, took a drink from one of the very attractive waitresses in a dashing black dress.

Mason turned around, eyes widening at the sight of the girls approaching. Vanessa wore a rose pink dress, the silk tight on her curves, but flattering, cut just above the knee. Her hair was curled, bouncing as she walked towards them, smiling with perfectly pink lips.

Alana wore a simple dark red halter dress showing her tanned arms and legs. Her unruly curls had been tamed and pulled back into a sleek pony tail, her eyes dark and enticing.

Beside her, Clara was wearing a elegant, strapless black dress. She wore a small silver bracelet and matching necklace, which twinkled charmingly in the chandelier light.

Lucas let out a low whistle and held his arm out for Clara; she took it gratefully and smiled at him.

"You look beautiful." He looked into her eyes and planted a kiss onto her lips. She looked at him playfully, intrigued by his affection.

"Okay well, let's get this party started!" Zach shouted and picked up Alana, twirling her around as she squealed at him to let her go.

" Wanna partner up with me cowboy?" Clara winked at Zach.

"Yee-haw!" Zach grabbed Clara's hand.

"If it's alright with you bro?" Zach asked Lucas.

Lucas smiled and laughed.

"Please get rid of her. "

"Absolutely, but um I'm leaving you this one right here." With his other hand Zach grabbed Alana and motioned her towards Lucas.

"Where to first?" Mason chuckled as the other four left. Vanessa waggled her finger out and stopped.

"That way, follow the finger."

"Very well." Mason took her hand and started walking towards the bar. They stopped at a machine and tried their luck with a few silver coins.

"Try this one." Vanessa motioned towards the end machine laughing.

Mason entered the coin, pulled the lever. The machine processed it and suddenly released dozens of silver coins.

"We won, we won!" Mason shouted and hugged Vanessa.

"It's only going to go uphill from here!" Vanessa shouted over the music coming from the machine.

"This way, no, no, this way." Clara shouted running in all sorts of directions with Zach. They ended up bumping into each other and glaring.

"Let's just walk onwards and stop at the first table we find." Zach said still laughing at their attempts to kick off the night in style.

"That's a deal. Let's go." Clara laughed and linked arms with Zach.

They stopped at a table which was nearly empty; a tall, skinny man was behind it shuffling a pack of cards. He was dressed in the hotel clothes and looked bored, anticipating the arrival of customers.

"The lady and I are in." He smirked and placed some chips on the green felt table.

"Lucas, come here, let's play poker!" Alana shouted and Lucas joined her and sat down on the high stool.

"I went to get us some drinks, here you are madam." He smiled and handed her the martini he fetched from one of the waitresses.

"Thank you, ahh look, there's Clara and Zach, you wanna play against them and beat them?" Alana sad pointing to where they were animatedly playing.

"Only if you promise not to hurt them." He nodded his head, indicating they move to sit opposite Zach and Clara. They both raised an eyebrow.

"Are you challenging us?" Zachary said smoothly and put a friendly arm around Clara.

"Please, there is no challenge here." Alana bit back.

They played the game for around half an hour including accidental spillages from Clara and glasses slamming on the table from Alana. Lucas and Zachary played good-naturedly and did not notice the crazed look in Alana's eye as she bet more and more each time.

"Woah, Alana - time for us to stop maybe?" Mason said as him and Vanessa joined them.

"Just one more game I swear." She said eyes glued to the

cards.

A slender, well-dressed waitress with caramel skin and almond shaped eyes came over with drinks and Clara noticed that Lucas' gaze lingered on her a fraction of a second longer than it should have and slapped his arm playfully.

"Lucas, come with me to the bar."

"Of course." He replied looking at her with desire as he rested his hand on the small of her back, leading her away.

"Well.... we were just ditched." Mason said and Alana laughed and ruffled his curls.

"No sweetie, you were just ditched. I'm moving tables." She announced, collecting her winnings.

"Yeah, I'll move games too." Zach said leaving Mason and Vanessa. Mason looked at Vanessa and smiled sweetly.

"You wanna watch movies at the suite?" He said huskily and she blushed.

"Your place or mine?" She replied and raised an eyebrow seductively. Mason grinned and walked up with Vanessa back to the penthouse.

Once in the penthouse, Vanessa got changed into yoga pants and a t-shirt, glad to be away from the noise of the casino. Mason was already lying on the sofa flicking through Netflix wondering what film to watch. He had taken off his suit and was just in his dress shirt and trousers. Vanessa arrived and jumped on the sofa smiling.

"Have you chosen something then?" She asked intrigued.

Mason leaned in and gently kissed her.

"How about we ditch the movie."

"I'll have another one of these, please."

"Right away." The handsome bartender replied to Clara, holding her gaze. He was tall and well-built; he had light brown hair and brown eyes. His name-tag read 'Ralph'.

Lucas noticed this interaction but maintained his cool, not giving her the satisfaction.

"So darling, enjoying Vegas?" He brushed her hair back behind her ear grinning.

"Yes, very much so, I love a good night." She charmingly slid her hand on his knee.

"Well then. Let's go have some fun!" He exclaimed and jumped off his seat. Clara followed him and waved goodbye to Ralph.

"It's always the bartenders eh? You can't resist them." Lucas laughed while walking through the casino with Clara following him.

"I don't know what you're talking about." Clara insisted with a slight sly grin.

"The lady in red wins again!" The man announced. Alana jumped up and high fived the crowd around her. She had managed to capture the attention of many people who were now cheering her on as she kept up her winning streak.

Zach smiled as she won again, he collected the chips. "Alright that's enough; you've won enough money to buy two new motorbikes. Let's go before you lose all of it."

"No, no! I'm on a winning streak Zachary." She said, the crowd around her encouraged to carry on but Zach was not ready to take no for an answer.

"Suit yourself." He left the table and walked a couple of metres to another table occupied by two tall blonde women speaking Russian to each other in hushed tones. Zach approached the two with a charming grin and offered them a drink which he had just picked up from the waitress nearby.

Alana walked up to where Zach and the girls were standing.

"Excuse me ladies, but I'm going to need to take this gentleman off your hands." She faked a grin, dragging Zach with her. Zach grinned triumphantly, but said nothing, having won over her attention.

"Oh, by the way, I got a text from Lucas asking if we wanted to join him and Clara at the club." Zach stated pretending to be uninterested.

"Are you kidding? Let's go now!"

"I knew I could get you moving" He smiled and directed her out of the casino.

They arrived at the club and found Lucas and Clara making out on one of the couches.

"Whoa guys, either keep it PG-13 or get a room." Zach said.

"You guys took your time to get here!" Lucas said smugly and stood up from the couch.

"Yeah sorry, I had to get Alana off the whole gambling thing." Zach said and ruffled Alana's hair who grunted obviously still bitter about her casino exit.

The two couples made their way to the dance floor and started dancing.

Over the noise and chaos the girls heard two voices which they recognised instantly.

"CLARA! ALANA!"

Their heads turned as did those of Lucas and Zach as they saw two tall figures approach them through the night club.

As soon as the girls recognised the two boys they hugged them, grinning up at their old friends.

"Alex, what are you two doing here?" Alana asked as the brunette boy's hands slid around her waist whilst examining her with his piercing green eyes.

"Details later, it's so good to see you." He said as he looked into her eyes and smiled. She held his gaze, taking in the familiar eyes, his boyish brown hair and chiseled jaw.

"Nicholas, I haven't seen you in ages." Clara hugged him tightly again, which made Zach and Lucas advance, intrigued. He had light blonde hair with radiant blue eyes, his dinner jacket was slung over his shoulder.

"Missed me?" He replied in a distinct English accent smirking before he kissed her fully on the lips.

10

A hand grabbed Nicholas' collar back forcefully and he was pushed back. Anger flashed on Lucas' handsome face.

"What the hell?" he said angrily and Lucas moved closer to him threateningly.

"I don't believe she asked you to kiss her." he said angrily through his teeth. Nicholas opened his mouth to retort but Clara pushed herself between the two boys and Alana tried to dragged Lucas away.

"Calm down." Alana whispered to him but he still looked furious.

"Lucas, this is an old friend, Nicholas, Nick, this is Lucas." Clara said hesitantly trying desperately to keep the peace.

Mason and Vanessa ran over to where they were, looking flustered.

"Your zipper's undone." Alana stated to Mason who turned a deep red and grinned in embarrassment.

"Your shirts not buttoned up properly." Clara teased as Vanessa quickly looked down at her shirt as the other two girls raised their eyebrows. Alex chuckled warmly.

"Still the same I see." and he curled his arm around Alana's shoulders. Nicholas put his hand on the small of Clara's back and Lucas prepared to lunge but Zachary grabbed his jacket and dragged him away, glaring at Alex.

"I'm going to ..." Mason trailed off pointing towards his brothers and went after them after giving Vanessa a soft peck on the cheek. Vanessa squealed with joy and hugged Alex and Nick tightly.

"So what are you guys doing here?" Alana said as Alex kissed the top of her head.

The girls had met Alex and Nick years ago in London. They had been childhood best friends, never knowing the truth about the girls. Then when the girls began going deeper into their training they had no time for friends or a life so they had not seen each other for years.

Then on a mission in Brazil a year before to discover the identity of a man selling tourists as sex slaves, they ran into Alex, Nick and their families again and that was the holiday that Alana and Clara got romantically attached to them. But as the agents they were trained to be, they had to leave them behind.

"We went through Vegas on a road trip with a few friends and were told this was the best nightclub by far." Alex said smiling sweetly.

"So how long are you beauties here for?" Nicholas asked.

"We're here until tomorrow lunch." Vanessa said as she sipped her drink. Alana was feeling restless, seeing Alex brought on a rush of affection and memories that she would rather not have to deal with right now. Mostly, she wanted to find Zach.

"I'm going to find the boys before they do something stupid." she muttered and rushed off to where the boys last headed.

Clara nodded absent-mindedly and she gazed at Nicholas, almost shyly. His blonde hair was so soft and she ached to touch its golden silkiness and his eyes were warm but calculating. He had a boyish cheeky smile that made her blush, but the thought of Lucas surprisingly kept popping up in her mind. When Alana reached the boys she found them playing a drinking game with some men near the bar. Mason and Zachary were completely wasted. She sighed irritably and went over to Zach. He looked at her and sneered drunkenly.

"Have a thing for tall green eyed boys then?" he slurred and looked shocked when he got a sharp slap on his cheek. Mason was laughing hysterically at a joke he'd told a tattooed bald biker man easily twice his size who looked ready to rip his head off.

"You guys are wasted, Lucas, you're still sober, take away their drinks, I'll get the girls, and please save Mason." Lucas nodded dejectedly and grabbed the boys' drinks away.

The girls left Nicholas and Alex for the night; as they were about to leave Alex pulled Alana towards him, leaning in for a kiss playfully. His hands found their way to her waist and she suddenly pulled away.

"Alex.. I have to go."

She pushed him away gently at last and turned to find a pair of green cat-like eyes staring at her. Zach stood uncertainly, clearly still drunk, but his eyes were sober, and green with envy.

When they arrived back at the hotel they slowed down as they waited for the lift and heard a sound of heavy footsteps. A man passed by them looked at Alana straight in the eye. No one besides the girls noticed a thing and it was only ones they were safely in their own suites that Alana brought out the piece of paper.

"The perfect brush pass." she muttered and passed the piece of paper to the girls. They opened it to reveal one simple emblem. A viper curled around a dagger and a series of letters underneath. Clara drew in her breath sharply and cursed. "That's the sign from group that attacked Zach and me." Alana said and her brow furrowed in confusion. Vanessa quickly jotted down the letters and began to try and decipher it. "Alana, The Vipers?! Don't you remember who they are?!" Clara's voice was louder and slightly frantic.

Alana suddenly brought her hand to her temple trying to soothe the throbbing pain. How could she forget?
She certainly remembered the significance of the Vipers, and felt quite stupid for not having remembered sooner.

"Your... your parents." Vanessa said addressing Alana and Clara.

Alana gave a short curt nod. The Vipers were the criminal group that killed Alana's parents and Clara's mother. That was the last mission they had worked on. They were lethal. They managed to track down Alana's parents, Lena and Carter Hilford and Clara's mother Elizabeth and Clara's aunt who was not much older than the girls then. Only one of them, Clara's aunt, had survived the mission.

"Let's work on the cipher." Clara said quickly.

"It's the chiffre indechiffrable." Vanessa said, dejectedly.

"The impossible cipher, great, that's going to take ages without a code word."

"Try vipera." Alana said, pacing the room.

"Why vipera?" Clara asked whilst Vanessa drew up a table to decipher it with the code work Alana gave her.

"It's Latin for viper." Alana said blankly.

After a few more minutes of excruciating tension Vanessa jumped off the sofa in joy and was about to say something when Clara clamped her hands over her mouth. Alana brought a finger to her mouth signalling them to be quiet.

Vanessa looked at them questioningly. Alana grabbed her hand and Morse coded on her palm.

'Man who passed note came from here. Room is bugged' the message said. Vanessa nodded once and passed Alana the paper.

Cub, Fish, Halo.

The three words were written underneath Vanessa's code breaking. Cub was a baby tiger. Sirens were part fish. Halo linked with Cherub. The message was clear. Clara shook her head. They knew everything. Including their code names.

"That's not possible. The only way they could know our field names is if they..." she trailed off.

Vanessa nodded.

"The agency has a mole." Alana finished with finality in her voice.

"So they were after you that night at the restaurant, not Zach." Vanessa said for clarification.

"I guess so, it was probably a warning, but ... wait." she frowned and continued pacing the room.

"Goats enjoy the rustic image, dinner out front but under garage stand." Alana said casually and Clara jumped up to her bags and brought out a smaller purple bag with her gadgets.

'GET RID OF BUGS." Alana's cryptic message had said, the girls just got the first letter of every word, it was a simple code they used since they were children, it gave them a little head start to jam the bugs before the listeners had time to enforce them. The device in Clara's hand beeped comfortingly.

"They're jammed, what did you want to say?" she asked Alana.

Alana bit her lip.

"Zachary didn't find the fact that the Vipers were after him such a surprise, this must mean he was expecting them, meaning the Vipers must be involved in the deal somehow, but not in the alliance with the DeRico's and Triad" Alana spoke quickly within the 20 second window the small signal jammer could provide. Clara let out an involuntary yawn.

"Let's go to sleep, we'll deal with this in the morning." Vanessa said.

"Drink water to prevent a hangover." Alana sang whilst going to the bathroom to brush her teeth. She leant her head on the cool porcelain and cleared her head. She looked at her reflection. Her face was blank and her eyes tired. The girls fell asleep as soon as their heads hit the pillows.

Clara groaned, rubbing her head and Alana joined in. Alana held a hand out and Clara passed her a pair of large face-covering sunglasses.

"Hey guys!" Vanessa said quietly.

"Shhhhh! Is there any need to shout?" Clara hissed and Vanessa giggled.

"Hangover?" she said, and Alana nodded.

"Perhaps a little bit." she said and slumped on the sofa.

She suddenly got up with an evil glint in her eyes. She motioned for the girls to follow her as they tiptoed to the boys' rooms.

Clara tiptoed into Lucas' room. She watched him sleep for a moment admiring his chiselled chest rise up and down and his hair over his face. She leaned in and pinched his nose closed so he woke up gasping and looking at her confused. He blinked a few times then smiled slightly which made Clara's heart skip a beat.

"Wha-" he started but was cut off by the feel of Clara's lips on his. He kissed back then stiffened remembering last night. She drew back sighing.

"Don't you have Nick for that?" he muttered and she frowned.

"That was an accident, it didn't mean anything." She said and Lucas gave her a long look but said nothing. Clara sat up and sighed, irritated.

"Okay, so you can have as many girls drooling all over you but I can't have one ex- boyfriend turning up and suddenly-" She was cut off by Lucas pulling her towards him. She smiled against his lips. Couldn't he take any argument seriously? She thought wryly to herself.

"Hey , Mase? Wake up." Vanessa said gently and Mason's eyes opened confused.

He took a few seconds to look at his awakener and a grin spread across his face.

"Morning beautiful." he said and shuffled over so Vanessa could squeeze in next to him. She rested her head against his chest breathing in his warm musky scent. He nuzzled her hair and groaned something like 'IIIIIII-mmmuuuuuuvv-oooooo'.

"I can't hear when you speak into my hair." she said smiling. He gently turned her head so she could look into her eyes.

"I love you." he said.

Vanessa's heart squeezed and a warm feeling spread throughout her body.

"I love you too." she said, knowing it was the complete truth, and knowing just how much trouble she was in for that.

Zach was mumbling in his sleep when he felt the ice cold water land on his face and soak his entire upper torso, t-shirt and bed sheets. He gasped at the cold and sat up to see Alana holding a now-empty vase.

"What. The. Hell." he said wiping water away from his eyes and glaring at Alana who was trying to contain her laughter.

"You wouldn't wake up on my first attempt." She shrugged putting the vase down.

"And what was your first attempt may I ask?" Zachary said, his teeth grinding together.

"Opening the door?" Alana said smiling wickedly.

Zachary smiled dashingly to Alana and she was caught off guard.

"You know, you look real hot in the morning ..." he said, voice husky, leaning towards her.

Alana opened her mouth to speak when she felt herself being pressed to Zach's hard chest. Then she felt an icy wetness seep through to her shirt and she squealed.

"ZACH! Let go of me!" she screamed but Zach just chuckled at her feeble attempts to escape his bear hug. She kneed him in the leg and they both toppled over onto the bed. Alana immediately grabbed Zach's wrists and restrained him.

Suddenly the door opened and Clara and Lucas tumbled in laughing, stopping at the sight of Alana restraining Zach to the bed.

"Oh er, sorry bro, we'll come back later." Lucas said containing his laughter as

Clara giggled whilst they backed out of the room. Zachary chuckled and Alana buried her head into his chest in embarrassment and laughed.

"Come on, let's go home." She said and pushed herself off him, holding his hand.

"Well that's pretty screwed up." said Beck after reading the debrief Vanessa wrote for him. Clara nodded and Alana paced the room expression grim.

"So what do we do now?" Clara asked and Beck shook his head.

"You have to continue as normal; I can't contact the Agency since we've been compromised. Just be extra careful, try and bring the current mission to a close."

"Well good news is we have a lead on Zachary's SIDE deal in a few days." Clara said and Alana scoffed, annoyed about how long this mission was taking, and how attached they were becoming to their new lives. They had to get in and out quickly, they couldn't afford distractions. She tugged her braid and sat down.

"We're in so much mess, fooling around with these boys isn't going to help, they won't tell us anything the whole school doesn't know, everyone knows they're criminals, they're just a waste of time." Alana muttered bitterly trying to evade the image of Zach's face from her head. Clara shrugged.

"At least we've met three super-hot guys who are obsessed with us." This induced a chuckle and the mood lifted slightly.

"Oooh I just remembered." Vanessa groaned. Everyone turned to look at her as she buried her head in the sofa cushion.

"We have advanced maths tomorrow." she sighed dejectedly joined by the groan of the other two girls and Beck's taunting chuckle.

"Why are you upset? You've done your homework nerd." Beck teased. Alana and Clara looked at each other in panic and rushed upstairs to complete their forgotten homework.

"OMG! I haven't seen you guys in ages. I've missed you so much!" Millie gushed before barrelling her small frame into the three girls for a group hug.

"It's only been a weekend..." Alana said laughing as Millie bounced around. She stopped bouncing and looked at them incredulously.

"YES! But you've been in an entirely different country!" she said twirling her hair, which was now dyed completely red.

"Different state-" Vanessa interjected but was cut off by Millie.

"Aaaaand you guys were with the super duper hotties! Tell me ALL about it!" Clara tried to get a word in but Millie gasped in shock as if just remembering something.

"You know what you guys need?! You need a party! Your house, Friday at 6? Awesome I'll tell everyone." With that she spun round quickly and dragged Tom and Fred with her who had come to say hello. Vanessa shook her head in amazement.

"There's no one quite like her is there?" Alana said laughing softly.

"She soooo cute!" Clara cooed hands on her cheeks.

Alana's and Vanessa's phones beeped and they rummaged through their bags for their phones.

"It's a text from you." Alana said looked at Clara who had her phone in her hand.

Vanessa opened the text.

'Party at our house, Friday at 6
V.A.C

Simultaneously all the phones around them either beeped and vibrated.

"Are we in an American chick flick or British spy movie?" Alana said incredulously.

"I guess we've got a party to plan then?" Clara grinned.

"Come on, we're late for gym class!" she said as they grabbed their bags from their lockers and scurried off towards the changing rooms.

"Hilford! Five fouls in a minute! Take a lap!" The burly female gym teacher bellowed.

"She got in my way!" Alana shouted back. Her curls were wild and her face was flushed from the rigorous hockey playing.

"Don't answer back! TWO LAPS!" the coach screamed again going a bright beetroot colour.

Alana sighed irritated, threw down her stick and began to jog around the pitch.

"Blake! Stop chatting and more playing." the gym teacher shouted at Clara who was discussing with Millie about how their team vests were completely the wrong colour for them and green did not evoke any team spirit.

Vanessa was absentmindedly skipping around with her hockey stick.

They were playing hockey outside in the sunshine for gym class. Alana had fouled nearly every player by whacking them with her hockey stick and the other two girls had too much on their minds to take the game seriously. There was so much to think about, so much to be aware of, they had to always be alert and on their guard, which is why they spotted the spy before he spotted them. The formation was silently agreed on. They knew they could not attack him since they would be compromised. Clara excused her to get some water and her and Vanessa headed to where Alana slowed down her jogging. The man in the cleaner's uniform had passed by 20 minutes ago in a long overcoat and walking stick. They always forget to change their shoes, she thought to herself. Out of her periphery she noticed Clara and Vanessa jogging towards her. They walked to the closest door in silent agreement to begin talking.

"He came alone, hasn't spotted us yet, we're safe for now, criminal groups wouldn't send spies alone." Clara said slightly breathless.

"He must be from the Agency, lower level clearance." Vanessa agreed.

The girls and Beck were the Agency's secret. Every other agent was above standard age of 21 but the girls being trained since a young age and having to take over their parent's job made them an exception. These girls were normal, with each other, but in the end they were just government weapons. Secret weapons, those were the most deadly. Only a select few had high enough clearance to know or come into contact with these girls; Beck being one of them since he too was trained young. Having an Agency agent here to spy on them could only mean bad news. Alana brushed her hair back, a sign that she was thinking and Vanessa pursed her lips before speaking again.

"We can't be compromised, we have to exit the field." she said quietly her eyes darting around.

Clara's eyes were wide and wary as she watched the man from the safety of the shadows of the building. Alana's face was cool and composed and she drew in a breath ready to give field orders.

"Siren exits building from front entrance, Cherub takes the fire exit on my cue. Don't meet at house, it's staked out, shadow my bike." she said quickly

"Wait, what's your cue?" Clara called after her but she had already left on her jog so it looked like she hadn't paused at all.

Vanessa kept an eye on the man who was now scrutinising the group of girls playing hockey. It didn't even look as if he was calculating every detail about the school, but Vanessa knew he was. He was good; she thought and turned to watch Clara disappeared as if by magic and Alana slink into the shadows like a cat. But we're better, she smiled to herself. Her smile widened when she heard the scream of the fire alarm. Time to go, she thought as Clara headed for the front entrance and Vanessa joined her classmates to confuse the enemy agent.

You can't fool a spy; she thought wryly, especially not three.

Mason and Zachary were in the labs when the fire alarms shattered their ear drums.

"Aww man come on! Can't they set it on vibrate or something?" Mason said covering his ears.

"No stupid. You wouldn't hear it otherwise." Zachary said

slapping a book over Mason's head.

Mason groaned as he grabbed his stuff and winced as a stabbing pain shot through his hand. He looked at the fresh wound which he got after a fight broke out yesterday. His mind wondered back to it.

It was in the shadows, Lucas negotiating with the other party and Zachary standing menacingly by Mason's side. They looked so calm and collected, power radiated off them and if you looked in their eyes, you wouldn't believe they were only 18. They had a haunted, knowing look in their eyes, as if they were shells of themselves, nothing inside. To everyone else the brothers were the hot bad boys in a gang. They assumed that they beat people up, did drugs, sold drugs and stole cars. Their 'gang' was one of the deadliest organised criminal groups. The boys were young, yet they were involved in something beyond their control.

Lucas had stopped talking and a silent nod from Zachary sealed the deal. Mason admired his older brother, stepping up and bearing the tough life. He dealt with the worst of it and protected his brother as did Zach. Mason looked at Zach. He was leaning against the wall gracefully.

Mason frowned slightly; Zach didn't have to do this. He had no blood tie to the DeRico's that bonded him to this, except his loyalty and pride. The three had been inseparable since the day they met as children. Things were so simple back then. Then Lucas and Mason were brought into the family business. When Zach was first offered he denied politely. Then his mother was killed. Any shred of dignity he had that stopped him getting involved was buried with his mother's casket. His father was close to Mason's and Lucas'. He was a respected figure in the DeRico clan. When Mason's father extended his offer to Zach again he accepted. His brothers were all he had now. His stepmother was nice enough, half his father's age but she was kind to Zach who was only 8 years younger than her. He adapted to the criminal way easily, everyone knew who they were and exactly how dangerous they were. But Mason didn't want it. Any of it. He wasn't like his brothers. Every time he caused pain he felt pain. Sure, it decreased over the years, but he still felt something. He savoured the feeling of goodness Vanessa brought to him with her large intelligent eyes that read him perfectly. As his thoughts began to wander he was jolted back to reality by Zach. They were outside.

Zach noticed Mason's distant look but did not question it. Mason was good at heart. He knew right from wrong even if he was powerless. Zachary on the other hand, just as Lucas, had learned to numb those feelings. They embraced what would be their lives. Had they any choice, then they may have chosen somewhere else, but this lifestyle fit them like his worn soft leather jacket. Out of the corner of his eye he saw the girls rushing off. Clara did not stop to check her reflection before driving, Vanessa didn't check her blind spots twice and Alana didn't even have her helmet or gloves on. Tell-tale signs like this screamed that they were in a rush, and it was not because of the fire. He contemplated following them. They looked like they were doing something urgent, important... suspicious.

"Hey I'll catch up with you at home." he called to Mason and kick-started his motorbike.

"Can I have three rooms for the night, with balcony?" Vanessa said handing the receptionist her card.

"Wait, we'll pay in cash." Clara said handing her some bills before she she could take the credit card.

They could not afford to be traced back by their credit card. They informed Beck as they went upstairs to their rooms. They decided staying at a hotel should throw the agent off their scent for a while at least. The rooms were spacious and decorated in rich gold and reds and they immediately flopped on the beds and switched the TV on. They all convened in Vanessa's room watching Paranormal Activity when they heard a knock on their door. Vanessa jumped slightly spooked by the movie and Clara rushed to the door. She looked through the peek hole and opened the door.

"Oh Zach! What a surprise." she said loudly and Alana

groaned audibly.

Vanessa stood up looking at him quizzically.

"How did you find us here?" she questioned harshly.

He shrugged and sat down on the bed next to Ana who was frowning at the TV intently trying to ignore his presence.

"I just followed you guys." he said casually and waved a hand in front of Alana, ignoring her blatant stubbornness. She looked at him coldly and turned back to the television.

He let out a low whistle and clasped his hands together.

"Whatever the reason you're here, I brought company!" He flashed a 1000-watt smile at the girls.

At that moment there were a series of knocks at the door. Vanessa sighed and opened the door to Mason and Lucas who bundled in like toddlers. Mason hugged all of them with a big grin on his face and bounced over to the music speakers, put on a song, turning the volume up to the maximum. Alana tutted, eventually jumping up on the large cushiony mattress.

"Let's play ..... TRUTH OR DARE!" Clara said, eyes gleaming with mischief and everyone agreed, sitting on the plush carpet in a circle.

After another hour of ridiculous dares the bottle landed on Zach.

"Hmmmm. Truth." he said.

"Okay, who do you fancy?" Clara asked deviously.

Zachary smirked and looked at Alana who had not spoken directly to him all night.

"Alana Hilford obviously." he said. The others gasped slightly, or giggled nervously. Alana rolled her eyes annoyed and stood up, walking out of the room. Clara inclined her head towards the door and Zach rushed after her.

"Alana, wait, stop!" he called after her, she stopped walking down the hallway and turned, her arms crossed over her chest.

"What?" she said coolly.

"What? You've been angry at me all day, one day you're all like, 'yeah we're cool' and MOST times you're like 'I hate you'. Now I tell you I like you. You're just really confusing." He ran his hand through his hair in frustration and her expression changed.

"You can't just TELL me you like me! You're trying to play me Zach. You think I believe any of that bullshit?" she yelled at him. He ground his teeth together. They were quite close now, close enough to feel the body heat radiating off each other.

"You're crazy, how am I supposed to-" he was cut off by Alana locking her hands together behind his neck and pulling him in for a kiss. He grabbed her by the waist, pulling her in tighter. Her hands slid under his t-shirt, brushing his skin lightly as the kiss deepened. She broke the kiss suddenly and they were both stood there in the hotel corridor breathing deeply. She ran her hand through his hair and tugged it softly and he tilted her chin up and kissed her softly on the lips. She smiled at him slightly, heading back to the hotel room, leaving Zach even more confused than he started off.

"I want to go outside." Vanessa gazed at the darkness beyond the window.

"It's like midnight... we can't go to the beach." Clara said and it clicked.

"Midnight swimming guys?" Lucas said raising an eyebrow.

The beach was dark, moonlight bounced off the water and the sound of waves rolling onto the sand was refreshing. Lucas pulled off his top and trousers so he was left in his boxers. With a whoop he ran into the icy water and dived under. The other two boys joined in and yelled at the girls to join them.

"TAKE OFF YOUR CLOTHES!" Mason yelled and they all looked at him, shocked.

"Not all of them I mean, just top layer..." he said thankful for the darkness to hide his blushing.

The girls stripped to their underwear, pelted by playful

wolf whistles from the boys. Alana dived in and swam over quickly to the boys. Vanessa skipped and delicately immersed herself in the water whereas Clara inched in and out of the water.

"Hurry up!" Lucas shouted at her, laughing at her yelps as the cold water flooded around her ankles.

"It's super cold okay!" she shouted back, arms crossed over her body.

Lucas got up and ran out of the water and Clara began shrieking hysterically. He grabbed her, flipped her over his shoulder whilst she screamed as he dived in the water along with Clara and she spluttered and splashed Lucas. He chuckled, kissing her on the nose playfully. This induced a huge water fight with a lot of attempted drowning. The water was dark and the moonlight was the only source of light.

"Guys, I hate to ask, but what are the sleeping arrangements?" Alana asked, floating on her back in the water. Zach swam to her and grabbed her waist up so she had to put her arms around his neck to stay up. She bit her lip and as he leaned in for a kiss she dived under and swam around him.

Clara laughed and grabbed Lucas' hand as they started heading out of the water with Mason and Vanessa.

"Mason with Vanessa, Lucas and I and Alana and Zach. Any objections? No? That's settled."

They ran off to their rooms with their clothes. Alana sighed, trying to ignore the jitters she was feeling.

When Clara and Lucas got to the room they got changed into their sleeping attires. Clara put on one of Lucas' t-shirts.

"Well hello there, handsome." Clara stepped out of the bathroom, greeted by Lucas spread across the bed, an impish grin on his face. It was like a constant game of Chicken with Lucas. A constant game she wanted to keep playing.

Mason pulled Vanessa closer to him, he breathed in the scent of her coconut shampoo which he could still faintly smell. She turned to face him and kissed his cheek and settled to sleep enveloped by Mason.

Around 10 minutes later, she heard a small buzzing coming from Mason's bedside table. She leaned over to him to turn the sound off when she saw the text message glaring at her.

"Had a great time last night, x" From Sophie. Vanessa dropped the phone and scurried back to her side of the bed hoping that she had mistakenly read the text or that she imagined it. Worrying about the text kept her up until she could not keep her eyes open a second longer, and fell into a deep, troubled sleep.

"You're sleeping on the floor." Alana slumped down onto the bed. She switched the light off and before she knew it she felt herself being dragged by her feet off the bed.

She squealed.

"FINE, FINE, fine. You can sleep on the bed. I'll sleep on the floor."

She got off the bed and made a huge fuss out of getting the spare blankets including audible sighs.

"I promise I won't make any moves, just sleep on the bed, your sighs are annoying me." Zach said smirking. She paused for a moment and dropped the blankets and crawled into bed. He instantly pulled her in and was surprised when she did not struggle. She lay her head on his chest, and settled to sleep.

"Goodnight Alana..." he said after a few minutes, her breathing was heavy and he thought she was asleep.

"Night Zach..." she murmured softly in return.

11

"Morning Becky!" Alana chirped as they all walked into the house.

"Morning. You girls look rough." he commented, noticing the bags under their eyes and how they dragged their feet around the house.

"Schools in an hour, wake me up okay?" Alana said and rushed upstairs to throw herself on her bed. Vanessa went upstairs to get ready and Clara headed to the shower.

Beck ran his fingers through his short dark hair. He looked a little more relaxed now the girls were home and safe. Although he knew all too well that when the time came for them to leave they would be heartbroken, no matter how many times they try to deny it.

The time came for him to go to work at the beach bar. The beach bar was an ideal place for a small job. The shifts were easy during weekdays, the weather was fantastic, breaks involved surfing of jet-skiing and Beck now had a collection of phone numbers from attractive customers. Not to mention, he had a constant supply of sources of information

"Can I get you anything?" he gave the tall, dark haired customer a dashing smile. She batted her almond shaped hazel eyes and smiled at him.

"Just sparkling water please." she said, her voice was slow and silky.

Beck gave her a wink and went to fill her glass. He placed the glass in front of her whilst she fiddled with the straps of her gold bikini. She paid Beck and crossed one long tanned leg over the other.

"So when's your shift over?" she said swirling her drink around.

"10 minutes, you wanna grab a bite?"

She smiled in return, signalling she'd wait for him by the beach, and sauntered away.

The girl's phone beeped in lesson and they quickly checked their messages under the desk.

'Training after school -B.'

"So Becky wants us to touch up before show-time" Alana muttered and went back to sleeping on her desk.

Clara fiddled with her bracelet and began texting. Vanessa paid attention to the lesson, making notes in meticulous handwriting, trying to keep her notebook away from Alana's sharpie.

The girls rushed home after school, grabbing their training gear.

"Oh hey Clara, what's up?" Vanessa looked up at her puzzled best friend.

"You haven't seen my cherry shaped earrings anywhere have you? You know the ones that go with the necklace Alana got me." Clara plopped herself on to the bed exasperated. Apparently her cherry earrings were essential for training.

Vanessa replied unenthusiastically, not paying much attention to Clara.

"Something tells me you're having boy trouble?" Clara cocked her head to the side smiling.

Vanessa's expression answered her question for her.

"Come on; spill the beans to the resident love guru."

"Well, when we were at the hotel, Mason fell asleep and his phone rang, it was a text from a girl sayi-"

"Omg what did it say?" Clara interrupted her eagerly.

"Saying 'Had a great time' or something." Vanessa said

softly.

"Mason is totally into you, it's probably nothing. Don't worry about it." Clara brushed off her concerns, glad to see Vanessa smile. If only he was more into Vanessa than being a pawn in his crime family, this mission would be a lot simpler, Clara thought to herself.

"Hey guys." Zach walked into Lucas and Mason's house and sat on the sofa.

Mason and Lucas nodded in acknowledgement, focused on the video game in front of them.

"Yeah not much, did you get Clara's text about the party tonight?" Zach said while

getting his phone out of his pocket. Lucas' head shot up at the sound of her name and smiled at the thought of seeing Clara again tonight.

"Yeah, half of California got that text." Lucas said mentally kicking himself for letting her in his brain. No one should have that much power over him, yet that night at the hotel, was more than just another one of his meaningless conquests. For the first time, it had meant something.

"Can't wait!" Mason said, full of excitement. Zach and Lucas both laughed and looked at each other.

"Yeah, it's about time you sealed the deal with Vanessa." Lucas teased jokingly.

"Lucas is right, you've got to give a girl what she wants." Zach added smirking.

"I don't understand, we've been official for a while now." Mason said innocently,

confused at what his brother was trying to say.

"That's not what we mean Mase." Zach laughed and was joined by Lucas' sniggering.

"But enough about that, we've got business to sort out." Lucas' expression turned serious.

"Who the hell are you?" Alana said at the girl waiting outside the house. Clara brushed past Alana.

"Zazzi!" Clara exclaimed and gave the girl a hug, having met her at an Agency event years ago.

"Hey, I'm Beck's friend, I'll be helping you with training today. Don't worry, I'm in on the secret."

"Wait, but where's Beck?" Vanessa asked.

"He has a date with some girl." Zazzi said with a shrug and smiled cheerfully at the girls.

"Wow, you're so happy." Alana shuddered as she struggled to braid her hair behind her back.

Zazzi walked up to Alana and took her hair gently. In a few seconds she had expertly weaved Alana's curly hair into a perfect french braid.

"There you go." she said securing the end of the braid. Alana felt the braid cynically and eventually grinned.

Zazzi drove the girls, chatting to them about school until they reached a large, empty field.

"Right, so we start with three laps to warm up, then we'll go over fighting." Zazzi instructed and Alana groaned audibly.

"Excuse me, I'm more of a lover than a runner." Clara raised a hand objecting.

Zazzi blew a whistle quieting Clara's objections and the girls began running without another word. After about six minutes they finished their laps, feeling their blood pumping and their muscles warmed up.

Zazzi smiled proudly at them.

Zazzi taught them how to hit places that could knock grown men out. She moved swiftly and fast, impressing even the girls. The girls practised sparring, not holding back, unleashing powerful kicks, flipping one another other over their shoulders.

By the end of the workout Alana, Clara and Vanessa were lying on the grass breathing heavily, hot and sweaty.

"You're crazy. You're trying to kill us." Alana tried to raise an accusing finger but she had no energy.

"Those criminals better watch out... we're absolutely lethal now." Vanessa said sleepily.

Clara was trying to get up and gave up, sighing and lying on the floor motionless.

"Is she dead?" Vanessa asked, gently prodding her.

"Cool down lap and stretch. GO GO GO!" Zazzi bounced around them, ignoring the groans and moans.

Friday afternoon came faster than expected. The girls were getting the house ready, locking away anything valuable and setting out drinks although they could count on the football team to bring the majority. Beck was out, on another date with this new mystery girl. They all rushed up to get changed. The doorbell rang and Alana rushed down to answer.

Clara looked around, impressed with how fast they got the house ready, to her surprise the first people in were Tom and Fred. They hugged Alana and Clara and Vanessa when she skipped downstairs. Vanessa shimmered on her way down in a sequinned pink mini dress.

The doorbell rang again and she threw open the door to allow a steady flow of high-school students to come in.

Clara quickly checked her reflection, she was wearing a cherry red strapless top and dark jeans. She had scraped her hair back into a sleek pony tail. Alana ran down the stairs, having just changed from her pyjamas to a plain black dress, naturally paired with her combat boots, 'just in case' she had justified to Clara. Clara threw a pair of heeled sandals at her as she ran past her.

"PARTY TIME PEOPLE." She yelled on the way down,

turning the music on to full blast as she sauntered past.

"CHUG CHUG CHUG CHUG CHUG CHUUUUUUGG." The crowded chanted and Zazzi slammed her empty beer can on the table.

"And that, is how you drink." She gasped, holding back the desire to projectile vomit. Clara shook her head at her disapprovingly from the distance.

Vanessa was wondering around looking to check if Mason had arrived yet. She fiddled around the room greeting people with a warm smile and sighed when she realised he had not turned up.

Millie ran to Vanessa, hugging her tightly and squealing with delight.

"Let's dance" Vanessa suggested, trying to distract herself.

"Totally! I love this song!" She squealed and they headed to make-shift dance-floor.

The party was in full swing by midnight. Most people had arrived, except for the brothers. The girls were having fun dancing crazily to the songs blasting through the house with their new high school friends.

Much to the girl's surprise Lania and Natalie showed up, with their quieter friend, Sophie. They walked in the front door looking around and sneering.

Alana looked to Clara as she tapped Vanessa on the shoulder. Vanessa sighed sadly and Alana cracked her knuckles. Clara rolled her eyes at Alana's dramatics.

"Look what the cat dragged in." Natalie glared at Alana who raised her eyebrows at her.

"You're in our house, or did you forget that along with the rest of your dress? "

"Who's the third stooge?" Clara said eyeing up the girl next to them with reddish blonde hair and a splattering of freckles and cat-like green eyes.

"This is Sophie. I'm sure your boyfriend knows her." Natalia said nodding towards Vanessa. Sophie smirked at her arrogantly. Vanessa pursed her lips, trying to stay composed.

"I notice they're not here. Don't blame them." Lania said, her voice drilling through the music like nails on a chalkboard.

"Please shut up. Your voice gives me a headache." Alana muttered, ignoring the expression on Lania's face.

"Make me." She replied.

"Trust me she will." Clara said, holding Alana's arm just in case she did.

People had started crowding around the girls and Zazzi joined them.

"We just came out to check out how lame this party is, and leave to go back to Zach Mason and Lucas." Natalie said smirking at the girls, eyes gleaming. Sophie stepped closer to Vanessa threateningly

"You might want to step back before I break your leg, slug." Alana said, and Eve looked at her taken aback. Vanessa too, looked at Alana, more taken aback by the use of 'slug' as an choice of insult.

"Don't try be a smart ass. In order to be a smart ass , you gotta be smart, otherwise you're just an ass." Zazzi said cuttingly. The terrible trio stepped back, and eventually made their way out, aware of the losing battle.

"Well that almost ruined my buzz." Alana turned away and shouted back- "ALMOST!"

Clara turned to the party, giving everyone a dazzling smile. She grabbed a drink from Zazzi, finished it in a gulp and signalled to the DJ to get the party started again.

As Clara was busy restocking drinks, she felt two hands slide around her waist in a warm embrace. Expecting to see Lucas she turned around slowly soon to realise Lucas was not the one behind her.

"You came." She said softly looking up into Nicholas' eyes.

"Well I couldn't miss out on a party, could I?" he whispered leaning in closer.

The thought was tempting but Clara knew better to fall into his arms again. She pulled away slightly.

"It's okay, shhh." He pressed his fingers to her lips and smiled.

"Details later, let's dance." He added and lead her to the dance floor. Clara had always admired his easy- going personality and the way he never worried about anything. Live in the moment, he used to tell her, and with that, they started dancing.

Alana shouted over at Alex when she spotted him across the room. Alex laughed easily, waving at her as she elbowed her way through the crowds of people to give him a warm hug. She seemed a little too relaxed and he wondered if she had a drink or two.

"You look intoxicating tonight." he said and she slapped his chest.

"I am not drunk." she replied indignantly.

"I said intoxicating not intoxicated." he said and flicked her nose gently. She looked at him blankly, then shook her head dismissively. His hand had not left the small of her back from the moment they had hugged.

He put both his hands around her, pulling her her close. She stepped back slightly and gave him a lopsided smile as she took his hand. He let her lead him outside to where a few people were out near the pool. Alana leaned towards Alex and eased her hands into his pockets taking out his phone and his keys leaving them on a stool. He got the point.

"3. 2. 1." she said and they both ran and leaped into the pool. She laughed, her teeth chattering as she floated on her back.

"Yeah, come on, let's get changed." Alex said putting his arm around Alana's shoulders.

"Okay, you may carry me up to my room." she said

seriously. Alex looked and her for a second and chuckled.

"If you say so Madam." and he picked her up and put her over his shoulder as she squealed, begging him to put her down.

He put her down once they arrived to her room. It was surprisingly clean and she was secretly glad it was not a complete mess. She remembered Alex being a bit of a clean freak.

"I'll go get something of Beck's for you to change into." Alana said, feeling quite sleepy and drowsy. She went to Beck's room and grabbed a spare pair of jeans and a t-shirt. Beck, Alex and Nick were once good friends too, the six of them had many good times together.

When she returned to her room she found Alex changed out of his wet clothes left only in his boxer shorts. She rolled her eyes and tossed her clothes to him and went behind the screen in her room to change out of her wet dress. She realised she had forgotten to bring her change of clothes, and asked Alex to pass them to her. She stepped out to grab her clothes, not caring if he saw her half dressed.

That was when the door opened.

"Are you kidding me?" Zachary spat taking in the sight of Alana with Alex, and minimal clothing. She stared at him shocked, not understanding the situation until she looked around. She pulled on her try clothes quickly and ran after him.

"Zach wait no, it's not what it looks like I swear."

"Well what is it then?" He said, he felt himself heating up with anger. Why did she provoke so many emotions in him?

"I was swimming." She explained, feeling the feebleness of her excuse.

Zachary laughed humourlessly.

"I'm getting out of here."

"Zach no." Alana said, she thought it strange she actually cared what Zachary thought of her.

She followed him out to the corridor.

"Trust me, it just looked wrong. There's nothing going on between me and Alex. Look at me." Zachary was facing away from her. He snapped his green eyes to her pleading brown eyes.

He sighed.

"Why should I care anyway? It's not like you're my girlfriend or anything." he said and mentally kicked himself. No, she's not your girlfriend, You just wish she was, he thought to himself.

Her expression hardened.

"You're right. Why should you care?" she said with a tone of finality in her voice and she turned away. She half expected him to stop her, but found herself walking away alone.

"You have three seconds to get away from my girlfriend now." Lucas snarled at Nicholas who was dancing with Clara quite intimately.

Nick smiled slowly revealing his perfect white teeth.

"Lucas, is it? Just back off man." Nicholas ignored Lucas simmering with anger. Clara panicked, trying to get between them. She tried to get a word in edgeways but the boys were too close and fuming, their expressions, lethal.

"Make me. I dare you." he said so dangerously Nicholas let go of Clara suddenly. Her stiletto heels provided no stability, along with being slightly drunk as stumbled back and tripped over a can on the floor.

She felt herself falling backwards and she tried to reach out and grab something but her hands caught thin air, and everything went black.

12

Clara opened her eyes drowsily. She brought her hand to her head to find it had been bandaged. Looking around she concluded that she was in her bed. The lights were dim, low murmurs were to be heard from downstairs. The party must be over then, she thought and sighed.

"Hello."

Lucas leaned in and sat on her bed besides her. He kissed her gently taking care due to her fragile state.

She responded by deepening the kiss, fragile or not, she wanted this boy. He broke away, gazing at her.

"Thank God you're awake." Lucas whispered in her ear and smiled.

"Lucas what happened?" Clara looked up and brought herself to kiss him again.

He cut off the kiss and his expression turned cold.

"You hurt yourself while dancing with Nicholas." Clara mentally kicked herself at the thought of dancing with Nicholas and her memories of the night came flashing back. Their sensual moves, the way their bodies became one on the dance floor. Before she could open her mouth to reply Lucas kissed her, grinning at her, erasing all thoughts of Nicholas.

A soft knock interrupted their kiss. They both turned around to face the door and Mason and Vanessa popped their heads through the door.

"Oh sorry, are we interrupting something?" Mason asked innocently.

"No it's okay, come in bro." Lucas smiled at the gentleness of his younger brother.

"You're alive!" Vanessa ran in and hugged Clara on the bed.

"Speaking of, why am I not in hospital." Clara asked clearly annoyed at the lack of attention.

"Trust me, you weren't the one who need to be hospitalised." Mason said hesitantly watching Lucas' facial expression turn angry.

"What's that supposed to mean?" Clara asked, worried about Alana and Beck. No one spoke.

"Will someone tell me what is going on?" She sat up in bed frustrated. Mason and Vanessa turned to Lucas motioning for him to speak.

"I may have had a bit of a scrap with Nick." Lucas said emotionlessly.

"He's in hospital. Alex, Zach and Alana are with him." Vanessa added hesitantly.

Clara jumped up to change, shouting at Lucas angrily.

"It was pretty bad, Lucas damaged one of his kidneys." Vanessa said shyly looking at the ground and holding Mason's hand, avoiding Lucas' glare.

"I'm going to see him now. Why did no one tell me? And you-" She said looking at Lucas in the eyes threateningly. She could not get a word out, her face a vision of fury.

She grabbed her car keys and headed toward the front door with everyone following close behind.

"You can't drive now. You were unconscious five minutes ago." Lucas said once they were outside.

"And you might be unconscious in five seconds if you don't get out of my way." Clara said furiously, revved up the car and sped away. Lucas considered his options and decided to drive home leaving Mason and Vanessa alone at the house.

Alex and Alana were both by the hospital bed on opposite sides, feeling the tension between the two boys. Zach was by Alana's side on a chair, eyeing up Alex dangerously. Nicholas was still asleep and the nurse has just finished checking up on him.

"I still can't believe this happened." Alana said saddened by the sight of one of her friends in hospital.

"You can't exactly blame Lucas." Zach said coldly, his gaze fixed on Alex who was clearly upset.

"Nicholas didn't do anything wrong." Alex spoke clearly, anger flashing in his eyes.

"Yeah, is that why Clara got knocked out tonight?" His tone furious as Alex defended Nicholas' actions.

"Guys." Alana shouted as she felt the tension rising. She stood up and paced around the room with her hand held up to her forehead. She could not take this foolish macho competition yet the thought of Zach jealous made her strangely happy. She glanced at Nicholas one more time before sighing loudly. Alex stood up.

"I'll go get us some drinks." He said leaving the room.

Alana sat down opposite Zach avoiding his eyes. When she brought herself to look at him he was smirking arrogantly.

"So do you like this Alex guy?" Alana leaned back in her seat and crossed her arms.

"What's it to you?" she said coldly and he laughed emotionlessly.

"Oh honey, I couldn't care less." He said harshly and Alana stood up suddenly so she was facing him.

"So why ask?" she said forcefully, they were almost nose to nose. He moved forward and kissed her before she could say anything. They jumped apart slightly when they heard someone clearing their throat.

"Is there a problem?" Zach asked Alex who was staring at them, eyebrows raised.

"Yeah, how about the fact that we're in a hospital because your stupid friend got jealous and possessive."

"For goodness sake, can you not contain your alpha male

bullshit until we're at least out of this goddamn hospital?" Alana started for the door but jumped back as Clara rushed in. She kneeled by the side of the bed, holding Nicholas' hands, the worry clear on her face. Nicholas began to open his eyes and smiled as he saw Clara next to him holding his hand.

Alana motioned for Zach to come outside and leave them some space.

"How are you?" Clara asked gently taking in his bruised eye.

"I've been better." He whispered softly his lips curved in a smile ever slightly.

"I'm so sorry about Lucas." She said and looked down sadly.

"Hey, don't fret it." He sat up and lifted her chin up so she was looking into his eyes.

They stayed that way for a while, slowly leaning in until their lips brushed.

"No. No. No." Clara stopped the kiss and stood up frantic. "Don't do this."

"Do what?" Nicholas looked at her innocently.

"You can't expect me to fall into your arms again and just pick up where we left off." Clara said firmly.

"Why not? It's got to be worth a shot." Nicholas responded, struggling to sit up. She shook her head, muttered a goodbye and left the room. She stormed past Alana, Zach and Alex, ignoring Alana as she ran after her.

"I'm sick of guys! I want to go back to London." She muttered angrily, getting into her car and driving home.

"Well, it's getting late." Mason said tiredly running his hand through his curls. They had spent the last few hours removing drunk high school kids from the house. The whole house was now spotless as they had both cleaned up, ignoring the drama that was going on that night. Beck had come in an hour ago and immediately ran up to his room when any mention of 'cleaning' came to the conversation. She let out a shaky sigh and leaned into Mason for a hug. His strong arms enveloped her and she leaned her head on his chest. He gently kissed the top of her head.

"Go, you must be tired. Thank you for all the help." Vanessa smiled sweetly up at him. He walked out the door with a wave and his footsteps were joined with Clara's as she came home. She let out a groan and ran upstairs to sleep off the night, and the throbbing headache she had picked up along the way.

Vanessa smiled and pulled her hair up to a bun, it was growing longer now, when she left London it was only up to her shoulders. She felt melancholy thinking about London and she missed her parents dearly. Then a thought suddenly struck her, it's my birthday in two days. She smiled to herself. Back home the girls and Beck would go out for Chinese food and rent cheesy movies or check out trendy new spot if they were up for it. They always made sure to make her birthday special.

She moved to sit on the couch where she planned to crash for the night when she saw Mason's phone. She ran outside to hand it back to him, hoping he had not left already.

She opened the door and shut it behind her remembering to bring her keys. Mason was nowhere in sight. It was dark save for a small sliver of glowing moonlight. She put her arms around her, protecting herself from the chill. She would just have to give him his phone tomorrow before they shadowed Zach. Vanessa turned to go back to the door but she went headfirst into a man standing behind her. She felt herself being dragged back by a two pairs of strong arms - a hand closing over her mouth. Her arms were locked behind her but she jumped up and kicked the attacker in front of her hard. He doubled over and heaved in pain. She lashed out desperately managed a small short scream before a damp rag closed over her mouth and nose. Vanessa's eyes widened in panic but then drooped shut as the chloroform did its job and everything went black.

Zach and Alana left soon after Clara, walking in the moonlight. It was colder than usual and Alana couldn't help from shivering. Zach noticed this and cocked his head to the side to look at her.

"Are you cold?" he asked teasingly. Alana jutted her chin out defiantly.

"Of course not, I just shivered in anticipation of getting home." This caused Zach to chuckled and put his arm around her shoulder pressing her closer to him. She hated to admit it but he was extremely warm and she cuddled closer to him.

"Better?" he asked and she shrugged moving slightly closer to him. She then felt a vibration in her back pocket and Alana pulled her phone out. It was a text from Clara.

'Vanessa's been captured. Come home now. Be careful, we've been compromised.'

Alana swore under her breath, her heart beating faster.

"Zachary, we have to get home now." She said and turned when she heard a few footsteps behind her. She looked to see three male figures dressed in black walking speedily towards her.

"Damn it Zach run!" She shouted and they began running as fast as they could. Adrenaline pumped through Alana as her feet pounded on the pavement. Zachary was a few feet ahead of her and he grabbed her hand dragging her forward. They had created some distance between them and the men chasing them but they had to stop. They were ahead by far and their lungs were burning. Zach spotted a secluded alley way and pushed Alana towards it and they both stayed there. They watched the three men run past confused as to which direction they went. Alana trying to quieten her breathing. Zach put his hand over her mouth gently willing her to be silent. The men were finally no where in sight and he breathed a sigh of relief.

"Would you care to explain what the hell that was?" He

said looking at Alana intensely.

"Well obviously those men were chasing us." She panted. Zach shook his head and rubbed his temple.

"I'm taking you home, and we're talking about this tomorrow." He said and she nodded tiredly. With the rush of adrenaline gone she was very weary, but she couldn't rest yet, not when one her own was in danger.

Clara opened the door for Alana having watched her approach from the hidden camera by the door. They couldn't leave anything up to chance now. Beck was also up and sitting on the kitchen counter.

"I just got chased, Zach too. Alex is with Nick at the hospital, they're leaving tomorrow. Tell me everything." Alana spoke fast, Clara was sitting on the couch with her laptop in her hand and her gadgets were arranged in front of her. Her hair was in a bun and her eyes were tired and puffy. She yawned widely and tapped on her keyboard.

"Vanessa disappeared about 20 minutes ago, I had just come home and Mason had just left, the video recordings I have here show that she went outside to give him his phone and she got taken away by these two men. No facial recognition, they weren't facing the cameras."

She said showing Alana the video recording. Alana ran her hands through her hair. There was no waiting in this situation. They had to do something and fast. The sun was almost rising, she noticed.

"I'll put the house on lockdown mode; we'll be safe for the night." He said, he hugged the girls tightly and went to adjust the security system. Alana went to get changed, and made them coffee to help work through the night.

"We need to re-watch the footage of the kidnapping." Clara took a sip of coffee. She didn't need it. Her fear for Vanessa was keeping her more awake than any coffees could.

Clara, Beck and Alana watched the surveillance tape closely. They watched Mason leaving the house and Clara walking past him furiously. Then a few seconds later Vanessa walked outside, closed the door and paused when she realised Mason had left. Then two big men came from the shadows. One came from a shrub by the door and the other from behind a parked car. Vanessa kicked into action but was carried away to a black car parked on the other side of the road. The clarity of the video was not good enough to identify either the men or the car plates.

"Let's go outside and see if we can find any clues." Beck said.

Clara and Beck went to where Vanessa was directly taken whereas Alana headed to where the mysterious car was parked. She examined the tyre marks closely, trying to make sense of the situation. There were distinguishable tyre tracks that had obviously left in a hurry. They headed south west. She thought back to the footage, trying to piece together the make of the car.

"The kidnappers were driving a black Audi R8. They headed south west and speeding. That's all I know. Beck, hack into traffic cameras and see if there's any trace of this car." Alana said hurriedly. Beck let out a low whistle.

Clara wondered around the shrubs the men came out of and noticed a glob of dry saliva near the door.

"Ew." she said but paused and thought back to the surveillance tape. Vanessa kicking her kidnapper, hard. He doubled over and spat on the ground gasping for air. Clara let out a gasp and bent down to the crucial piece of DNA. She opened her little case and brought out a swab. She ran it through to be tested and went to Beck who was on his computer, waiting for results.

"I have DNA...." She said in a sing song voice and Beck's eyes widened.

"Are you serious?" he said and gave her a bear hug which left her gasping for breath. He then turned to his laptop as he heard a beep signalling his hack was successful. He tapped a few codes in and an image of the car and its drivers came up. He clicked print and Clara jumped up to get the printed paper. The men were both bald with scarred identical faces; they were twins. They ran the faces through their recognition database as well as the car plates.

"This car is registered to a Mr Primuzes who owns a supermarket chain, a big baller, one of his 10 cars he keeps around. As for his ugly henchman- Arthur Gingrich, ex-con, arrested for petty crimes, theft, and carrying offensive weapons." Beck reeled off the information in front of him.

"Do we have an address?" Clara prodded and Beck nodded.

"Just one second... Ah yes, he lives in Fresno, California, owns a mansion, tight security." He printed off a map and Clara collected that as well.

"Well from Los Angeles to Fresno that would take over an hour. We need to call Mason."

Clara said and stood up to call Alana, but there was no sight of her.

"Alana? ALANA?!" she shouted and began panicking thinking of all the terrible things that might of have happened. She ran around along with Beck looking for her, however she was not to be seen anywhere.

"WHAAAAT!" Alana shouted right by Beck's ear causing him to jump slightly.

"Where the hell were you?!" Clara said angrily. Alana held up the doughnut and looked at them confused.

"I was hungry."

They told her about what they found and she nodded, mouth full of doughnut.

"Okay so we know it's not the agency, otherwise they would've been a bit smarter than tweedle dumb and tweedle dumber. " Alana quickly said.

"Not the DeRico's either since we would've known and it's not the Vipers, must have been the Triad, this Mr Prismusousyes guy must be a pawn." Alana said and Clara brought out her phone.

"Tell your brother to come over now, alone."

Mason was dragged by his collar into the living room where he was pushed into a chair.

"What the...?" he started but shut up when Beck, Alana and Clara circled him.

"Vanessa's been kidnapped, because of you. We need you to

tell us everything you know or else you won't make it out of here alive." Clara said coldly. Mason made a move to get up but a knife landing in between his legs into the chair made him sit back.

"Next time, it'll be higher." Alana growled and Mason let out a choked laugh.

"You guys are joking right? I don't know why Vanessa's been taken!"

"Does the name 'Primuzes' ring a bell?" Beck said and Mason froze.

"This can't be happening..." he said and shook his head running his hands through his curls.

He looked at the girls and Beck who were looking at him expectantly.

"Erm, well we haven't been entirely honest with you guys. Damn, I shouldn't be saying this but we're part of these illegal doings and my side tried to back out when we realised another party was muscling in, Vanessa's a pawn, they're trying to get me to persuade my father to hand over what they need. It's complicated, but Vanessa's safe for the moment. I'll call my dad and get her, I'm so sorry guys." he said, looking like a lost puppy.

Clara nodded once and brought out her phone. She quickly sent Zazzi a message and nodded at Alana when she received a speedy reply.

"You can go Mason. Do what you have to do." Beck said and Mason left.

"Okay, we have a deal to shadow this evening, stay home and rest, make sure you're ready." Beck said and the girls nodded, they would have to do this mission with one less person.

Vanessa's eyes fluttered open. She looked around confused and tried to remember what happened but with the splitting headache she had she found it hard. She brought her hand to her head and felt a lump, she pressed it gently and winced in pain. It all came back to her. The sickly smell of chloroform. Waking up in a strange car and being knocked out. Now this. She looked down at herself. She was in a chair and a strange man was sitting right in front of her gazing at her intently. He was Asian, thin and tall and he was dressed impeccably neatly.

"Such a pretty young lady, it's a shame the young Mr DeRico left his girlfriend unprotected." he said. He pulled a cigarette from behind his ear and whistled as he lit it, blowing the first puff of smoke in her face.

"Do you know why you are here Miss McCloud?" he asked her. Vanessa shook her head softly.

He chuckled to himself humourlessly.

"Your boyfriend's criminal father refused an offer with the people I work with. Until they are back on track, you will be staying here. Soon you can meet your fellow inmate. Quite a nice chap, found him trying to get into our databases so we caught the spy and he's been here for a while it seems now." He said looking at his watch. He blew out smoke again, his signet ring glinting under the light of the bare lightbulb.

Vanessa tried to get up but the man gestured for his henchmen to come and drag her. She calculated the odds and didn't resist, there was no visible escape and too many people. The only way for her now was if she was rescued, and she was sure there would be someone on their way now. A sack was put over her head and she was taken down some stairs. The sack was removed as she was facing an old, heavy, oak door. She noticed the several locks on the door. One padlock, two tumbler locks and a code. The door opened creakily after being unlocked and she was pushed into a dark musty room. The room was lit by a dim, naked light-bulb, it looked like a basement, one door, no windows, brick walls like the old part of the mansion and a bare stone floor. She noticed an empty chair with leather straps by the legs and arms and then her gaze fell upon the occupied chair.

She gasped and her mouth opened in shock. He looked up at the gasp and faced Vanessa. He knew who Vanessa was. Vanessa knew exactly who he was too. But his face registered no sign of recognition and he looked at the men holding Vanessa coldly.

"Oh, so you think she's an agent too?" he spat out and the men laughed deeply.

"No. She's the lady friend of the young Mr DeRico. She's here for a short stay. Unlike you." They sat Vanessa down onto the sturdy chair and tightened the leather straps over her slender wrists and ankles. They checked to see she was secured before leaving the room and locking the door.

"You haven't been compromised yet Vanessa? I knew you girls were good." He muttered once they had left.

"When did they catch you?" Vanessa asked, her voice was soft and sad as she took in Bandy's appearance.

"The day I left. I haven't revealed anything to the Triad yet. I hope they rot in hell." He paused and sighed.

"I've missed you girls." he said. His right eye was swelled shut and his cheek had a nasty cut on it. He was visibly tired but determined. His wrists had cuts and bruises from where he tried to pry his hands out of the tight leather straps.

"We've missed you too Bandy." Vanessa choked out, staring at the blank wall in front of her.

Zach arrived at an old factory and he slipped into an alleyway nearby. There were already about six men waiting for him, usually he wouldn't go alone but these men were on their side. There should be no trouble, he hoped.

One of them held out a small brown envelope for Zach to

take. They began mumbling something and Clara inched forward to get their conversation in range of her listening device.

"Is this it DeRico?" Zach asked and one of the men nodded.

"Give it to your father. It's very important. This video will be enough to convince any interested party in our... product shall we say. Keep it out of the wrong hands." The man said and Zachary nodded.

Clara pulled Alana and Beck back when Zach left the group and they held their breath in silence as he walked precariously close to them. The girls and Beck decided to stay and find out some more information about the group of DeRico's.

Suddenly Alana was dragged back by her hair. She elbowed her attacker in the stomach. He groaned in pain which caused Clara and Beck to snap their heads towards them. This, however also drew the attention of the DeRico's.

One of the men shouted a command and the three agents were now surrounded. They quickly sprang into action. Clara went for two smaller men, Alana went for the big one whereas Beck fought off two at a time. Their kicks and punches were mostly blocked but they did manage to get a few hits in. At the same time everyone drew their guns.

"Put down your weapons little spies." One man said cruelly pointing his gun at Alana who was pointing it back at him.

"One shot and everyone dies." she said coldly and he chuckled. All of a sudden another man came behind Alana, yanked her pony tail back and pressed a knife to her neck. The positions of the guns changed as Alana dropped her gun and Beck and Clara looked at her helplessly. Her hair was being pulled so tightly her eyes watered slightly and she felt a trickle of blood as the knife pricked her skin.

"Shoot and she dies." The man behind her snarled next to her ear.

"Take me. Leave them. You want answers don't you? Take me." Alana said through gritted teeth. The man chuckled.

"But why little one, take one spy, when we could have three?" He sneered in her ear. She recoiled at his voice.

Alana looked at Clara and Beck. They shook their heads.

"We're not leaving you behind." Beck said firmly and Alana looked at Clara pleadingly.

Clara looked conflicted but she understood Alana's wishes. She was doing this for their good; they couldn't risk it all now.

"Come back for me okay?" she said before she kicked her attacker and began fighting to give Beck and Clara a free exit. As soon as they were out of sight she surrendered.

Two men grabbed her arms and pulled them painfully behind her back. She bit the insides of her cheeks, trying to stay composed. Alana felt alone and way out of her depths, there was no knowing what these men do to spies, but it could not be good. At least the others had a chance to make things right, she thought.

The leader of the group stood in front of her smirking nastily.

"Well little one, this may hurt a bit." the man said and the last thing Alana saw was the butt of the pistol smashing into the side of her head and she passed out.

13

Zazzi had been driving for an hour and she was getting impatient. She was a young agent and this was only her second mission. She had to excel at this so she wouldn't end up being backup. Plus she couldn't bear to think of what might happen to Vanessa if she didn't get there in time. Every few seconds Zazzi would glance at the red dot on her navigator. 5 miles to go... 4 miles... 3 ... 2... 1...

Zazzi stopped her truck in a public library car park and decided to walk the rest of the way. She brought her gadgets and concealed them on herself. Slowly the iron wrought gates came into view and she smirked, counting off security cameras and calculating the camera blind spots. The security was tight but it was not impossible.

The inside of the mansion was large, Zazzi had snuck in through a back entrance and entered into what looked like a huge kitchen. Kitchen staff were working busily in the steam and the hustle and bustle of work so no one noticed her entrance. She quickly looked around panicked and made a dash for a door which led her to a small corridor full of hangers and clothing on them. Zazzi quickly spotted a maid uniform and smirked.

The mansion was gigantic, gleaming halls filled with ornate carvings, artistic statues and rows of paintings hanging on the walls. Silent. Watching.

Zazzi adjusted her uniform as she walked past a couple of men talking in hushed ones. She lowered her head and they paid no attention to her. She slowly paused to hear what they were saying.

"So far he's not said much, but we'll get him to crack or we will have to dispose of him." One of the men said and the other chuckled.

Suddenly the man turned, spinning on his heel, his long coat swishing behind him. He spotted Zazzi and clicked his fingers. She froze and mentally prepared herself for a fight.

"Ahh, bring up two whiskeys to the game room would you?" he said in an haughty tone and walked away with his accomplice. Zazzi let out the breath she was holding and turned around. She saw another maid holding a tray of food and she followed her silently. The maid looked over her shoulder every few strides, a tell-tale sign she was doing something suspicious. Zazzi followed her in a disorientating array of hallways until she reached some steps that led her to an oak door. The maid put the tray down including a kitchen knife and turned around suddenly. Zazzi quickly faced away from her to walk straight into someone.

A tall, bony woman in the same uniform as Zazzi was staring at her intently, her eye s burning holes into her.

"Who are you? You're not on our staff." she said coldly taking in Zazzi's appearance. "I'm aahhh!" Zazzi gasped as she felt a knife being pressed against her neck. The wary maid had come up behind her with a kitchen knife.

"ARMAND, WE HAVE AN INTRUDER" The bony woman screeched and Zazzi swore under her breath.

She ducked under the blade pushing the maid down the stairs and she punched the bony woman in the face. She turned to run and collided with a tall burly man.

Oh, so this must be Armand she thought bitterly. She

smiled nervously and tried to run again but Armand had other ideas. He grabbed her and put her over his shoulder as if she weighed nothing. She pushed her knee forcefully into his chest and he grunted but didn't move. She struggled against him but gave up, she was compromised. After a while she was taken down the stairs and pushed forcefully down them. The bony woman whose nose was gushing blood, fumbled with some keys and a code which Zazzi tried to get a glimpse at. She gasped at the sight in front of her. She was handcuffed into a wooden chair and Armand lumbered over her.

"Who are you." he said it in a thick French accent as a statement, not a question.

"I'm a reporter, my name is Zelda North and I work for the Daily Gazette." she said calmly but her fingers trembled slightly. He ripped off her apron and searched her finding a few knives, listening devices, bugs, decoders and a stun gun.

"Reporter you say?" he said, baring his yellowing teeth at her. She glared at him and looked at Vanessa who looked at her worryingly, her big brown eyes red and watery. Her bottom lip trembled and she let out an involuntary whimper. Armand turned to face her glaring at her. She glared at him back and he faced Zazzi again.

"Well I guess we have another spy in the building. You're going to regret ever thinking about infiltrating this place." he said, splaying spit onto Zazzi's face. He left and locked and bolted the doors.

"Hey, my name's Bandy." Bandy said smiling weakly at Zazzi who chuckled dryly and smiled back.

"It's just a big old party isn't it." she said rolling her head back.

"What the hell are we going to do now?!" Clara said furiously slamming her things on the counter. Her hands we shaking with rage and her eyes were watery. She rested her head in her hands.

"In the matter of two days I have lost my best friends; with two agents down how the hell am I supposed to do this?!" her voice shaking with anger.

Beck stood by her and she turned to hug him.

"It's going to be fine, we know the Triad won't hurt Vanessa, she's safe for the moment." Beck said soothingly but the question that hung thickly in the air was voiced by Clara.

"Yes, but what about Alana?" she whispered but Beck said nothing. They both knew how spies were interrogated.

"The agency won't let us get her back, if it puts us in danger. So what I suggest is we throw protocol out of the window and get her back." he said firmly.

"Okay where do we start?" Clara said hopefully but the hope disappeared when there was silence again. The fact of the matter was that there was not much to work with at all.

Beck sighed. "I'll look at some databases for DeRico members and see if we

recognise any of them."

He walked over to his computer and Clara slumped on her sofa settling down and getting some rest.

"If anyone can bring them back it's us." he said softly and Clara smiled hugging him tightly. They were interrupted by a knock on the door.

Clara jumped up and ran to the door, in secret hope of the return of her two best friends. She opened the door and was greeted by none other than Zach and Lucas standing nonchalantly outside.

"What do you want?" Clara asked eyeing out the two guys in front of her, her expression cold and motionless.

"To catch up." Zach said flashing a fake smile at Clara who

was contemplating on whether or not to close the door in their faces.

"Where's Alana?" He asked slightly stepping in to look behind her for Alana.

Clara stood in his way.

"She's out." She looked at Lucas who was avoiding eye contact and looking at the ground.

"You know when she'll be back?" Zach spoke again, louder this time hoping to get a more detailed answer.

"Who knows?" Clara said and looked down at the ground, sadness flashing through her bright blue eyes. She brushed her long hair back off her shoulder and looked up at Lucas.

"Is there anything else I can help you with?" Clara cocked her head to the side.

"Are you alone?" Lucas asked ignoring Clara's question.

"No actually, I'm with Beck."

"What about Vanessa?" Lucas questioned further. Zach returned to his car, waiting for Lucas to come back.

"Nope, she's out too. It's just Beck and me." Clara shrugged looking back at Beck who was on the sofa filing through some paperwork. After finally persuading them to go she slammed the door, walking back to the living room. She rubbed the back of her neck tiredly and felt the small lump of her microchip tracker.

"Beck. Alana's microchip! We got them installed when we were 14! We can trace her location!" She exclaimed and they ran towards Beck's computer. He quickly opened the program and typed in a series of coding until the screen began loading.

"It's going to take three minutes. Just wait and sit tight, we'll get a signal." He said and Clara paced the room in anticipation.

1 minute left.
20 seconds.
10.
9.
8.
Clara moved closer to the screen.

7.
6.
5.
4.
3.
2.
1.

The screen showed a map with a red dot. Beck quickly noted a street name down but the screen changed again.

[MICROCHIP DEACTIVATED] the screen flashed a few times and Beck slammed his fist onto the desk.

Clara groaned in frustration.

"We were so close!" She screamed and she slapped the counter.

"Wait, how would they deactivate the microchip? The only way you can is to do it from the agency system or extract it from its setting ..." Beck trailed off when it sunk in. Clara stared at him horrifying, her mind reeling with thoughts of what they were doing to her friend.

"She's in for it." Beck said gravely.

Alana slowly came back to consciousness. She was handcuffed to a metal chair and he feet were tightly strapped to the legs. Her head ached where the gun handle had struck her head and she opened her eyes to a man in front of her. He had a mop of white- blonde hair, a bloated face and small eyes set far apart from each other.

"Nice of you to finally join us." He said, his voice was fast and robotic. Alana smirked back ironically.

"Nice of you to have me here." She said and he chortled. He had two other men in the room with him who were standing by the door. He faced Alana again not even remotely shocked at how young she was.

"We have a few questions we need to ask you little spy." He said, his mouth near Alana's face.

"First of all, you need a breath mint." She said turning her head away from him. He smiled cruelly. She watched him warily. He took a step forward a backhanded Alana across the face. Her head flew to the side as he left a red welt on the side of her face.

"Who do you work for?" He snarled and she glared at him, ignoring the sting of the slap.

"You'll get nothing out of me." She growled back and spat in his face. He returned this by swinging his chubby fist right at her face. She bit her lip as she felt one side of her face throbbing.

He croaked a laugh and grabbed her hair dragging her up.

"Had enough little spy?" He said and she growled at him.

"Is. That. The. Best. You. Can. Do." She said in between gritted teeth, feeling her scalp bleeding as he pulled her hair.

He shook his head. One of his minions wheeled in a table full of surgical instruments and knives. He stopped the cart right by Alana's torture chair. She gulped silently but tried to maintain a calm air about her. She couldn't let them scare her with a display of glorified cutlery.

The man brought out a long, thin jagged knife and he held it up to the light bulb for a while. He slowly dragged it hardly across Alana's forearm and she struggled in her chair as blood flowed all over her arm. He laughed deeply at her pain and put the knife to her cheek again leaving a mark.

"Still silent little one?" He said digging the knife deep into her cheek. She whimpered slightly and one of his henchmen spoke up.

"You might want to check her for implanted microchips. We removed everything she had on her but most agents have some sort of tracking." He said.

"Oh well aren't you a smart ass." Alana spat at him and the mans hand went around her throat tightly, his nails digging into her neck. She made a small choking sound as his fingers pressed the back of her neck feeling the lump.

"Knife." He said holding his hand out for one of his henchmen to place a blade in his pudgy hand. He pushed Alana's head forward and dug the knife in deeply cutting out the lump. Alana screamed out when she felt the blade dig into her and she spasmed in pain.

"NO NO NO STOP." She screamed and he stamped on the bloody microchip killing its signal.

"Now will you tell us who you work for." He said getting angry. Alana felt tears running involuntarily down her cheek.

"I already have a team coming to get me and when they find you, you will wish you never laid a finger on me." She screamed at him and he replied with another punch causing her lip and nose to bleed. He smiled, his yellow teeth poking out from his thick lips.

"I don't see any team around."

14

Bandy struggled against the bindings around his wrists. If he could only slip through it, then he could escape. He looked at Vanessa who was trying to look for a way out. Her calculating eyes searching for an exit from the gloom. The other agent in the chair opposite him looked collected but something was troubling her. Bandy watched her closely. Vanessa had told him she was on their side but he doubted that the Agency would send an agent to help a mission that seemed to be going fine.

His musings were interrupted by the door clicking open and food being brought in. Or something resembling food. Finally, he thought, feeling the emptiness of his stomach. Vanessa scrunched her nose at it and Zazzi sighed audibly.

He noticed a bone in the small sliver of meat he had and he took it. It could be useful. He put it in his mouth and began sharpening the end of it. The bone was soft - pretty soon he'd be able to chew it into a sharp point. Then they could break out. Bandy smiled to himself and Vanessa noticed.

She hoped he had a plan, she'd been looking around for ages and found nothing, there was 24 hour security and the guard left his post for 10 minutes maximum. Even if they broke out of their bindings, there was no way out except for the door with multiple locks. She could pick some of the locks, maybe find the code too but it would take at least half an hour. She prayed that her friends were after her. Zazzi had come but she had gotten caught, she wondered if her friends would follow soon after.

Armand came in. It looked like he ran the household and the illicit activities that came along with it. He muttered something in Mandarin to one of his accomplices who left the room hurriedly. His Triad tattoo was visible, his shirt sleeves rolled back. Vanessa looked down trembling, playing the role of Mason's terrified girlfriend and Zazzi shifted in her seat. Bandy kept a brave face on but even fear was beginning to show.

Armand grabbed Bandy's collar with a beefy hand.

"Have you been talking to the DeRico girl?" He snarled at Bandy and he raised a hand to hit him.

"No stop!" Vanessa shouted and did not lower her gaze at his glare.

"What do you want from us?" She said softly, a tear rolling off her nose.

Armand bared his teeth.

"You are getting an upgrade by orders of Mr DeRico."

Vanessa shook her head.

"N-no no thanks. I'll stay here until I am released." She said and he glared at her.

"You will regret it."

Mason paced around his bedroom impatiently. Anger was gushing through him, tearing through him. He fought to control it but it possessed his every move. His sweet, intelligent Vanessa was being held captive with two other spies. She was not a common criminal, she did not deserve it.

He had not talked about what he was going to do with his brothers yet, he didn't even know himself. He just couldn't stay there helpless. He picked up his phone and rang his father.

"Dad, any word?" he said into the phone containing his anger.

"Mason I can't call them until the deal is over; then we can get her back safely." Mason's father said through the phone and Mason growled.

"That's in 2 weeks. She needs to be back now. Her cousins won't take it well that she's missing."

Mason's father sighed irritably.

"Well maybe you shouldn't have gotten close to her. Now go, I have work to do." And with that he hung up.

Mason swore loudly and threw the phone on his bed. No. He wasn't going to stay put. He would save her himself.

Clara typed furiously into her computer. She had her glasses on scrutinising every detail on the screen. Beck was also on several devices. Clara was looking for Vanessa. Beck was looking for Alana. Zazzi hadn't called in which only meant one thing. Well two things. Either she was caught, or her phone ran out of battery. It was most likely the former.

"Anything?" Clara called out after a while. Beck shrugged.

"I have a tracing but it's too general, it just highlights east California, so she seems

quite far away." He said and Clara sighed.

"Well we know where Vanessa is but if Zazzi was caught we can't risk going there. Perhaps we should call the agency?" She said but Beck snapped his head towards her.

"We can't trust them with information. There's a mole and until the mole is gone, then we can trust them." He said coldly and Clara raised her eyebrows.

They spent the next hour trying to do something but failing. Clara checked her phone. She had several missed calls from Millie and a text from Lucas which she didn't open. She also had a text from an unknown number which piqued her curiosity. She tapped the screen and opened the text message.

It was blank. She reloaded it but there was nothing to see. Just a blank text message.

Probably some stupid joke, she thought and proceeded to delete it but paused. No one would take the time to send a blank text message to a number and bother to make their number private. Clara tapped her finger on the desk and walked up to her room, hoping for any inclination as to why someone would send her a blank text message. She laughed softly remembering when Alana accidentally sent her a photo of her elbow by leaning on her phone. It was only ages later when she realised she had sent a photo of her elbow. Her mind wandered over to a lesson they'd had during training about using mobile cellular devices. They were being taught on how to download a software to make their phones and their targets phones as listening bugs. The target' phone would be completely controlled by their phones, the phone could turn into a bug at the entry of a few codes.

"Damn, I would HATE for that to happen to my phone." Clara had said, fiddling with the spy-phone. Vanessa was at a ballet exam so it was just Clara, Alana and their teacher, Mr Ritzer. He was a fun teacher, young, good looking and had a great sense of humour.

"Ooh I know a way around your texts being hacked! You could make the text the same colour as the background! Then it would look invisible!" Clara said typing something into the phone. Mr Ritzers phone beeped and he took a moment to change the colour.

"No no no that wasn't meant for you." Clara said blushing furiously.

"Mr Ritzer is a slice of hotness." He read out and chuckled. Alana's eyes widened and Mr Ritzer winked at Clara who wished the earth would open up and swallow her. The invisible text messages. The only people that knew about

them was Alana and William Ritzer. Clara squealed as these memories rushed back to her. She fumbled with her phone, finding a way to change the text colour on her highly specialised phone and cried out in relief.
'You're not safe. Spies everywhere. Be careful. Don't call. Don't debrief. Just get
out safe.
-W.R'

Clara smiled but felt a sense of dread overcome her. They really were alone now. The only people she had were Beck and William who was probably thousands of miles away, as was her Aunt.

She ran downstairs to Beck who was working on the what could have been in the envelope Zach received.

"Beck." She said and he turned his head towards her.

"We're going rogue."

She couldn't take it anymore. She was very quickly losing her mind. The walls felt like they were closing in on her. Alana tried to breathe closing her eyes and lying down on the straw mat her interrogators had so kindly provided her. Her wrists were cuffed together as were her feet and she was kept in a small closet-like room with not much except toilet breaks and water. They didn't give her food. They needed her weak, but alive. Her long hair was messy and matted with blood. The back of her neck hurt horribly from where they had dug their knife in to rip out her tracker. Her face was bruised and she was sure she had a cracked rib. One thing was for certain, these men weren't planning on keeping her alive after they had found out what they wanted. Which they never would, she resolved.

But she had found out what they wanted.

When she was fading in and out of consciousness they had

been discussing what Alana had come on this mission for. The deal. Not an 'it' they were trading, but a 'he'. It wasn't an object the two groups were dealing with, it was a person. More specifically, the information this person was in possession of. Dr Brian Dallow was their captive. A very valuable, and highly sensitive captive. She did not know what information he knew just yet, but what she did know was that he was highly sought after by many criminal organisations, and international governments.

They had a matter of days until what Dr Dallow knew would be sold to the highest bidder, and the Vipers were there to make sure Dr Dallow went to no one but them. She had passed out before getting any more details and later cursed herself for being so weak.

She felt her cheeks moist with tears and Alana wiped them furiously. She had to get out of here. Her next toilet and water break was in 12 minutes. For those twelve minutes she decided to prepare herself. She knew she was acting in the spur of the moment, but at least she would prepare for those 12 minutes. Alana instantly went into a few exercises to keep her as awake as possible. She braided her hair and secured it with a piece of ripped fabric. 5 more minutes.

She looked around for a weapon but found nothing except a cigarette stub. She stood up shakily and whimpered in pain as she felt sparks of agony shoot through her body from multiple places. They had tried to hurt her in excruciatingly painful ways and she didn't know if she could stand it any longer.

The door creaked open and a maid came in looking at Alana cautiously. Alana followed her until they reached a room. Alana took a gulp of water feeling instantly more refreshed. Quick as lighting she turned and smashed her fist into the maid's nose and swiftly smashed her palm into the side of her head. She felt bad for hurting her but it had to be done, she broke into a run out of the room, adrenaline pumping through her veins. The place she was being held at had long, dark stone hallways and her footsteps echoed through the darkness. Her breath came out in ragged puffs and she could feel the warm wet stickiness of blood as the wound at the back of her

Party Crashers

neck opened up again. Voices and footsteps echoed and she slowed her pace and her pounding heart.

"Damn it." She muttered under her breath searching for a place to hide. Right beside her was a wooden door and she twisted the knob praying it was open. She felt relief flood her when it opened with a small click. The door closed and the men passed heatedly discussing the difference between beer and lager. Alana set off again, she needed to find a phone or something, she looked at the room she was in and she gasped as her eyes adjusted to the darkness. The room was security central, there where screens everywhere showing another corner of the place she was in, also the outside. She sat down on the chair quickly trying to figure out where she was when she noticed, too late, a steaming cup of coffee and a jacket hung on the back of a chair.

The sound of a throat clearing turned her towards a tall, attractive man. He smirked at her as she looked around frantically. Alana grabbed the cup of coffee and threw it at him and tried to run but he grabbed her arm and pulled her back from the door. She turned around and swung at him but he deftly caught her hand and twisted it painfully behind her back causing her to bend over. She kicked him in the groin area and his groan confirmed she had found her target. She broke into a run again, running purely on the adrenaline of danger.

The running footsteps of the man could be heard close behind her so she ran for the closest door and locked it, hoping it would buy her some time. She looked around and nearly collapsed with happiness. There was nothing but a desk with some papers on it, but what made her ecstatic was the computer. She opened it and almost laughed with joy when it wasn't locked. No footsteps could be heard from outside, she had time. Alana almost laughed when she spotted the Skype icon in the corner and logged on hurriedly, her hands fluttering over the computer shakily. Then came footsteps, they were near the door. She quickly opened a video message and clicked record. The man on the other side tried to the knob and found it locked. This was followed by some heavy pounding as he tried to force the door open.

Alana looked straight into the camera.

"Clara, Beck, I don't know where I am, I hope you're safe." He voice broke weakly and she quickly said what she needed too.

"I know what they're dealing. It's not an object it's a person. Dr Brian Dallow. I don't know what he knows. But it needs to be kept away from the Vipers, from any of them, before they sell to the highest bidder. They want to use it for something bigger, I didn't find out what. You need to stop this. I love you-" she was cut off by the door slamming to the floor and a group of men swarmed into the room grabbing Alana by her limbs. She struggled weakly but there was nothing she could do anymore. It was in Beck and Clara's hands now.

"Clara your computer beeped! I told you to get off Facebook!" Beck shouted to Clara who had popped into the kitchen for a snack. Clara walked in, staring at her laptop curiously.

"That's not my Facebook sound, that's my Skype sound." She said slowly.

Beck sighed still typing furiously into his computer.

"Tell your friends you're busy." He said gruffly and was cut off by her cry.

"I only have you, Vanessa and Alana on this account!" Clara said rushing to her laptop. Beck jumped up from his seat and rushed to her computer screen. She gasped.

"It's from Alana." Beck said and Clara opened the video message.

Alana's blurry face showed up on screen. Fear showed in her eyes even through

the bad quality and they could make out the bruises and

dried blood on her face.

Her voice came out weak and crackly but the pain rang through clearly. Clara looked at her best friend's face, her heart slamming against her chest. Beck and Clara both leaned closer when she started talking about the deal. Clara heard the thumping and they both saw the men come and grab her. Before the video call had ended they heard Alana shout out and the screen went black.

Clara looked at Beck, his handsome features contorted in frustration. He brought his laptop next to Clara's and began typing furiously.

She smirked.

"Can you trace it?" she said and he nodded with a small smile.

"She's not getting rid of us that easily." He said smirking back and Clara gripped his arm in happiness. They were interrupted by a knocking on the door. Clara ran up to open it, checking through the peephole first, it was Mason.

"Mason, what are you doing here?" She said confusedly. He looked troubled and had dark circles under his eyes, his soft curly hair was in disarray and looked like he had run his hands through it one too many times.

"I'm going to get her. Don't tell my brothers where I am."

"Not your smartest move little one." Alana's torturer said condescendingly. Alana was once again strapped into a chair but in a darker room with one window which was boarded up with. Alana said nothing but her heart was crashing against her ribcage and she was shaking with fear as her façade fell and the table with surgical instruments was wheeled in.

"You told someone a very important secret, now I will need to find out yours..." the man said and gave a cruel short laugh.

Alana shook her head violently.

"No no, please." She sobbed watching as he took out a hammer from the table. He fiddled with it in his hands twirling it through his bulky fingers and he went to Alana. She bunched her hands into fists but with he forced her hand to open. Alana opened her eyes confused as to what he was doing when he brought the hammer down hard on her middle finger, instantly breaking the bones. She let out a piercing scream and writhed in pain in the chair thrashing around. Her hand was bleeding and tears flowed down her face.

Her screams were cut off by a backhand to her face causing her to spit blood and her right eye started to swell.

"Who do you work for?"

"I'm too young to be a spy." She whimpered feeling her body course with pain and fear.

"You're also too young to hold under torture so tell us, who sent you and who else is there?" he said and he brought out a thin sharp knife.

Alana froze at the sight of the knife. "W-what are you doing with that?" she stammered nervously and he chuckled.

"I'm going to re-adjust your face, maybe make your smile wider, you look a bit glum." He mused laughing at his own joke.

"Okay I'll tell who I work for ..." She paused catching her breath. The man halted watching Alana closely. She lowered her voice and he leaned in to catch what she was trying to tell him. As soon as he was close enough Alana head butted him forcefully and he yelled again, slapping her sharply against the face. She shut her eyes, preparing herself for the pain. Her head was restrained by a man behind her and he brought the knife to the middle of her bottom lip, his lips flecked with spit as he glared at Alana. With a slow, deep press he cut her lip open and she felt the warm moist blood flow down her chin slowly and she squeezed her eyes shut tightly groaning in immense pain.

"So, would you rather die painfully, or tell me what I need and die swiftly? I can't promise I will make it painless." He sneered at the snivelling Alana.

"I'll tell you nothing." She said spitting out blood.

"Then, I'll kill you." He replied, wiping the knife and picking up another tool from his selection.

"We're here." Beck said opening the door to his jeep as he and Clara got out. She looked up at the large castle-like mansion.

"Doesn't look like its 5 stars but I guess it'll have to do." She said sarcastically and loaded her utility belt with her gun, some knives, her lock picks and other gadgets. She also brought Alana's utility belt and Vanessa's remained n the car. They ran towards the mansion, laying low, saving their energy for the big showdown. The mansion was monstrous in size, and far away from Los Angeles so the Jeep was their only getaway. Beck and Clara headed towards the mansion but they couldn't find one entrance that was not protected by guards. Beck looked at Clara and at the windows with large ledges, big enough for two nimble spies. Clara nodded and they reached for what they needed in their utility belts.

"Happy Birthday Vanessa." She muttered as they set off.

"Zach we have a call and Mason's nowhere to be found." Lucas said storming into Zach's bedroom. His room was impeccably tidy and plain being trained as a solider since he was old enough to walk. Zach was lounged on his bed cat-like throwing darts at the door and one narrowly missed Lucas' head.

"Yeah I got the call too. Some interrogation I heard, this should be fun, haven't had one in ages." He said, not sounding very excited at all. He got up off his bed with a sigh and grabbed a white t-shirt and his jacket. Lucas chuckled.

"You wouldn't want to wear white on interrogation days, blood stains are hard to get out." He said and Zach nodded knowingly.

"Thanks bro, black shirt it is." He said with a cruel smile and they both left the house taking Lucas' car.

"It's a long ride, we have time to try and reach Mason." Lucas said as Zach strapped himself in.

"Or we could work out how we're going to make this one talk." Zach said darkly.

"Oh, happy birthday Vanessa!" Zazzi said brightly at the tired Vanessa.

"I want to go home…" Vanessa whimpered drowsily. Bandy was fiddling slightly and suddenly let out a gasp.

"Guys I think..." He lifted his right hand which was no longer attached to the chair. The guard had taken his break which had given him an open window to break free with the bone he had managed to chew into a point. He ran over to Vanessa and hurriedly unbound her. She flexed her arm enjoying the feel of her stiff joints being stretched. Bandy moved over to Zazzi's bounds when the keys jingled from outside and Bandy rushed back to his seat as him at Vanessa readjusted their bindings. The thick, burly guard entered and sat on his stool staring at them, leering at Vanessa and Zazzi.

"Didn't know teenage girls were your thing." Bandy said dryly and the guard snapped his attention to Bandy with a growl. He got up and sent a swift backhand to Bandy and the connection of the slap echoed in the room followed by silence. Bandy glared at the man as he walked over to Vanessa who started trembling with fear and looked down. He grabbed Vanessa's throat and lifted her by the throat turning to grin at Bandy with his face almost touching Vanessa's.

"Problem, spy filth?" He gloated turning back to Vanessa only to feel himself being dragged back and thrown on the floor. He shouted out in surprise as Bandy roundhouse kicked him in the face and he spat out blood, staggering backwards. Vanessa jumped up to help the weak Bandy fight off the larger man.

The man was strong but had no skill. Vanessa pushed him forcefully against the wall where Bandy began punching him, one blow after another. With one last kick to his stomach the man slid to the floor with a thump, unconscious. The noise of the fighting attracted attention and the door swung open with another two guards. Vanessa ran to the smallest with a side kick causing him to lose his footing as well as her. She was weak but she would fight them all anyway- anything to get out of there. Bandy struggled from his lack of combat skills but together they knocked out one of the men. The other grabbed Vanessa by the hair and held a gun to her head. Bandy instantly stopped fighting as Vanessa felt her head throbbing with pain. One of the men on the floor began regaining consciousness and he steadily rose to his feet.

"Big mistake." He snarled and Bandy lifted his chin defiantly.

"I've made bigger mistakes." He retorted and Vanessa whimpered as the man pulled her hair tighter.

The man laughed dryly. Bandy was breathing heavily and looked Vanessa straight into her eyes.

"Vanessa...I need you to get out of here. Do it for me. Do you promise me?" He said, big brown eyes staring into hers.

"SHUT UP." The man shouted pointing his pistol at Bandy.

"PROMISE ME VANESSA." Bandy shouted the air of urgency increasing.

"I promise." Vanessa said softly as the gun shot echoed through the room. She never left his eyes. Not even when he slumped to the floor, his chest pooling with blood as his head smashed onto the floor. A shot through the heart.

Vanessa's vision swam with tears as she screamed. She began violently shaking and she fell to the floor beside Bandy's body, pressing down on his wound to stop the bleeding. His breath rattled out weakly and he looked up at her before his eyes glazed over. He was dead. She tried to choke out words but nothing came. She felt as if she was far away, watching this from another place, it was a dream. A nightmare. He couldn't be dead. She extended her trembling hand to shake him awake.

He was just playing games, he wouldn't die here, not like this, he would die safe and happy when he was old, when he lived his life. They would be friends for years, he would get to see his children grow up. Not die after weeks of torture in a dull basement. She didn't hear or see anything else except Bandy's still body. He was gone. All the times they'd spent together. Taking pictures, high school, when they found him at the beach party, his laptop. All the images flashed through her mind, each with stabbing pain. She couldn't stop her body shaking with heart wrenching sobs and she was screaming with grief.

She sobbed out in pain, trying to shake him awake violently, and hugging his dead body close to her, hoping for him to hug her back. But all she got was the dampness of his blood and his dead weight. The only movement was her uncontrollable sobbing.

The men lifted her up, dragging her away from Bandy, back to her chair, re-adjusting her bindings. One of them kneeled down to her level, looking right into her wide teary eyes.

"So you knew the spy. It seems that the DeRico's girl isn't actually their girl at all. She's one of them." He said looking at the other men and they got up to drag the body away. Vanessa thrashed in her chair when they took him out of the room. She struggled against her bindings so forcefully she thought her hands would fall off.

"NOOOO, DON'T LEAVE ME, BANDY DON'T GO!" She screamed out, until her vocal chords couldn't scream anymore.

"I promise." She whispered softly making a vow to get out for Bandy.

15

"Well there's like 1000 windows, which one do we jump?" Clara said, as she looked up at all the windows and the possible entrances; if they could catch on to the ledge on the second floor then they could swing into the first floor window and work from there. Her thoughts were interrupted by Beck pulling her behind a bush as a car pulled up by the castle. Neither Beck nor Clara managed to get a glimpse of the car and they were thankful they parked the Jeep out of sight. Clara tapped Beck's shoulder gently and he turned to where she was pointing. A small window on the third floor that appeared to be boarded up.

"Well I guess we have no choice, let's check it out." Beck said, flashing a perfect smile as they took their wires and swung it so the claw gripped at the ledge about the boarded window. Slowly and quietly they levered themselves up read to swing back and do a classic bit of breaking and entering.

"Mr DeRico, Mr Rufus, how are you today? Where, may I ask is Mr Mason?" The boys were greeted by one of their men at the door.

"I don't see how that is any of your concern." Lucas said coldly as they walked towards the usual room. They opened the door but it was empty.

"What the-" Zach started and the butler stepped up.

"Oh, she was trouble so we moved her to the third story interrogation room." He stammered and Lucas' eyes widened.

"She? A girl? That's unusual." He said slowly as they headed towards the room. Zach opened the door to reveal a girl strapped in the chair. She was bent over, curly brown hair matted with blood hiding her. Lucas stepped forward and was in front of the strange girl in an instant. He put his hand under her chin, lifting it up slowly to reveal her face.

"Alana?" he gasped as her eyes fluttered open and closed again. Zach stepped back, horrified.

"This is a mistake, she's my girlfriend, not a spy-" He was cut off by the boarded windows flying into pieces.

The cardboard ripped apart. Beck and Clara speedily recovered from their entrance and everyone brought out their guns. Everyone held one another at gun point and it was only then that they realised who they were facing.

"Oh... maybe she is a spy..." Zach said taking in Clara and Beck's entrance.

"Clara?" Lucas looked around dumbfounded.

"No. It's Tarzan." She said sarcastically and Lucas' gun switched from Beck to Clara, his eyes full of cold rage.

"Who the hell are you?" Lucas yelled at her and Beck turned his gaze to Zach. He looked troubled and kept looking from Alana's still body to Lucas and the DeRico men that joined them. Silence hung heavy in the air, guns ready to kill. Zachary nodded to himself as if rounding up a conversation in his head and turned his gun away from Beck to Alana's torturer.

"Zach man what are you doing?" Lucas hissed.

"Put your gun down now or I will kill you Rufus." The man snarled but Zach held his gun assuredly, a mad look in his eye.

"Lucas. Get. Alana." Zach said before shooting the spot above the man's head diverting his attention. He kicked the man powerfully in the best causing him to crash into the wall. His minions started firing blindly and Beck unarmed one of them swiftly knocking him out with an elbow to the side of the head. Lucas looked torn but ran over to Alana and tried to undo her bindings. Clara came behind him with a knife and quickly cut her free without a word. He turned to look her in the eyes but she was attacked from behind. Lucas quickly lifted Alana over his shoulder, she didn't move or react. Clara punched the man and turned to yell at Lucas.

"The windows! Our wires are still attached!"

Lucas quickly saw the wires and nodded.

"See you down there bro." He shouted to Zach who was fighting off two men and with Beck.

Lucas took a leap and managed to grab on and keep Alana on his back.

"Hang on little one." He said as they slid to the floor heavily. Lucas had a deep burn mark on his hands from the wire but ignored the pain as they landed. Alana moaned faintly and Lucas felt his t-shirt damp with blood.

"Shit." He muttered and he laid her on the ground. He was joined a moment later by the others. Lucas looked at Clara and felt his emotions in turbulence. What the hell was going on, he thought;.

"To the Jeep." Beck ordered and Zach reached down to pick up Alana and he cradled her as they ran to where Beck hid the jeep. He quickly unlocked the car and they scrambled in as Beck started the car and sped off down the dirt road.

"Wait! My car is back there!" Lucas said and Zach slapped him over the head from behind.

Lucas sat next to Beck in the passenger seat and Zach sat at the back with Alana's head in his lap. Clara looked at her frozen, shocked at the state of her best friend. No one said anything for 10 minutes.

"So where are we going?" Beck said.

"Hospital." Zach said at the same time that Clara said "Motel."

"Motel it is." Beck said calmly.

"What?! Alana needs to get to a hospital immediately!" Zach shouted heatedly.

"If we go to a hospital we all die. The authorities are probably alerted about us and your people will head to the closest hospital first thing. Our Agency has gone rogue. You've gone rogue." Beck replied coldly. He paused.

"How is she?" he asked more gently, wanting to ask what the Agency was. Both Clara and Zach looked at Alana. She was deathly pale under the had blood on her face along and large blackish bruises. Her fingers were broken and swollen. Clara lifted her t-shirt slightly to reveal serious bruises, more cuts and even burns. Her lip was still bleeding and she didn't stir at all. Zach stared at her wondering how Alana could still look so broken yet so beautiful.

"We need to tend to her but we'll do it ourselves, you've got the kit right?" Clara asked Beck and he nodded. A few more moments of silence followed.

"So, you're agents?" Lucas said coldly clearing his throat. Zach silently stared at the beaten and bruised Alana.

"Yes." Clara replied shortly. Lucas nodded.

"Why are you in California?" He asked icily, he turned his handsome face to look

outside.

Clara began to speak but Beck cut her off.

"We can't tell you. " He said curtly. Lucas looked furious but this time Zach spoke up.

"It was the deal, wasn't it?" he said slowly. Beck did not reply, but his knuckles whitened as he gripped the steering wheel. Zach nodded, he knew he got it right. They drove for an hour creating a distance before stopping at a motel. It was clean at least, and perfect for laying low. Beck went inside and paid for the two rooms in cash. Zach lifted Alana whilst Clara gathered the weapons. The receptionist didn't even look up as the team trooped in. When they got to their rooms Zach lay Alana on the bed gently and Clara brought the medical kit. She took a knife and cut off her clothes leaving her in her underwear. She still didn't stir. Clara motioned to Zach to help her and he took some bandages out of the kit.

After they had managed to wash most of the blood off Clara brought out a needle to stitch the deep wounds.

"Woah woah woah. Do you even know how to use that?" Zach asked before Clara began stitching the gaping wound.

"Of course I do." She sighed irritably and she stuck the needle into Alana's skin. Alana immediately started stirring and her eyes snapped open.

"Zach restrain her!" Clara said urgently and Zach covered her mouth gently and held her down as Clara stitched her up as fast as she could. He whispered in her ear, telling her it would be over soon. Alana closed her eyes and started whimpering and breathing heavily as if trying not to cry. Clara bandaged her up, put some clothes she brought for her on and told Zach she was going out to get some food for all of them. When Clara left, Alana shifted and tried to sit up. Pain coursed through her body and Zachary rushed to her side when he heard her gasp in pain.

"Lie down, you're hurt." Zach said gently putting his hands on her shoulders. Alana looked at him blankly. Zach straightened up as she finally sat up. For a while neither of them said anything. Alana's face was stony and her eyes were devoid of any emotion. She lifted the covers off her, confused as to why she was wearing a blank tank top and combat trousers. Clara, she thought and she smiled slightly at how much she had missed her best friend. Even her leather jacket and combat boots where tucked away in the corner.

"You need to rest Alana, you need time to heal." Zach said and she flinched as he came close to her.

He reached his hand out to her and she instantly recoiled, backing away from him.

"Alana?" He asked confused as she tried to get up and walk away but nearly passed out. Zach rushed to her but again she flinched away and Zach was shocked at the expression on her face.

Fear.

She started visibly shaking and backed herself into a corner. She was shaking her head and Zach stepped towards her slowly, one step at a time. One side of her face was badly bruised and her lip was swollen.

She looked at him with burning hatred and Zach felt as if he'd been stabbed. He reached out to her but there was nothing there. She was a shell of what she used to be. She looked at his hand forlornly and stood up. Zach stopped her from falling to the ground and lifted her up gently putting her back on the bed. She crawled to the edge of the bed, grabbing the lamp nearby defensively.

"Come on little one, I won't bite." He said trying to ease the tension. Her eyes widened at the use of the name her torturers used and she dropped the lamp and started crying uncontrollably.

She began screaming hysterically and Zach panicked, utterly confused. Clara ran in and took in the scene. She glared at Zach.

"What did you do?!" She screamed angrily.

"Nothing! I don't know why she's screaming!" Zach said holding his hands up, stepping away from the screaming Alana. Clara ran over to Alana hugging her tightly as she cried into her shoulder.

"Zach, it would be best if you just go." Clara said and Zach sighed and left the room running his hand through his hair. Clara gently settled the now calm Alana down on the bed and snuggled in next to her.

"Clara?" She whispered her voice scratchy due to her over-used vocal chords. Alana stayed silent for a moment.

"We need to get Vanessa back. Then get the hell out of here." She said softly before falling into a deep sleep.

"Up up up! We've got to move. We're wanted by everybody. Beck get Alana, she's still sleeping. Lucas you drive and Zach get the weapons." Clara said after they finished breakfast. Their next step was to find Vanessa and Mason. They needed to take this one step at a time.

They all got into the car, Beck carrying Alana and Zach watching her closely. Clara got in beside Lucas and avoided his eyes. She passed him a slip of paper with the address of a hotel and their fingers brushed lightly. Ignore it, she thought as she quickly drew her hand away and Lucas began to drive.

It was around late afternoon when they got to the hotel. Clara went to her room and put down her stuff along with other things she had brought. She walked over to the mirror to readjust her hair when the door clicked open and Lucas walked in.

She turned to face him and crossed her arms over her chest.

"We need to talk..." Lucas said. Clara shrugged and sat down, motioning for him to sit down.

"So..." he started.

"So?"

He paused for a moment, gathering his thoughts.

"Were you only getting close to me for your mission?" Lucas blurted out. Clara averted her gaze.

"I was doing my job." She said softly. Lucas sighed and stood up and Clara felt her heart sink.

"Lucas no. Wait." She said grabbing his hard. He looked at her so coldly she almost flinched but she kept her grasp on his arm and looked straight into his blue eyes.

"At first it was about the mission, but then, I got to know you, and Lucas I swear, I didn't mean for you to find out this way." She paused and bit her look looking at him with her big blue eyes.

"You make it so hard for me to hate you Clara." He said, hurt, torn. She said nothing, just looked down.

"You came to destroy me, you've made me an enemy of my own family."

"Lucas-" she started.

"Don't. You're an agent. You used me Clara. All these things. But, I just can't help it Clara, you make me so…"

Lucas ruffled his hair frustrated. She pulled Lucas towards her, laying her head on his firm chest.

"Just say it." She whispered, holding her breath as she waited for him to speak.

"I love you." He said softly before kissing her gently.

Zach knocked on the door and Beck swung it open. Alana was sitting up on the bed and she stiffened when she saw Zach.

"How is she?" He asked Beck.

"She heals fast, she's much better. But she still needs time, to heal, psychologically…" Beck said looking at Alana worriedly.

Zach walked in gingerly.

"I'll give you guys a minute…" Beck said leaving the room.

"Alana." She turned her head away from Zach, getting up off the bed.

He stepped forward to help her and heard her breath catch in fear.

"Damn it Alana! Why are you scared of me!" He shouted and grabbed her by the shoulders looking into her face which had a bit more colour in it.

"I would never hurt you. Never." He said, holding her small shoulders gently, feeling his heart pang when she stepped away.

"You're one of them." She said shakily and he felt heartbroken when she looked at him like he was a monster.

"You're a criminal." She pointed to her face.

"You do this to people. You kill people. Innocent people. If it wasn't me in that chair, you would've hurt them like they hurt me."

"I've hurt people, and it makes me feel terrible. Cold. Heartless. You hurt people… and you don't even care." She said, her voice now a whisper, her face filled with pain. Zach reflected her pain.

"Alana, I-"

"Don't!" She shouted "Don't say anything!" She angrily tried to wipe her tears. "Just don't tell me I mean something to you. Don't tell me you actually care. Just leave me. I don't want to see you."

He sighed, desperate to make her see his side. His eyes were bright and he stepped closer. She looked up at him, at his beachy blonde hair, his soft green eyes, and his handsome face gazing at her worriedly.

"Alana you have no idea what you mean to me. You have no idea what I would do for you. I don't want to care, but I have no choice." He paused, watching her face for any sign of expression.

"You're not making it easy for me. I know I'm not a good guy, but I can't leave you." He stepped closer to Alana and took her hand and ran a finger along her jaw gently. She closed her eyes as a tear rolled down her cheek. She leaned into his chest.

"I want to kill the person that hurt you like his. I would do anything for you Alana, but I would never leave you. I need you." He said looking at her earnestly. She snapped her eyes open looking into his sea green

eyes. Zach leaned in and kissed her cheek gently.

"Zach?" she said softly, as if she wasn't sure it was him. He murmured in response, kissing her neck lightly.

"I want you to go. I never want to see you again." she whispered feeling tears run her face and down Zach's back. He stiffened and drew away.

"I'm not going anywhere Alana."

Alana woke up. She checked the time, it was late afternoon, she'd slept so deeply throughout the whole night. She looked around, Clara was gone and there was a leather jacket on the armchair beside her bed. Zach, she thought and ignored the aching pain that came with the thought of him. She stood up and winced at the torturous walk to the bathroom. She had a shower, got dressed and brushed her teeth. Only after she was done she looked into the mirror and saw her reflection. Alana let out a piercing scream when she saw her face. Zach ran into the bathroom at Alana's scream where he saw Alana stood holding her face, crying in shock at her reflection.

"That's not me!" She shrieked, touching her face and breaking into hysterical sobs as her eyes looked at him wildly. Her lip had a large cut down the middle, her bruises were dark and large and she had cuts all over her. I look like a monster, she thought.

"Alana come here." Zach said worried about the unstable Alana but she was not listening.

"My face…" she said softly looking lost, her eyes filling up with tears as she was transfixed by the mirror. Before Zachary could stop her she punched the mirror shattering in into pieces. Zach grabbed her hands which were bleeding before she could cause any more damage to herself and pulled her towards him, crushing her against his chest. She was shaking but seemed to relax in his arms as she breathed in his scent which smelled like the ocean. Zach kissed the top of her head gently holding her tight.

"Who? Who could ever want a face like that?" She whispered every so softly into his chest but Zach heard. He drew away from her so he could look into her eyes and saw the pain in her face, her face had healed considerably but she had been badly hurt.

"I can." Zach said sternly looking into her eyes. She gazed back at him. She looked so vulnerable and sad that he leaned in and kissed her softly. She closed her eyes and kissed him back but suddenly he felt a knife against his throat and he stepped back.

"I can't let you hurt me Zach. I can't let you hurt anyone else." She said. I can't be weak again, she thought. Her eyes were steely, any vulnerability gone but her hand was shaking visibly. Insanity showed in her face. She was not Alana at that moment.

"Alana... Alana you don't want to do this. You can trust me." Zach said stepping back but she moved closer to him.

Her jaw was clenched and she had a stronger grip on the knife. Her hand started shaking and her face crumpled with sorrow.

"I can't do this." Zach stared at her blankly.

"I can't hurt you Zach. Without you... I feel like I can't..." She closed her eyes and drew in a shaky breath, and Zach stayed silent watching her.

"Shhhh." Zach said coming closer to her.

"I can't breathe..." she said and Zach enclosed his strong arms over her as she
cried into him, her arms pulling him close to her.

Lucas' fist swung towards Clara's face, she quickly dodged his forceful punch easily and kicked his bicep causing him to take a step back. They had been sparring for the past hour as Beck had ordered them to keep on top of their training.

"When and why did you become spies?" Lucas asked as he punched Clara's hook and jab pads.

"We started training when we were 13; our parents were all spies too." She replied and slid down to the ground and kicked Lucas' ankle forcing him to topple over. He laughed and he got back up onto his feet.

"You were trained well." He smiled and approached her seductively sliding his hands around her waist.

"Nuh-uh, our training session is not over." She smirked and held out her palms for him to punch.

"If you insist," he winked and began hitting the large pads on her hands. "So where are your parents now?"

Clara looked thoughtful.

"Both Alana's parents died in a mission, along with my mother. I never see my dad due to his job, and Vanessa's parents are in hiding at a safe house. We live with my aunt Jenny." She looked down and
   sighed, nostalgically remembering her parents.
   "Come here." Lucas said and held Clara close to him. He cupped her face in his hands making her look into his deep blue eyes.
   "I think this session is over, don't you?"
   "Yeah okay but Beck's going to kill us when he finds out we only did an hour of training." Clara laughed and Lucas put his arm around her as they walked back to the house.
   "I think I can handle him." Lucas smirked, and Clara smiled.
   "Yeah but can you handle Alana?" she smirked back. He let out a low whistle.
   "Even injured she can still take me." He winked and they walked inside. Lucas' phone rang and he answered it. After a while he turned to Clara.
   "We gotta move. We're meeting Mason and Vanessa at another hotel." He said and she nodded running off to tell Alana, Zach and Beck.

"Damn it." Mason said as he was fighting off the guard. He punched him but missed the gut and ended up hitting him in the chest instead. Mason grabbed the guards head and brought it down to his knee hard. He repeated the action and finally got the upper hand by grabbing the guards head and smashing it into the wall. The guard was instantly knocked out and Mason rummaged for the keys, ready to open the door.

When the door swung open his eyes were instantly drawn to Vanessa. She looked up at him, blinking a few times and her mouth opened in a silent gasp. Mason didn't get a chance to say anything as the guard assigned to the room instantly attacked. Mason stepped back and kicked the man powerfully. He ran over to Vanessa to cut off her bindings quickly.

"Oh Vanessa, I'm so so sorry." Mason said hurriedly and he freed her, he leaned in but was dragged back by his attacker. Mason pushed him against the wall and kneed him in the groin. After making sure he was passed out Mason ran over to Vanessa and hugged her tightly. She drew away to look at him and felt tears welling up in her eyes. Zazzi cleared her throat and Vanessa rushed to unbind her.

"Come on, let's leave." Mason said and they all quietly opened the door. The hallway was silent. They tiptoed through the hallway. Vanessa reached out blindly and knocked down a vase which fell to the floor with an ear splitting crash. Mason winced and Zazzi groaned in annoyance. They waited in silence and stood absolutely still. A large booming voice shouted out, bouncing off the walls.

"Who's there?"

Mason looked around searching for a way out. They heard footsteps.

"Ahh screw it." Mason muttered and ran to attack. Zazzi shrugged and ran after him diving headfirst into battle. They both moved fast and gracefully but even more guards joined them.

"Vanessa- get out!" Mason shouted back at her and she ran to get past the battle. They were clearly overpowered. Mason and Zazzi were in combat with four guards and Vanessa felt helpless. She tried to kick someone in the back but ended up stumbling and falling backwards, grabbing onto a curtain for support which went down with her. She proceeded to get up but instead was dragged up by Mason's strong arms. He grabbed her by the shoulders.

"I need you to be safe okay?" He said and she nodded, shocked at the fire in his expression.

"Go!" He urged and Vanessa ran for the exit. She spotted Mason's car parted outside and scaled the gate landing shakily on the gravel. Vanessa ran to hide behind his car and waited.

A few minutes passed. It felt like hours when she heard scuffling footsteps. She froze but breathed out a sign of relief when Mason popped out at Vanessa.

"Come on! Get in!" He said looking behind him unlocking the car.

"What about Zazzi?" Vanessa stuttered. Mason looked guilty and waited until they were speeding away from the oncoming guards.

"I had to leave her, they overpowered us, I swear, I tried to help but they took her away." Mason's big blue eyes were wide and pleading.

"Shh shh, it's okay, we'll come back for her." Vanessa said softly and sadly hoping she was okay. She stroked Mason's cheek gently. He gave her a long smouldering gaze and she looked down at her hands.

"Mase... I need to tell you something." She said breathing in deeply. He rested his arm on her knee.

"Anything."

Vanessa breathed out and shut her eyes. When she opened them again she had the strength to tell him everything. The whole story.

Her heart sank when Mason took his hand off her leg. Mason's expression turned stormy and he gripped the steering wheel tightly.

"Oh." He said after a while.

Vanessa's jaw fell open and she turned to look at him but his eyes were fixed onto the road ahead. She felt her anger sweltering, she never usually got angry but her emotions were all over the place.

"Is that it?! Oh?! That's all you're going to say?!" She said loudly, her voice rising in pitch.

"Well what am I supposed to say Vanessa?!" He yelled

angrily and she looked at him in shock saying nothing. He ran his hands angrily through his soft curly hair.

"I thought... I thought I finally found someone who saw me as something other than just ... just a criminal. Turns out, that is all you saw in me. Is that what you want to hear? Whatever Vanessa. I just don't care." He said and stared back intently at the road. Vanessa looked at him for a moment, drinking in his features, longing to kiss the curve of his lips but she turned towards the window and felt the tears softly run down her face. Mason fiddled and brought out his phone and dialled a number.

"Hey it's Mase... yeah yeah I'm sorry....yeah she's here. Tell them she's safe... Hey Lucas... oh you know? Oh okay ... right, see you there." He said and hung up, chucking the phone in the glove compartment angrily.

"You'll be with your fellow operatives shortly. Alana's been interrogated so she's in a bad condition but she's getting better." Mason said briskly tone. Vanessa nodded, her lip trembling and she faced away from him.

"Is it over? With us I mean." Vanessa said hesitantly, dreading the answer, still looking away from him. Mason waiting for a moment before replying.

"It's over."

When they arrived Vanessa got out of the car as fast as she could. She saw Clara, Alana and Beck waiting for her and she ran to them. They all enveloped her into a bone crushing hug and she draw back smiling at them, happy tears running down her face. Mason walked over to his brothers, not even looking at Vanessa. She looked at Alana and gasped, running over to her, fretting over her injuries and gently touching her face. Alana grinned easily, her eyes shining.

"I'm alright Vivi don't worry." She smirked. Vanessa hugged the girls again.

"My years of professional medical training came in handy." Clara added jokingly.

"What years of medical training?" Alana and Vanessa asked

simultaneously.

Alana turned to the others.

"You guys get settled down, meeting in my room now." She said.

In the girls' room, Alana was resting on the bed with Vanessa, Beck and Lucas at the table and the others pacing around restlessly.

"So what's our next step?" Clara smiled at Alana as she sat on Lucas' lap. Alana spoke from her reclined position.

"We work together to stop the deal." She said shortly and Lucas didn't respond, holding her gaze.

"Deal?" She said more harshly but there was still no response.

"Look if the Vipers get a hold of Dr Dallow they will be in possession of a lot of important information and I still don't know what it is…"

She paused, waiting for one of the boys to give her an answer, but none of them spoke until Beck broke the silence.

"I think we do. Dr Brian Dallow went missing a month ago. He was a government technician and world renowned scientist. Which means, whatever he knew was something concerning the US Government." Beck looked up from his computer screen and to the boys. Lucas sighed.

"He's world renowned also for his photographic memory. Dr Dallow knows the US Government' nuclear launch codes and access." Lucas paused, letting that sink in as the girls and Beck stared at him, stunned.

"The Triad captured him, and are working with the DeRico's connections to arrange a sale to the highest bidder. Turns out a lot of international governments would want access to the US's nuclear launch codes. The Vipers have caught wind of Dr Dallow's capture and want the codes for themselves." Mason continued.

"Why not just get the codes out of him, why are you keeping him alive?" Vanessa questioned.

"Because he's more valuable and reliable alive. He can be

put back into the field as a double agent."

Clara looked at them disgusted. This was bigger than they had ever imagined.

"How could you do this?"

The boys looked up at her, shifting uncomfortably under the glares of the others. Clara gained momentum and continued.

"This is nuclear warfare you're playing with. You're risking millions of people dying! This is a man's life you're putting up for auction." Her voice was rising to a scream.

"Hey ease up, we were just doing what we were told." Zach interjected.

"We were told that this was just a political asset, that no one would dare use the launch codes, just use it as a bargaining chip." Mason added, trying to calm Clara down.

Alana slammed her palm onto the table loudly, silencing everyone.

"Enough."

She looked around at the boys, maintaining their eye contact.

"You have a chance to make this right. You have a chance to help us save the world. Are you going to take it?"

They nodded solemnly.

"Fabulous. Okay first, we need to get our supplies." Clara ordered, clapping her hands together enthusiastically.

"Then…" Alana started.

"Then we go to London. We have a mole to catch." Clara finished.

"Let me go!" Zazzi shouted, struggling as she was held by two

guards. One of them
chuckled at the absurdity of the command.

She sighed and elbowed one of them in the stomach causing her to be released from his grip.

"Zazzi Kingsley Viper Agent, my identification is in my pocket." She said at them and reached for her credentials. The men looked at each other and nodded, allowing her to walk free.

"Don't judge a book by its cover." She snarled at them and took their phone to dial a number.

"Zazzi here. I lost the girls. I'll get them back don't worry, I'll bring them to you."

16

"The plane leaves in two hours, we have a long journey ahead of us!" Vanessa said cheerily and the troop stood up.

"Are you sure we won't get caught? By the authorities or something." Zach asked lightly. He was ignored.

Clara checked her watch and got up brushing Lucas' shoulder lightly with her hands.

"Shhh…." Alana hissed at Mason who crushed leaves under his feet audibly.

"Sorry!" He whisper-shouted back, earning another glare from Alana and Clara.

He still felt uncomfortable around the girls; he didn't trust them at all and was shocked at how his brothers gave themselves up to them so easily without a care that they could destroy them.

"Remind me again why we're creeping through your own back yard?" Lucas asked. Alana let out an irritable sigh.

"Because it's not our back yard, this house was given to us by the Agency." Beck said quietly as he motioned for them to follow him. They followed silently until they all arrived below Alana and Clara's shared balcony.

"Okay, so we should probably try-" Lucas started, formulating a plan but was cut off by the girls throwing a rope down at him from the balcony.

Lucas looked around dumfounded, he looked at Zach who shrugged and climbed the rope. Mason stumbled slightly and Vanessa held his hand to steady him before her eyes widened and she snatched her hand away. He cleared his throat awkwardly. They entered Alana's room quietly and paused to listen. Silence. They moved throughout the house quietly checking every corner for someone until they gathered in the centre of the living room in the darkness.

"Okay, Clara and Lucas, you get necessities, Mason and Vanessa keep lookout from the balcony and Zach and Alana you get the weapons, I'll get everything else." Beck ordered. Alana opened her mouth to speak before she was grabbed around the throat by a strong arm and dragged her back. She let out a strangled cry before elbowing her attacker forcefully in the stomach. Meanwhile Vanessa and Mason tried to fight off another attacker as Lucas tackled the last one.

It seemed the place was filled with spies but luckily there were only three. Once Alana managed to loosen his grip she slid down and lifted her leg to kick her attacker in the face. This gave Zach time to grab his collar smashing him into the wall.

"Don't you ever touch her again" He growled in the man's ear before Alana knocked him out against the bannister.

A loud smash caused everyone's attention to turn to Vanessa who was standing above one of the attackers lying on the floor with bits of smashed vase lying around him.

"Oh man, I liked that vase." Clara crossed her arms. They turned to leave, grabbing their bags.

"Wait!" Vanessa called out and everyone snapped their attention to her.

"I need to tell you guys something." She started -her voice soft and sad as her eyes glistened. Mason avoided looking at her knowing that if he did, he would not be able to stop himself from kissing her.

"What's wrong?" Clara asked. Vanessa bit her lip, not knowing how to start.

"Can we hear it today?" Alana said impatiently and Beck swatted her.

With tears falling freely down her cheek Vanessa told them all about Bandy's death, how it happened and why. She finished finally and the girls and Beck stared at her in shock. Clara's mouth hung open and her eyes shone with unshed tears. Beck's forehead wrinkled and he turned away rubbing his temples. Alana stood deathly still with her arms crossed and a grim distant expression on her neutral face.

"Let's split." Clara said finally and the others hesitantly shuffled away.

Clara and Lucas headed for Clara's room first. Clara walked into her closet collecting everything quickly and she felt Lucas' arms massaging her shoulders.

"You okay?" He mumbled against her hair. She shook her head softly and went to Vanessa's room then to Alana's. She got on her knees before leaving the room and began rummaging for something under Alana's bed.

"What are you going?" Lucas asked and Clara got out from under the bed holding a sharp knife with a squirrel shaped hilt. Lucas looked at her confused.

"Alana would've killed me if I forgot Mr Pointy." Clara shrugged zipping up the duffel bag and grabbing Lucas' hand.

"Here." Alana said coldly, throwing the box of weapons at Zach. He grunted as the heavy box landed in his arms.

"What you got in here, guns?" Zach said and rolled his eyes at Alana's glare. They headed out of the attic until Zach stopped in his tracks.

"Shhh! Do you hear that?" he said setting down the box softly his eyes wide and serious. Alana frowned slightly trying to listen, one hand reaching for her knife. Suddenly she felt Zach pull her from behind and pin her against the wall, her breath caught at their close proximity and her eyes fluttered closed when his lips brushed her neck. His body was pressed up against hers and his green eyes looking into her golden ones, burning with passion.

"You can't pretend you don't like me." Zach said in a low voice before releasing her. She said nothing as he picked up the boxes, his arm muscles tensing and walked out of the attic.

"So…. How have you been?" Mason said uncertainly after spending an awkward few minutes pacing the balcony in silence with Vanessa. She looked away from him brushing her brown hair back from her face.

"Oh now you care?" She crossed her arms, avoiding his eyes.

"Of course I do Vanessa." He mumbled softly turning away shaking his head. She looked at him. He would break up with her one minute and now he says stuff like this. Was he trying to make her crazy? Vanessa cleared her throat.

"Obviously not enough to be with me." She said softly and felt her cheeks burning when he looked at her.

"I didn't break up with you because I don't love you. I broke up with you because you don't love me. You just used me for your mission. You don't care." He muttered angrily and turned to face the sky.

Vanessa exhaled angrily and turned to face him, her newfound braveness pumping into her.

"If I didn't care why would I even bother arguing about this with you? I could've left you ages ago but I didn't, and you know why Mason DeRico? Because I love you. You can break up with me, but it's not going to change that one fact." She said and starting to blush uncontrollably at Mason's intense glare. He took a stride forward and held her hands whilst lifting her chin so he could look into her eyes.

"Vanessa! Curly! We're off, hurry up! London's waiting!" Clara called from downstairs and broke the moment. Vanessa's shoulders slumped and they headed downstairs.

A figure slinked into the house silently, unnoticed by anyone, hiding in the shadows. The figure had watched Vanessa and Mason absorbed in their own lives and slipped inside. The figure heard everything. Knew everything.

"Agent Zazzi here. They're going to London."

They stepped off the plane, the bus ferrying people to the airport leaving, and another pulling up for them. It was beginning to get dark. They took their hand luggage with them and looked around, noticing they were the only ones that were left. Then a man in an airport vest came up with them with a big grin that didn't quite reach his eyes.

"Hello! Come with me, please board the bus." He said but was stopped from saying anything further by Beck's throttling grip around his throat.

"Or you can fast track us through passport control." His dark eyes blazing.

"You'll never get out of here alive kids." The man bared his teeth and Beck punched him, knocking him out.

"We have to get out of here NOW!" Beck shouted as they saw another dozen people approaching them, all on quad bikes. Lucas swore under his breath and Vanessa tied up her hair delicately in preparation.

"Home sweet home." Alana muttered.

"So Beck, not to sound pushy or anything but have you got

a plan or are we just going to stand here and die." Clara asked sweetly, watching the hoard of men approach them with murderous looks, engines revving violently.

"Yeah and hurry up about it." Alana added.

Beck ran his hand through his short hair and looked around, noticing the bus driver leaving the drivers seat, gun pointed at them. Vanessa noticed and kicked his elbow, the gun flying out of his hand.

"The bus!" She yelled, elbowing the bus driver in the back as he tried to get up. She kicked him, shoving him to the ground as they all ran to the bus. Zach ran to the drivers seat as everyone jumped off. He spurred the creaky bus into action and swerved the corner. The team of attackers on quads began to approach them as Zach veered the bus around a sharp corner, taking out two of the attackers.

The bus jerked to the left suddenly and Clara stumbled, crashing into the window.

"OW! Watch it!"

"Sorry! I forgot I have to drive on the left here!" Zach shouted panicked. Alana walked up to the front of the bus, holding on to the seats as Zach weaved away. Beck trained a gun on the wheels of the quads following them. The quads moved out of the way of his shots and sent some back.

Alana reached Zach, directing him to a way out.

"We need to get to the airport, we can blend in there"

Vanessa suddenly yelled, crashing to a floor as one of the attackers crashed in through the open bus doors. Clara grabbed the attacker, dragging him to the floor and kicking him in the gut. Two of the quad drivers grabbed onto the side of the bus and made their way to the roof. Everyone ducked as gunshots rang out from above. They were shooting through the roof.

Vanessa got to her feet and looked at Clara. Clara nodded and headed for the open doors of the bus with Vanessa.

"Alana-"

"I'm on it" she replied, climbing over Zach and going for the bus driver's window.

Alana pulled herself up to the roof, quickly rolling out of

the way of one of the biker's fists. She kicked his leg out from under him and quickly stood up. Clara, Vanessa and Alana stood in a triangle on the top of the bus, arms out balancing each other. They drew their weapons but the guns went flying out of their hands. Clara grabbed one of the men, pulling his arm back and dislocating his shoulder. Vanessa sent a swift kick to his back and he stumbled off the roof of the bus with a yell. Alana was punching the other when she got shoved back. She rolled off the roof, grabbing onto the edge. With a yell she pulled herself back up, and leapt into action.

She tackled him, but he tossed her aside. She kicked him before he managed to hit her again and he suddenly toppled off the bus as it screeched, turning tightly. The girls held on, lying low. The airport was in sight. The bus stopped and the girls climbed down. Everyone ran out of the bus into the airport as their attackers dismounted their bikes. They walked into the airport, but it was too late. They had disappeared.

"Do you see them?" One of the men working in the CCTV yelled to the other.

"No, but what danger are these three teenage girls?" The man asked looking at

the many screens showing the main parts of the airport.

"A lot. Damn it! There's too many people, I can't see them." He said angrily

slamming his fist onto the table.

"Wait, wait, isn't that them?" Said the CCTV man pointing at screen 8.

"Yes. That's them." The man said, anger consuming him, turning his face and neck a

deep purple as he watched the screen intently.

The black seven seater car flew out of the car park, the tires screaming as it turned away from the airport. Mason and

Vanessa gripped the side of the car being flung from side to side as Alana swerved dangerously causing the tyres to skid noisily.

"And this is why she's the getaway driver." Clara laughed, feeling the adrenaline of the fight still coursing through her.

"Uh-oh." Alana said looking out the window.

"Ohhh please be a good uh oh. Like, uh-oh we have too much chocolate." Clara whined as Beck shook his head.

"More like Uh-oh the barriers are down." He said as Alana slowed down.

"Don't slow down! Kill it!" Clara said to Alana and she laughed as she slammed her foot on the pedal accelerating towards the barriers. The car was heading for a ramp at increasing speed.

"Oh no no no no" Vanessa said shaking her head and squeezing her eyes shut. The car hit the ramp and there was a few moments of silence at it flew over the barrier and landed heavily onto the tarmac. Alana built up speed again as everyone in the car shouted and whooped with joy.

Lucas whooped in excitement and Zach ruffled Alana's hair. She responded by swerving the car causing him to topple.

"Well, what a welcome home that was…" Beck muttered as they drove off to the distance.

"Hey auntie we're home." Vanessa said as she unlocked the door to their house. Mason, Lucas and Zach walked warily through the house, treading silently, checking the rooms one by one as Beck, Vanessa, Alana and Clara stared at them curiously.

"Okay, all clear." Zach finally said as Lucas nodded and Mason looked around cautiously, checking the rooms for intruders and signalling covertly to each other. Beck, Alana, Clara and Vanessa stared at them in silence before bursting out in laughter. They were doubled over, their shoulders shaking hysterically.

"They-they-they-" Alana could not finish her sentence. Clara finally managed to stop laughing.

"This place is like, impossible to get into unless you're us… you guys were-" She started laughing again as they shuffled on their feet feeling stupid after checking to see if the safest place they could be was safe.

"You could never be too sure." Mason mumbled and they giggled at him.

"Don't worry curly, you were cute." Clara said ruffling Mason's hair. Vanessa looked on at him with a pang, noticing how he didn't meet her gaze.

"Well I guess we should formulate a plan?" she said softly not looking at Mason but feeling his soft blue eyes looking at her. She saw him run his hands through his hair from her periphery and she focused her attention to Alana who had managed to find an old packet of sweets somewhere and was pouring them into her mouth.

Alana mumbled something, mouth full of sweets that no one seemed to understand.

"I believe what my charming friend here was trying to say is that we should have a sleepover." Clara said.

Zach looked at her in confusion. "Well unless you were planning on kicking us out then yeah we are sleeping over…"

"Oh no no, one of our sleepovers." Vanessa smirked as the girls ran for their rooms.

Beck chuckled and shook his head.

"Brace yourself boys."

"Pick a hand." Vanessa said to Lucas as she held two DVD's behind her back and
a cheeky smile on her face.

"No way, I'm not watching any soppy movie." He shrugged and Clara sat next to him kissing his cheek.

"Pick a hand, it's either Titanic, or Grease ." Alana said as she lay down with her head on Zach's abs as he flicked through an old photo album.

"Fine, this one." He said motioning for her right hand.

"Great! Titanic it is! I'll get snacks." Vanessa chirped putting in the Titanic DVD and skipping to the kitchen to get snacks.

"So what's the plan for tomorrow?" Mason said lounging on the couch lazily.

"We'll be infiltrating the Agency's archives, which are underground." Beck said casually.

Zach nodded. "Let's see if we can make it past Jack dying."

"Is this the place?" Zach whispered into Alana's ear causing her to shiver at the feel of his breath on her. She nodded gravely and sent a signal to Vanessa who was located behind the building.

"Siren here, I never would have thought we'd have to infiltrate this of all places." Clara huffed through the communications unit. Alana chuckled and took a good look at the building. The Agency. Tucked away behind a busy street in central London, hidden in plain sight with thousands of secrets. Underground tunnels and chambers, gleaming stylish offices, armouries and training rooms.

"So why are we here again?" Vanessa said through her comms and Alana fiddled with her ponytail.

"Find anything that could help us get out of this mess and find the mole." She said simply.

"Okay, we're going in." Beck said and the way for the boys to follow. A series of vibrations reached the girls once they were inside and Clara brought out her makeup kit to check who they were coming from.

"Curly. Stop playing around. This is important." Clara hissed angrily and the vibrations stopped.

"Sorry... this is fun." He giggled sheepishly.

"Wait!" Alana hissed holding out her arm to stop Zach from crossing the room once they descended to the archives. Alana brought out her keychain and shone a light by the door revealing faint laser lines.

"How typical." Lucas muttered.

"Come on bro, let's James Bond it." Zach said as they advanced towards the lasers

weaving through gracefully.

Clara sighed and walked over to a wall and pushed in a code causing the lasers to disappear and all security alarms to turn off.

"What?" Zach started looking at her incredulously.

"We work here remember?" Vanessa giggled as the boys relaxed.

"Oh, yeah, well that makes sense." Mason said and shuffled awkwardly.

Vanessa brought out her keys and opened the doors. They descended a set of dark stairs leading to even more darkness so they all brought out their torches. The air hung heavy with tension and nervousness.

"What is this place?" Mason asked softly, his hand resting gently on the small of Vanessa's back, without thinking.

"It's all of the Agency's secrets." Clara replied.

The archives would have all the information they needed. Computers with all information ever stored in it were there along with paper copies of everything on the computers for back up. Whatever the girls needed would be there, it was up to them to find it. The second those files left the room, however, they disintegrated.

"We have half an hour before they are alerted that security is off. GO." Alana said looking at their watch and they all dispersed.

Vanessa wandered over to the filing with every mission brief. Alana was right by her looking at the organised crime section, rifling through sheets of information. Clara headed over to the list of agents and brought the names over to the computer doing quick background checks on all of them. The boys were spread around the huge room keeping guard and looking for anything.

Vanessa scanned through the information but frowned puzzled. There was no mission brief for their mission.

She looked through it again and went on to a computer looking through the folders thoroughly. Nothing. Their mission was not listed.

"Alana... come here." Vanessa said and Alana walked over looking at the screen.

"Our mission isn't listed anywhere, the whole thing was a set up. It says here that the CIA are working on the deal bust but there's no account of us doing so. Wherever the mission brief came from wasn't the Agency, someone made us specifically go on this mission."

Alana frowned.

"Well who could it be?" she said and Vanessa shrugged.

"Someone that wants something from us, someone able to get a mission through to us." She said and she went over to tell Clara and the others. Alana walked back to where she was looking up any files and history about the Vipers. They were thriving up until their 'mysterious' downfall which was down to the girls' parents but they slowly began to rebuild their organisation, becoming even more deadly than ever.

The last Viper agent to be taken in mentioned something about domination on a larger scale than before. The Vipers had tried to take control of South America organised criminal world before they were destroyed but a larger scale could mean anything anything. Lucas had told the girls all they knew about the deal. The DeRico's and the Triad would be bringing a new player with deadly information into the market soon. The Vipers were trying to stop it, put it in their control, and use Dr Dallow's information for themselves.

According to Vanessa's information the CIA were on this case, and not the girls. Who would want them to get involved? It didn't make sense that the Vipers would want the girls to get involved in busting the case.

"It's a trap. It was from the start." Vanessa said out loud.

"Okay, I have blacklisted eight agents in this Agency who are likely to be the mole." Clara announced walking over to Alana waving a few sheets of paper. She skimmed over the papers looking for something.

"Clara, this is your list of the hottest Agency agents." Alana said shaking her head.

"Oh right sorry, here you go." She said handing Alana another pile of papers.

She looked at them and found Clara to be right, there was definitely something wrong with their agent database. They were blank. No records other than names.

"Okay, so these are from this country, what about others? Try the American branch." Alana said and Clara walked over to the computer again as Alana looked for the others.

They had less than five minutes left, she realised when she looked at the watch. Time flies when you're having fun, she thought bitterly and she reached the tall figure by the door.

"Zach..." She started reaching her hand for his shoulder when he turned around revealing himself. Oh, not Zach, she thought.

"Who the hell are you?" Alana said before the man's fist slammed into her face.

"Son of a-" she swore as she felt blood dripping onto her lip. She spun and kicked him forcefully and he reached for a bookshelf blindly in the dark and threw it at her. The books managed to slow her down and he began to run away.

Oh no you don't, Alana thought and she began sprinting after him. She was close behind him so she leaped on his back flooring him and she pinned him down to the floor. Drawn by the commotion Zach and Lucas ran to them and Clara left the printer printing out names to find out what was happening.

"Woah, didn't know we were seeing other people." Zach laughed.

"Shut up and get him up." She said brushing herself off as Clara rushed to inspect her nose.

"It's fine it's fine." She said, gently swatting Clara away. Suddenly the room started flashing red and sirens began blaring.

"Oh darn it." Vanessa sighed delicately and they all began running for the exit.

"Okay, we know what we need, let's go back to our place and get a plane back to LA." Clara said and she suddenly slapped her forehead with her palm.

"Oohhh damn it, I forgot the list of potential moles from the American branch, Its still in the printer, I have to go get it." She said and hurriedly heading back to the building.

"No! Don't! They're coming!" Vanessa hissed but Clara kept running. She leaped through the door and slowed down when she reached the door leading to the archives. Silence. Gently she creaked the door open and descended the stairs one at a time. One of the steps creaked and she held her breath listening to the silence but there was nothing. She let out a sigh of relief and she tiptoed down the stairs and into the archives room which was still dark. Silently she slipped past book shelves and stacks of information and reached the printer. Nothing. The sheets that had been here a few moments ago had disappeared, she looked around her. Silence. She felt an eerie chill creep up on her and decided to make a run for Beck's car. Only once she was safely in the car and driving away she let out a sigh.

"Did you get it?" Alana asked, fingers tapping on the steering wheel.

Clara shook her head and gazed out of the window.

"Someone beat us to it."

"Home sweet home." Zach said as he lay down on his bed stretching like a cat. Lucas threw a pillow at him as the girls settled around his room.

"We need you to tell us all we need to know about everything." Beck said bluntly and Zach made a big deal of sighing and standing up.

"Firstly, we don't NEED to tell you anything." Zach replied, green eyes blazing.

Beck took a step forward threateningly, as did Lucas.

"You're agents or whatever, but we're a crime family, we have different rules." He said forcefully.

Alana stepped forward angrily.

"You said you would work with us. Just because you're a criminal doesn't make you as bad as you think you are. You know the deal needs to be stopped but you're just too scared to tell us any more information we can use. There must be something we can use to stop this. We need to know where Dr Brian Dallow is." She said, all with one breath, her arms crossed and her stance demeaning.

Lucas looked to Mason then to Zach looking torn.

"Believe me when I tell you, we'd be dead if anyone knows we tell you. But... we'll tell you." He said slowly and Clara nodded slowly.

"Well..." Zach started.

"Are you kidding me? This. This is where you have all your information?!" Alana hissed at Lucas and he shrugged casually as he took a USB stick out of his locker.

"It's the safest place for us." Mason replied and Vanessa sighed.

"Oh boy." sighed Alana.

A small whirlwind of red hair and pink dress came hurling at the girls.

"Guys! Where were you?! You haven't been here in ages, are you guys okay? Are you guys coming to the Winter Ball?" Millie's facial expressions changed from surprise to confusion to excitement.

"Alana's Chihuahua farm back in England had a bad case of smallpox." Clara said patting Alana lightly on the shoulder, feigning sympathy.

Millie nodded wisely. Lucas looked at her incredulously and Zach turned away to hide the laughter. The bell rang and Millie jumped slightly and clapped her hands together.

"I've got class." she chirped and they joined her on the way to their classes.

17

A sleek black car pulled into the school parking lot, braking violently inches away from the boys. Lucas leaned on his car as Mason got out and crossed his arms. Zach was hiding with the girls at a distance which allowed them to hear and see most of what was happening. A man who was almost completely bald except for a small patch of hair at the side of his head stepped out of the car followed by a short, stocky man. Lucas stood up to his full height and met the man in the middle.

"Why call DeRico? We heard you've been assisting others." The short stocky man said in a strong Spanish accent. Lucas held his gaze. His companion stayed by the car.

"You're lucky we kept you alive after the stunt you pulled in Montenegro." he replied harshly. The man shuffled embarrassed, and drew himself up to his full 5 feet and 4 inches.

"Then why call for me?" he said annoyed and Mason snorted.

"Our father wanted us to confirm you knew exactly where the deal was going to happen and when. We cannot let the weak links ruin this." Mason said in an authoritative tone, looking down at the man in front of him with disdain. The man shook his head in disbelief, palms out in front of him imploringly.

"Of course I know." he said, voice tinged with incredulity. Mason shrugged, his expression unchanged.

"Let's hear it then."

That was all it took for the man to spill exactly what they needed to know. As the men turned back to their car and drove away, Alana, Clara and Vanessa walked out from their hiding place. Clara crossed her arms looking particularly pleased.

"Thanks for the help sweetie." She said to the car driving into the distance as she brought her phone out to call Beck and update him.

Alana stretched out her arms and smiled lazily.

Mason suddenly turned towards the girls blocking their way. His face was contorted with anger and he ran his hand through his hair angrily.

"That's what its going to be like with us isn't it, you'll use us to bust the deal then arrest us, won't you?" he yelled. Lucas and Zach turned to face the girls, curious as to their response.

"No that's not true-" Clara started.

"That's pretty much the deal," Alana said at the same time and Clara slapped her arm immediately.

"Since you've aided us in catching a bigger fish we will probably be able to let you get away free of charge." Vanessa said diplomatically, reaching for Mason's forearm to calm him. Alana kept his gaze as he saw their worry dissipate.

The boys nodded and they all headed to finish their classes. Walking back to their lessons Alana leaned over an whispered to Vanessa and Clara.

"Are we still going to that Halloween party tonight?"

Clara turned around to look at her incredulously. "Hell yeah!" she said at the same time Vanessa said "Hell no!"

They stood there looking at each other in silence before Vanessa rolled her eyes, conceding.

"So how are you?" Mason asked Vanessa awkwardly. She rolled her eyes subtly and crossed her arms over her chest, the pink tulle skirt looking ridiculous to her at that very moment.

"Fine, you?" She replied shortly.

"You wanna talk about it...?" Mason said. Vanessa turned to face him angrily but saw he was grinning childishly.

"You..." she started but was cut off my Mason stepping forward.

"You." He said before pulling her to him and closing his mouth over hers.

"Tell us again why you guys have to come with us to this party?" Clara asked the brothers sighing. Mason shrugged, his knight armour clinking.

"We were invited." Lucas said simply and adjusted his superman cape before kissing Clara on the cheek, much to her pleasure. Zach entered the room with the flourish of his own black cape.

"And what are you supposed to be?" Clara asked him and Zach held up a finger motioning her to wait while he fiddled in his black trousers for something.

He put his fangs on and gave them all a wide, plastic, fanged smile.

Alana burst out laughing. She walked up to him and put her hands on his shoulders.

"I think you look sexy." she drawled and his face lit up.

"Really?"

"No.." she said giving him a kiss on the cheek. Lucas cleared his throat and swished his cape giving them a full view of his superman costume as he patted his slicked black hair, waiting for a compliment.

"I don't know about you but Mason looks the worst," he said with a cough and patted Mason on his armour, which threw him off balance.

"I am an honourable knight! Come on, this is totally hot..." he said brandishing his sword. Zach and Lucas nodded vigorously.

"Yes yes, completely." They said with a serious expression. Zach clapped his hands and shooed the girls.

"Your turn to get changed, go go go!" He ushered them out.

"Ready!" Clara jumped inside and flicked her hair over her shoulder and put her hands on her hips showing them all her wonder woman costume. She strutted out of the changing room and walked over to where the boys were standing, with a flirtatious smile on her face. Lucas nodded in agreement and she walked to him and placed her hand on his muscular chest.

"So its official, we're matching costumes." and Clara leaned up to kiss him.

There was a small knock on the door and Zach snapped his fingers.

"That's Vanessa, Alana wouldn't have knocked," he said smiling to himself, his fangs baring over his lip, giving him a slight lisp. Vanessa tiptoed inside and smiled sweetly. She was wearing a pearly pink corset with a matching tulle skirt and a sparkling tiara making her a perfect princess. She blushed slightly and Mason chuckled taking her hand and kissing it softly, twirling her.

Suddenly the door swung open and Alana stepped in dressed in cargo trousers, black vest top, combat boots and a utility belt. Her hair was pulled back into a braid. She adjusted the crucifix necklace around her neck and fixed them a serious stare before breaking into a grin.

"Aw man, did no one tell you it was a dress up party?" Zach mumbled and Alana smiled.

"I did dress up. I'm a vampire slayer," Alana said drawing out a stake from her belt. Lucas laughed quietly and Zach's eyes widened slightly as he shuffled away from her.

"So I guess we're not all matching costumes..." he said and Alana shook her head. They headed for the door but were interrupted by Beck walking in dressed as a US marine solider. Mason poked his machine gun gently and his eyes widened.

"Is that..."

"Real? Yup." Beck replied patting the gun softly.

"Ooh man why are you coming?" Clara huffed indignantly. Beck faced her with an eye roll and poked her gently in the ribs.

"I'm coming to protect you girls," he said saluting her army-style.

"We can handle ourselves perfectly fine without a babysitter ." Clara replied, jutting her chin out.

"Not in those heels you can't!

"Watch me." Clara winked and they walked off ready for the party.

"This feels wrong, partying while our teammate is dead and getting no further in on the case. Not to mention Zazzi is still missing." Vanessa said softly so only the girls heard her. Alana rubbed her shoulder and smiled assuring her that they were on the mission. She handed Vanessa her phone. Vanessa looked at it and her brows creased with confusion. It was a list of three names.

"You sure they're going to be there?" she asked Alana. "Of course I am."

Thudding music. Dancing bodies. The sound of laughter. Masks, feathers, sparkles.

The girls jumped up and down to the music. Millie also came over to join them, jumping up and squealing in delight at the girl's arrival.

"You guys came!" She said and hugged them squeezing the air out of them. Alana laughed and took Millie by the hand. Millie had dressed up as a clown with rosy cheeks, white face and a comic colourful dress which she twirled around in.

"This will never get old." Clara shouted over the music.

"Until we get old." Alana shuddered and excused herself to go get them some drinks. Vanessa and Clara danced to the music for a few more minutes when Vanessa tapped Clara lightly on the shoulder.

"Look who's here." she said and Clara smirked adjusting the cape. Three asian men with suits rolled up to reveal their Triad tattoos had entered the club, looking around like snakes searching for prey. They looked like they were in their early twenties and walked with an air of authority. Zach popped up behind the girls and tapped Clara on the shoulder.

"Who's here?" He said loudly baring his fangs. He was swatted and shh'ed angrily by the girls.

He noticed the men and his expression darkened underneath his pale makeup.

"Triad." he growled and pushed past the girls to get to the men.

"Zach no!" Clara hissed but Zach ignored her. She tried to grab him but he escaped before she could. Mason's attention drew towards Zach and he dragged Lucas over to Zach.

"Zach man don't.." he said but it was too late, they were spotted. The men looked at each other and laughed to themselves. The girls quickly rushed over to the group that had now formed and Vanessa messaged Beck to stay hidden, there was trouble brewing.

"Well well, look who's here." One of the men with crystal

blue eyes said, his arrogant face smirking. He snapped his attention to the girls and his smirk deepened.

Suddenly he grabbed Vanessa's hand and pulled her towards him. Her brow furrowed in polite distaste. She tried to pull away but the man pressed a gun to Vanessa's corset. She took a sharp intake of air and her mouth set in a firm line, her cheeks turning a delicate pink.

"Who's this, your girlfriend?" he said cruelly to Zach but before Zach could reply the man turned around to the gentle tapping of his shoulder.

"Nope, I am." Alana said and slammed her elbow into the man's face. Mason pulled Vanessa away forcefully and the man fired his gun blindly. The party atmosphere seemed to freeze at the gunshot and panic ensued as the action played out.

The other two men muscled in on the fight. Beck jumped in taking out one of them. Clara slammed her palm into one of the men's noses, elbowed him and threw him to the ground keeping him there with her heel pressed at his throat as he struggled against her lock.

Mason spat out blood and kicked the gun out of the main man's hand. Lucas rolled over and got the gun. He looked around and the people from the party who were in a state of panic screams everywhere, but also curiosity. It seemed they had an audience. One of the men grabbed Alana's petite frame and threw her over his back so she was arched painfully, facing the ceiling. She shouted out in pain as he bent her body even farther back. Reacting quickly before he broke her spine she reached for her utility belt and brought out the stake driving it into the man's arm causing her to be released quickly with a crash to the floor knocking all the breath out of her. She crawled away from him, the other two in control, and Beck

"The police will be here in 5 minutes to arrest you for the murder of Bandy Marsoti." Clara said to them, her voice quivering with anger. While Alana brought out handcuffs the crowd that had formed around them began to clap and cheer for the girls

"Great Show." "So realistic." "You girls are hot!"

The sound of sirens and the flashing blue lights made the girls, Beck and the brothers run for the door, escaping the questions they would not be able to answer.

"Bandy's revenge, almost done." Alana said with a smirk.

"What do you mean almost done?" Mason asked as they got into the car and drove away to a safe house where their vehicles were hidden in a garage.

"Well once we find out who the agency's mole is and clear our names then I will make sure that we are the agents to deal with his murderers." She said with a smile and turned up the radio.

Suddenly she gasped and her tyres screeched against the tarmac as she stopped the car, her eyes wide and her mouth open at the person who was standing in the road. Vanessa smiled and jumped out of the car soon to be joined by the others.

"We thought we'd never see you again..." Clara said shocked.

"We've missed you!" Vanessa said, grabbing their surprise visitor in for a hug.

"Welcome back Zazzi." Alana smiled.

Zazzi released herself from Vanessa's hug and smiled widely at them all.

"I'm so glad you're safe!" She said enthusiastically.

"How-how did you get out?" Vanessa asked dumbfounded.

"Where were you all these days?" Alana questioned and Zazzi smiled warmly, grabbing Vanessa's hand and squeezing it.

"It's late… how about we get back to wherever you guys are hiding and we'll talk about it over hot chocolate and doughnuts." She laughed, the girls smiled at the familiar bubbly laugh.

"Ugh, no thanks, too many calories, but this beast needs food so let's go." Clara said patting Alana on the shoulder.

"She's right." Alana shrugged and they all walked off. Mason remained behind. He had not moved but rather was staring at Zazzi, brows furrowed in confusion. She turned, noticing his absence and her face went blank at his expression.

"How did you know we were hiding Zazzi?" he asked, his angelic face stony with contemplation. Zazzi paused.

"I checked in at my agency and they said you guys had disappeared so I went looking for you." She said simply and they kept on walking, arm in arm with Vanessa and Clara as Alana chattered happily.

"Come on, the hotel is about ten minutes from here, I booked two suites under an alias."

"Ohh is it 5 star?" Clara said as the girls rolled their eyes. Alana's reply was her motorbike speeding off.

"You can come with me Zazz." Clara said, opening the door to her Mini.

When they got in Clara connected her phone and played music loudly, singing along and flicking her hair.

Zazzi reached into her pocket discreetly, turned on a recording device and cleared her throat.

"So did you guys find out anything interesting?" she shouted over the music. Clara spilled everything they found out and had happened to them the past few days, leaving out a few details, she turned down the music as she pulled up outside a discreet, but fancy hotel.

"Okay, we're here let's go!" she said perkily and Zazzi hopped out of the car looking up at the hotel letting out a low whistle.

"Swanky."

Clara's phone buzzed.

"Oh its Beck, he says he's at the safe house getting some

stuff together, he thinks he's close to something." Clara said and Zazzi nodded absentmindedly not listening but concentrating on the glamour of the hotel.

When they walked into the gleaming lobby Zazzi excused herself to go to the bathroom whilst Clara went up to meet the girls in the suite along with the boys.

Zazzi checked all the stalls. Empty. She quickly went into the last one and locked the door getting her laptop out from her backpack and plugging the recording device in. Once the file downloaded she sent it directly to her Viper boss and packed her stuff away quickly. Her phone shrilled and she fumbled to pick it up.

"Is this some sort of joke?!" Her boss yelled through the phone. Zazzi winced at the noise and her brow furrowed in confusion.

"What are you talking about?" she replied incredulously. She heard him sigh heavily through the phone.

"Listen to the file you sent me." He said shortly and Zazzi turned on her laptop and clicked on it. It was 10 minutes of Britney Spears songs.

"I- " she started

"No. Just lead them here, soon. That's all we need." The call ended and Zazzi let out a breath she'd been holding in.

"Where's Zazz?" Alana asked and the door opened.

"I'm here!" Zazzi said jumping in front of Alana knocking her backwards straight into Zach who pulled her to him and kissed her softly on the lips. He grinned cheekily and the room erupted with wolf whistles and whooping.

"Guys let's check out the other suite!" Clara said and everyone stood up to follow her.

"No no no, we don't all need to go, Zach you stay here with Alana, secure the perimeter, we'll go." Clara said, her voice lilting with innocence as they left the room of the suite sniggering. She winked at Alana before leaving and closed the door behind her.

Alana looked at Zach from the corner of her eye until they burst into laughter.

As the others entered the other suite they set their bags down and looked around. Mason stumbled on the handle of Clara's bag and crashed into Vanessa. He quickly grabbed her round the waist to stop her from falling. Her breath caught at the close proximity and the others watched their brief contact.

Clara clicked her fingers as if just remembering something.

"I lost my earring, Lucas, Zazzi, would you help me look for it?" she said feigning worry, her voice rising a couple octaves. Mason blushed slightly and Vanessa's eyes widened.

"Awww man, I just got comfortable." Zazzi groaned from the couch and both Mason and Vanessa seemed to exhale in relief.

"Zazzi, I REALLY need your help!" she said widening her eyes with implication.

Zazzi sighed and got up dragging her feet and Clara shut the door behind her.

Clara and Lucas walked down the stairs discretely with Zazzi following them. They directed themselves to the lobby bar to kill time and keep Zazzi company.

"You're so cute when you play matchmaker you know that?" Lucas said and Clara smiled deviously. After a pause Zazzi gasped with realisation.

"Ohh so that's what you were doing!" She said bursting into her contagious bubbly laughter.

"Hey I'm going to go to the ladies' quickly." Zazzi instantly said as they sat down. Before she even had to time to finish her sentence she was on her feet walking away. Lucas nodded and swing his stool around to face Clara.

"What do you want to drink?" A flirtatious smirk on his face.

"Hmm.. I'll have a cosmo." She replied sliding her hand up his leg seductively.

He winked and motioned to the barman before placing his order.

Four drinks later, Zazzi came back only to find Clara and Lucas kissing passionately unaware of her arrival. She sat down and ordered a drink.

"Goodness where the hell were you? Does is really take half an hour to go to the toilet?" Clara said interrupting the kiss.

"Yeah well I find it better to be in there than here and have to watch you two eat each other's faces." Zazzi snapped defensively.

"I liked it better when you were gone." Clara said jokingly too caught up in the moment to care.

"Let's take this upstairs." Lucas whispered in Clara's ear. She smiled as they left, unaware of Zazzi's glare.

"So how are you?" Mason asked Vanessa awkwardly. She rolled her eyes subtly and crossed her arms over her chest, the pink tulle skirt looking ridiculous to her at that very moment.

"Fine, you?" She replied shortly.

"You wanna talk about it...?" Mason said. Vanessa turned to face him angrily but saw he was grinning childishly.

"You..." she started but was cut off my Mason stepping forward.

"You." He said before pulling her to him and closing his mouth over hers.

"You know they did this on purpose." Zach said and Alana rolled over onto the bed groaning.

"Really?!" she said sarcastically. Zach walked up to the

foot of the bed and grabbed Alana's ankles and pulled her. She squealed and kicked out but Zach released her and leaned over her with his arms on either side of her head. He leaned in close and gazed at her, taking in her golden brown hair spread out in tumbling curls, her deep eyes which hid so much, and the sly curve of her lips, like a cat. He breathed heavily and felt himself stir with an unfamiliar feeling. Just admit it man, you got it bad, he thought to himself.

"Alana I think-" Alana put a finger to his lips. "Don't say it."

"I'm in love with you." he said, his voice deep and serious. The corners of her mouth twitched slightly into a genuine smile.

Zach leaned forward and kissed her hungrily, loving the feel of her soft lips against his. He nipped at her neck gently, trailing kisses along her jawline. Everywhere he kissed left searing heat and she reached for him, pulling his body as close to him as he could. His hand reached the skin under her vest and he caressed her, joining her on the bed.

"Zach I lo-" Alana started breathlessly but was interrupted by a knock on the door. They looked at each other and Alana pushed him off her and they walked towards the door. Before Zach could answer it Alana grabbed his shirt pulling him towards her to kiss him roughly on the lips before releasing him, dumbfounded.

"I'll get the door." She said with a smirk and he grinned back, his green eyes twinkling, his short hair mussed and his cheeks slightly flushed.

"Hey, who are they?" Clara said to Lucas signalling to the four men outside the suite Alana and Zach were in. Lucas shrugged but he stiffened as he focussed on who they were.

"They're trouble."

18

Alana opened the door but before she could react the men grabbed her by the arms and covered her mouth with a grey rag. Chloroform. Alana's eyes widened as she struggled to hold her breath. Zach jumped into action punching the man with the rag but he barely reacted to his fist. Alana squirmed trying to get out of their grip, her lungs bursting for air. Suddenly Lucas jumped one of them from behind as Zach began fighting with another. When Clara kneed the man with the rag in the back he dropped the rag and Alana gasped for air whilst kneeing him in the face hard.

"We have to get out of here." Lucas said.

They ran to the room Vanessa and Mason were in and ran in to see Vanessa standing by an unconscious body, her arms crossed over her chest. A stray hair had come free of her perfect up do and Mason stood by her, his arm lingering by her waist.

"Come on, let's go." Clara said, her voice cool and commanding as she tucked a lock of hair behind her ear. They ran out of the hotel straight for the car park. Alana stubbed her toe and knocked over a vase causing the entire lobby to stare at her.

   Clara glared at her and Alana shrugged, embarrassed.

   "Go go go go go!" Zach ushered the girls through the doors.

   "Alana hurry up!" Lucas shouted pulling Vanessa into his car as Mason got in.

   "Zazzi come with me." Clara said hurriedly and Zazzi jumped in. Zach grabbed Alana towards his Harley. She hesitated.

   "I don't want to leave my Ducati." She said glancing at her gleaming black bike. Zach sighed and grabbed her arm towards his bike ignoring her many protests and revved the engine. Alana wrapped her arms around Zach tightly as the wind blew through her hair. She breathed in the smell of his worn leather jacket enjoying the speed when she felt his phone vibrate in his pocket. She pulled it out of his pocket and answered it. It was Vanessa telling them where to go. Alana replied and ended the call so Vanessa could call Zazzi and Beck.

   Alana heard another engine besides their own, she turned to see another two motorbikes closely behind them. Alana swore under her breath.

   "Zach we have two tails." She said and flinched when she heard a gunshot.

   "And they're armed?" Zach finished for her with a hint of a smirk.

   "Side bag." He ordered and Alana turned to rummage in the leather side bag when she pulled out two pistols. Zach didn't slow down, so Alana put one leg over another, slowly turning her back against Zach's. Gripping with her thighs she brought out the guns, one in each hand and aimed. She fired two shots from each gun aiming at their tires but they swerved out of the way. They sped up and sandwiched the Harley in-between them causing Alana to lose her balance. She managed to grab onto Zach's jacket. She let out a torrent of swearwords and fired again, the gun sending vibrations through her arm. They dodged her bullets and moved further away.

   "Speed up Zach!" She shouted over the roar of motors .

   "Hold on." Zach said with a short laugh and Alana leaned

over the seat bracing herself as Zach took a sharp turn towards a busy street. Alana quickly put the guns in her pockets and held on as Zach expertly weaved through the traffic but their attackers did not let up. Alana got up and steadied the guns and fired quickly hitting both their front tires. Their bikes instantly swerved out of control and collided together. Alana gripped onto Zach's jacket as he sped off.

"I know your secret Zazzi, the jig is up." Clara said as she observed Zazzi while driving from her periphery.

Zazzi felt her heart begin to race in shock, how could Clara know?

"What do you mean Clara." She shuffled in her seat, uncomfortably while Clara was speeding down the motorway awaiting Vanessa's directions.

"Come on there is no way, those nails are real." Her frown turned into a smile as her head nodded towards Zazzi's hands.

"Oh haha, you caught me. It's the salon down the road from your school, miracle workers." Relieved, a small chuckle escaped her mouth.

Zazzi felt her phone vibrate and she reached into her pocket and checked caller ID. Vanessa. She held the phone up to her ear.

"Hey Vanessa, where we headed to? Ok, yes, I know it. Okay see you there." Zazzi
ended the call and faced Clara with a warm smile.

"We have a 2 hour drive ahead of us, why don't I drive so you can catch a few moments of sleep." She said sweetly. Clara frowned slightly, not sure about letting Zazzi drive but Zazzi was right, she was exhausted. She pulled over and got out pulling her hair back into a ponytail and doing up her seatbelt. She instantly shut her eyes as Zazzi started the car, the motion of the car lulling her to sleep.

Vanessa inserted her key and opened the door letting out a shaky breath as she looked around. Mason and Lucas stepped in cautiously.

"What is this place?" Lucas said looking around at the cardboard boxes with wires and computer hardware. Vanessa smiled sadly at the clutter. No matter how hard they tried to redecorate he had always managed to clutter it up again.

"This is a good friend's apartment."

"Where is she?" Lucas said walking towards the window.

"He's dead." Vanessa said with a note of finality. Images flashed in her mind. The gunshot. The sound of his body thudding onto the floor. Her screams, her crying, willing him back to life.

She shook her head and went over to shut the curtains before turning on the light as she told the boys to rest. Soon after they sat on the couch Mason and Lucas fell asleep. Vanessa checked the clock on the wall. It was almost 3 am. A knock on the door made her jump but Lucas and Mason didn't even stir. She looked through the peephole and gasped when she saw an eye pressed up against it. She opened the door to reveal Alana and Zach. Alana grinned.

"You always freak when I do that, got any food?" She said and paused when she realised where she was. She turned to Vanessa who shrugged.

"I didn't know where else to go." She said in a small voice. Zach took off his jacket and stretched lazily. He got a glimpse of his reflection in the mirror, pausing to check his angles.

Alana yawned and tried to hide it.

"Go to sleep you two, you must be exhausted, I'll wait for the others." Vanessa said.

Zach kissed Vanessa on the head gently wishing her goodnight. He took Alana's hand and led her away.

"I don't know what's taking them so long; it was a 20 minute drive from the hotel." Alana said sleepily. Vanessa nodded softly and headed towards the couch being careful not to wake the boys up. She stayed awake for as long as she could but her eyelids began to feel heavy and she couldn't stay awake any longer. She fell into a deep, dark sleep filled with shadows and nightmares.

Bandy fell to the floor. Vanessa rushed over shaking him. Her hands were red with blood. Bandy's eyes shot open.

"Vanessa!" He called.

"Vanessa!" She could feel herself shaking. "Vanessa!"

Vanessa's eyes shot open. Her dark eyes met Alana's golden ones, light streamed in the room from the gap in the curtains.

"It was a nightmare." She breathed out and realised she was drenched in sweat. Alana was still holding her by the shoulders and looking at her with concern as if she would break into a million pieces.

"You okay?!" Alana said and Vanessa nodded, blinking.

"Yeah, yeah I'm fine." Vanessa looked around to see that Beck had joined them

but two were missing.

"Where's Clara and Zazzi?" Vanessa murmured shaking some consciousness into

herself, still sleepy. Alana looked at her strangely along with the others.

"Wh-y- you mean they didn't come home last night?" Alana asked, a sense of urgency in her voice.

"No- I mean, I waited for them until around 4am but I must

have dosed off." Vanessa said, her eyes widening.

At that moment Vanessa's phone rang, all of them turned to look at it on the side table. No one made a move until Beck stood up and picked up the phone and answered it.

He said nothing for a while until he heard a whimper on the other side.

"Vanessa?" Zazzi's voice came out tearful and hushed.

"Zazzi. It's Beck. Where are you? Are you with Clara? Are you okay?" He rattled off the questions, his voice tinged with worry. Zazzi sobbed through the phone.

"I managed to sneak away but they're coming to get me. Help us Beck. Please." Beck heard a commotion on the phone, a short scream, then the line went dead. He put the phone down and faced the others.

"Another rescue mission team."

Zazzi hung up the phone and put it in her pocket. She spun around on her heel, her long black braid swimming over her shoulder.

"That was almost too easy, don't you think?" She said smiling cruelly at Clara. Clara struggled against her bonding, her angry screams muffled by the rag tied tightly around her mouth.

"What's that? I didn't quite hear you with that thing." Zazzi said pointing at her mouth mocking confusion. She shrugged to herself and walked off laughing loudly to herself.

"This is where the phone trace led us?" Mason asked, looking up at the castle in
    awe.

"Why the hell is there a castle outside LA?" Lucas mumbled.

Zach leaned back on the car, hands dug deep in his jacket.

"Showdown's always in a big castle isn't it?" He said smirking and proceeded to walk until Alana dragged him back.

"Idiot, it could be a trap." She hissed and he shrugged.

"So let's walk right into it and see what they want. I'm fed up of being chased. At least this gives us a chance to chase them back." He said, a mischievous glint in his eye.

Beck flexed his muscles.

"Time to roll." He said wearily. Once they got closer to the castle they reached a lake.

"Well, now we know where to hide the bodies." Zach said dryly.

Vanessa looked closely at the castle, her forehead wrinkled in confusion.

"Wait, this castle looks too familiar." She mused and Beck rubbed her shoulders ignoring Mason's glare.

"Yeah, it does, maybe we covered it in training?" Beck said searching for a clue in the building.

"Wait- I have a plan." Beck said and they gathered around to listen to him. He looked at each of them as he gave his instructions.

Lucas shrugged after listening.

"Let's go in and get them back."

They wandered into the dark, stone hallway. They walked in with ease, the castle had no guards, it was too easy for them to get in. They stopped halfway down the hallway when they saw Clara and Zazzi tied to a horizontal pole above them, duct tape over their mouths so they couldn't speak. Clara's eyes widened and she went crazy, her screams muffled. Zazzi copied her actions and Vanessa and Alana ran over to get them down whilst Lucas and Mason remained where they were looking around for a threat. Zazzi got down first. As she pulled off the duct tape covering her mouth, barely hiding a smile.

Clara shook her head and they looked around to see ten guns pointed at them. Slowly they put their hands up in surrender. A slow but loud set of footsteps echoed around the room as a man entered. He was in his early thirties, hair greased back and a smarmy expression on his face. He brushed the sleeves of his expensive suit and smiled at them.

"Welcome children. Something tells me you walked right into this one didn't you?" He said, circling them slowly. Zach rolled his eyes and sighed in exasperation.

"Get to the point." He groaned crossing his arms. Vanessa giggled slightly and all the guns turned to her.

"Wha-? She giggled and you're going to shoot her?" Mason asked in disbelief. The man looked visibly impatient.

"I see your friend Beck isn't with you." He said stroking his chin, his dark eyes glinting. Lucas looked around, feigning shock.

"By God he's right!" he said sarcastically and the guns turned again to focus on him whilst Clara groaned through her bindings.

Zazzi suddenly began walking towards the man, her heels clicking on the marble floor.

"Zazzi what the hell are you doing?! You'll get yourself killed!" Vanessa hissed but Zazzi ignored her as she reached the man, her hips swaying as she walked.

"Antonio." She purred, wrapping her arms around his neck.

"Izabelle." He said as he leaned down and kissed her fully on the lips.

The others stared at them in complete shock.

"You- you're a double agent?" Vanessa said, her voice tinged with hurt. Alana shook her head slowly, eyes burning.

"No Vanessa, she's a bitch." She said icily.

With a growl she ran and tackled Zazzi to the ground, pinning her down to the floor with a loud thud. Zazzi tried to claw at Alana's face but Alana was pumped by anger as she punched Zazzi blow after blow in the face until she felt herself being dragged back by her hair. She struggled until the pulling stopped and she looked up to see Lucas slamming his fist into Antonio's face. Alana jumped up as the others prepared to fight but froze when she felt the barrel of a gun pressed sharply into her back. She looked around. They were trapped.

They later they found themselves tied by the wrists on the pole next to Clara. Someone had also decided to remove Clara's mouth binding.

"You are in so much shit. My lawyer will hear about this!" She shouted at a passing guard. She huffed, struggling in her bindings.

After a few moments of silence she spoke again.

"My arms are killing me." She said plainly and Mason chuckled. Antonio flounced in with Zazzi on his arm and an arrogant smirk on his face.

"I bet you're all wondering why you're here." She said, his eyes glinting.

"What I'm wondering is how Zazzi's face is doing." Alana said, winking at Zazzi who had an ice pack pressed to her face. Antonio chuckled and continued to talk.

"Well you see, we wanted to deal with three agents. Three very specific agents. Legacies in fact. Vanessa McCloud. I trust your parents are well. Safely in hiding I assume. Mm. Alana Hilford. Your parents didn't end up too well did they? If I remember correctly, they ended up just like Miss. Blake's mother."

"You son-of-a-bitch. I will KILL you." Alana spat but he just smiled shaking his head.

"The Agency makes the same mistake every time. Trying to train children to repeat the mistakes of their parents." He chuckled. Clara was fuming with anger, breathing heavily. Antonio's expression went from suave to angry in a second.

"A long time ago the Vipers were the most powerful criminal organisation in all circles. We had everything. Connections everywhere. We had a plan to create complete world chaos and domination and from that chaos we would emerge as leaders. World leaders. But all our plans were destroyed by a certain group of agents. So, we killed them. We also brought their children along to kill as well before they tried to take us down again but not before they found out a little information to help us get a little something we need to fulfil our plan. Oh and do remember, we shall also make you suffer and know exactly what their parents tried to stop."

Clara muttered an insult that was all-too audible.

Antonio ignored them with a scowl and continued.

"I've talked too much-"

"Damn straight." Zach snorted, interrupting him.

"May I remind you it's only the girls we need, we can kill and or torture you boys whenever we like. As I was saying, I've talked too much, I'll let the Boss speak to you." he said before backing out of the room.

"Oh boy…" Vanessa sighed looking up at her bindings, trying to scan her mind for any sort of plan.

"The Boss?! What is this, some low-budget mafia movie?!" Clara yelled at the door.

"I will bet you any money he's bald." Alana said and Clara snorted with laughter.

Lucas looked at Zach in disbelief and Vanessa giggled whilst Zach rolled his eyes.

"There's a 99% chance we're definitely going to die and you guys are laughing?!" Zach asked incredulously and Alana and Clara promptly shut up. Sharp footsteps snapped their attention to the door as a man entered, a man the girls never expected to see.

He greeted them with a cold smile and rolled up his sleeves. Clara gasped. The word barely forming in her mouth as she stared at the man in front of her.

"Dad?" she choked out.

"Hello Clara." He said, not at all surprised at all that his daughter was hanging from a pole.

"Is this some sort of sick joke?!" she screeched angrily but Mr Blake just shook his head. Clara, for once, was at a loss for words. He was tall, and handsome. Clara's features were obvious in his face, but twisted with cruelty and deceit. His hair was flecked with grey, and his skin was tanned and healthy. He gave them a brilliant, white toothed smile.

"You're the Viper boss?" Alana asked and Mr Blake laughed in response, looking at his expensive watch, rubbing a speck of imaginary dirt off his sleeve.

"Oh Alana, so witty, just like your parents. Shame about them really..." He paused, his shiny black shoes taking pointed steps around the room.

"But then again, not so much."

Alana scowled at him furiously.

"You're brave when I'm all tied up aren't you." She muttered angrily.

"How could you do this?! You made them kill mum... Alana's parents..." said Clara, her blue eyes wide and sad unlike her father's icy gaze. She found it hard to form any clear thoughts as she started at the face she had always admired, depended on. Loved.

"Lena and Carter had to die, they played too big a part in my downfall, whereas your mother... Elizabeth didn't have to die, if only she hadn't taken the bullet for her sister…" Sadness flashed through his eyes but it quickly disappeared. He clasped his hands together, a chunky gold signet ring catching the light, his long, neatly manicured fingers meeting at the fingertips.

"Now, I believe you've found out where the deal is going on am I right?" he said with a smile. No one said anything. Clara felt her heart breaking as he walked up to her.

"Come on daughter, tell your old man what he needs to know before I kill you." He spat and Clara glared at him.

"You. Are. Not. My. Father." She said holding back her tears. She had never been close to her father but he was the only thing she considered family except for Jenny, the girls and Beck.

"You robbed us of our childhoods; we never had parents to raise us, just Aunt Jenny. You've ruined her life too. I hate you for that. I always will." She said strongly.

Mr Blake just looked at her hardly.
 "Quiet." He said loudly and brought out a tiny silver gun from his waistband wiping it down with a handkerchief delicately.

 "Ooooh he's bringing out the big guns." Alana said sarcastically. Blake smiled and turned the gun to her.

"Alana. Lovely, mouthy Alana. Have you got any information for me?" He asked, his voice sugar coated.

"No." She said equally as sugary as him and he clicked the safety off. Her smirk disappeared she tensed. He looked at the others.

"Any of you want to spare her life and tell me everything you know?" He asked. They decided to call his bluff, not believing him and said nothing. A shot echoed through the hall and Alana screamed out as the bullet tore through her leg. Her body convulsed in pain as she cried out, yelling.

"God don't do this to me again." She screamed scrunching her eyes shut in pain.

Vanessa whimpered as the gun was raised back to Alana

"Now, any information?" He said preparing to squeeze the trigger.

"Shoot her again and I'll kill you myself." Zach shouted furiously. Mr Blake laughed humourlessly.

"Stop!" Vanessa shouted. Mr Blake turned to look at her amused, raising an eyebrow.

"Yes Miss McCloud?" He said smugly.

She bit her lip and looked at Clara mouthing 'sorry'.

"I know where it is, I know everything and I'll tell you everything." She blurted out.

"What?!" Mason hissed and Clara sighed and groaned.

"She's lying, she doesn't know anything!" Lucas said desperately but Mr Blake smiled, satisfied.

"I've always liked you, you were never a disappointment like Clara." He said whilst Clara muttered 'asshole'. Instantly he raised his gun and shot Lucas in the thigh whilst Clara screamed "NO!".

"Apologise to your father Clara." He said calmly, wiping the gun with his embroidered handkerchief. She shook her head violently, tears forming in her eyes as Lucas cursed. Blake shrugged.

"Very well." He raised the gun again.

"Ok ok I'm sorry! There. I said it." Clara screamed angrily, her blue eyes aflame.

He smiled and clasped his hands together.

"Now, I have a very important meeting to attend to and I will be seeing you later."

He said pointing to Vanessa who nodded solemnly. Once he left Clara turned her head to look at Alana.

"Alana, you okay?" Clara asked, her voice trembling slightly. Alana nodded. "Yeah it just brushed my leg, I'm fine. Your dad's a bad shot thankfully." She breathed out shakily as blood dripped onto the floor.

"Lucas?" said Mason.

"It's okay, hurts like a bitch though." He said through his teeth.

"Vanessa what the hell?! You can't lead him to the Deal, imagine what he would do with that sort of power, he's crazy! No offence Clara." Zach said angrily offering Clara a small smile but Vanessa stayed composed.

"I can't let him hurt any of you and he won't stop until he gets exactly what he wants." She said, her voice betraying nothing but her eyes giving Zach a look they understood completely. She had a plan. Zach nodded once in understanding and Mason looked over at Clara.

"Clara, I'm sorry about your dad, you don't deserve this." He said softly and Clara smiled through her tears, ignoring the dull ache inside her. She met his eyes with gratitude.

They hung there for about an hour and noticed how late it was getting when they all began yawning and dozing off. Suddenly they heard a loud grumbling like a dying whale and they looked around in shock. Vanessa met their questioning gazes, blushing wildly.

"Sorry that was my stomach." She said, much to their amusement.

They all fell silent as one of them spoke up.

"Mr Blake requires you all to attend dinner with him tonight, in the correct attire." He
said and with a signal of his hand they all felt themselves crashing to the floor, released from their bindings.

"THAT was my BUTT." Clara complained loudly but they were promptly lifted and taken away at gunpoint by the guards. Lucas and Alana groaned in pain as they limped out of the great hall along with the others.

"I'm not wearing that." Alana stated, glaring at the dress in front of her. Vanessa lifted her light silver couture dress. Alana pushed the box away whilst Clara emerged from behind a screen dressed in a metallic blue dress. She slid on a pair of silver Jimmy Choo sandals and stood up, her face grim.

Vanessa went to put on her own dress and Alana took her

shimmery gold dress to change. Her leg had been bandaged up and they had been given a selection of make-up, perfumes and jewellery.

"Why may I ask, does your father want us to wear designer party dresses?" Vanessa asked delicately once she got dressed and put her hair up. When they had all gotten dressed they went to their awaiting escort of guards. They had a role to play if they were going to survive it. The least they could do was play the role to the best of their ability.

"I'm a prisoner in my own castle." Clara mumbled. They were taken to a grand dining hall where a string quartet played delicate music and silver platters of food were laid on the large oak table. The chandelier spread warm glowing light all over the grandly decorated room. The girls would have appreciated the glamour of it all if it wasn't thwarted by Mr Blake sitting at the head of the table scrolling through his emails on his phone. The girls heard a sound of heavy doors being opened and the boys stepped in. They wore black tuxedos with black bow ties, all scrubbed up and impossibly handsome in their dark, criminal way. They stood behind the girls protectively.

Clara put her hand on Lucas' shoulder gently, leaning up to whisper in his ear.

"How's your leg?" She asked and he gave her a small smile.

"Better, don't worry about me." He said, giving her a soft kiss on the cheek.

"I'm sorry-." She started, looking down miserably.

"This isn't your fault Clara" Lucas said firmly and grabbed her hand as she looked up at him.

"I love you."

Clara put on a brave face ready to confront her father.

Mason brushed a stray hair from Vanessa's face and she leaned into him slightly.

Blake looked up from his phone screen and smiled.

"Please, sit. Ladies may I say you all look exquisite." He gestured to the seats and the place-cards.

The girls were sitting on one side with the boys opposite them, spaced out evenly along the long oak table. They sat down cautiously, no one saying a word. Clara was sat the closest to her father.

"Eat! Eat!" Mr Blake said, smiling graciously to his guests, motioning to the food. No one made a move until Alana groaned in exasperation.

"Don't need to be told twice." She said, tucking into the food on her plate. Clara rolled her eyes and the rest of them began eating. They spent a good half an hour stuffing themselves with food, ignoring Mr Blake's attempt at small talk until Zach spoke up, a conniving glint in his sea-green eyes.

"What game are you playing." He asked coldly, narrowing his eye. The others stopped eating except for Alana who did not realise there was a world outside of her and her plate.

Blake smiled to himself and cleared his throat.

"Mr Rufus, what makes you think I'm playing any game?" He said and Zach scoffed.

"You're a criminal Blake, I think I should know how they work." He said bitterly and Blake nodded to himself impressed. He signalled to a waiter who brought out gleaming plates of cheese cake. Alana and the boys hoovered up their plates instantly whilst Vanessa delicately ate hers, watching Blake warily. Clara hated cheesecake and barely touched hers at all but whenever her father glared at her she pretended to take a bite and pushing it around her plate.

"I'll tell you the outcome of the 'game' and that is... you will all die." He laughed jovially at the serious expressions around the table and waved his hands.

"Of course I am just indulging in a little dinner-time humour. I will of course, spare my dear daughter." He looked at each of them, the silky smile not fading.

"Now for the game. You have all thoroughly enjoyed your cheesecake-" he was interrupted by Alana choking, reaching for her throat. Her hand reached out for water but she knocked the glass over. The others watched as she began choking violently and Zach and Clara got up and rushed over to her.

"Alana? Alana!" Zach shouted but she'd passed out completely in his arms.

"What did you do to her?!" Clara asked panicked when Mason began choking
  too. Mr Blake smiled, his expression snake-like.

"Your cheesecake had been drugged. You will fall into a deep sleep in around 20 seconds, then you will then be ready to tell me where the Dr Dallow will be handed over to the DeRicos. After you do that... you will be dead." He said to no one in particular. The choking had stopped and the six unconscious bodies were slumped over the table, unmoving. Blake took a sip of his wine, placing the glass down onto the table with a clink of finality.

19

Zach was the first to wake up. He looked around disorientated and felt his arms aching. He looked up; they were all tied to the bar again. Clara was already awake as she had been for the past thirty odd hours, hanging on to every word being said around them.

"Clara?" Zach mumbled sleepily. She looked fatigued, barely staying awake.

"Oh good you're awake, the others should be awake soon." She said weakly. In the next half an hour they all gradually work up. Mason blinked confused and looked around.

"Why am I here? What day is it?" he slurred, his eyes puffy with sleep.

"It's deal day." Vanessa said grimly as Clara nodded to herself.

"Alana wake up!" Clara hissed at her, looking around. Alana made no movement, her head slumped. They were back in their own clothes after their black tie dinner. The main doors opened and Blake walked in. He was dresses as formal as ever in a dark grey suit and a crimson red pocket square.

"Good morning!" he said brightly in his crisp British accent.

Alana mumbled still half asleep.

"I said good morning!" He bellowed and Alana jerked awake blinking rapidly.

"Morning." She said forcing her eyes open.

He smiled coldly and turned to face Vanessa.

"I believe you have some information for me." He said making a hand signal so that Vanessa fell to the floor with a thud. She was instantly swarmed by two guards but she refused to move.

"No. I need to tell you in private, we talk outside, alone." She said and he nodded, amused.

"Very well." He said and left her outside. She took one last look back at her friends before turning away to follow Blake.

Vanessa and Mr Blake walked out to the castle grounds which were blooming with colourful flowers and delicate fragrances.

"Clara never got to experience her own castle. She has no idea of what I had planned for her. Until that damn Agency got a hold of her. All you girls, I could've trained you to be my greatest asset." He mused as they walked on the cobbled path. A soft breeze blew around them.

"We would have never worked for you." Vanessa said quietly. He laughed heartily at her.

"So moral, just like your parents. How are they by the way? I hear Brazil is nice this time of year." He said lightly, his lips twitching into a cruel smile. Vanessa felt the blood in her veins turn to ice and her heart began pumping wildly.

"You know where my parents are?" she was horrified but did not dare to look at him. She felt as if he could see straight through her.

"Oh yes, I know exactly where they are and all it takes to kill them is one very quick phone call and you can join Alana in being an orphan." He said. Vanessa's mouth was set into a straight line.

"I told you I would tell you everything I know, leave them out of it." She said in a small voice.

"Yes and I will make sure you tell me everything when I bring you along. If I find out you're lying not only will I kill your friends and your parents but I will also make you watch every second of their deaths. So, what was it you were going to tell me?" He said menacingly and Vanessa paused.

After she told him all he needed to know he tapped his chin thoughtfully.

"What an ingenious idea. Who would imagine?" He said sarcastically and looked at Vanessa who was fixated on something in the distance.

"Better get ready then." He said and clapped his hands as they turned to walk inside. Vanessa allowed herself one small smile as she took one last look at something in the distance before following him in.

"They'll be there. The man you're looking for is George Blake. The girls will come through, I'll make sure of it."

Beck hung up the phone as he saw Vanessa retreating back into the castle with a final glance at him.

"We are leaving, please try not to do anything stupid while we're gone." Blake said to the remaining agents strung up in front of him, giving them a condescending smile, as if they were toddlers he was leaving in a room for a few minutes.

"Hurry back." Zach said sarcastically with a smirk. Blake glared at him venomously.

"If they try to escape, kill them." He called out to the guards before heading out, dragging Vanessa with him.

As soon as he left, the guards slumped their shoulders, lighting their cigarettes and turning their attention to their phones. They lazed around barely even glancing at the group. An hour passed and they began to get bored.

"Let's head to get some lunch; I'm starving." One of the guards said and the others nodded mindlessly in agreement and headed for the door. One turned towards Clara, Alana and the boys leering at them.

"Don't move." He said wagging a thick finger at them. Once they left Alana sighed.

"So what do we do?" Clara asked and Alana looked up.

"Well if I can reach the bar with my legs I could undo my binding." She said dreamily. Clara stared at her expectantly.

"So do it!" she prompted and Alana groaned.

"Too much ab exercise…" she grunted and Clara kicked her shoe at Alana.

"Ow! Okay fine FINE." Alana growled and took a deep breath. Slowly she began lifting her legs and felt the burn in her lower abdomen. She puffed out air, still drawing her legs up, scrunching her eyes shut and resisting the urge to give up. With one final push she hooked her feet onto the bar above her. She breathed out a sigh of relief as she adjusted her legs to pull the rest of her body up. Once she was balanced on the bar she fumbled with her wrist ties and managed to take them off. Her wrists were red raw and bruised. She rolled her shoulders feeling the delicious release in tension.

She sat back on the bar with her legs hooked on so she was hanging upside down. Once she got a good hand hold she moved herself towards Lucas and pulled herself up to undo his ties. He landed on the floor steadily and looked around to see if anyone had heard whilst Alana finished up untying the others. Finally she jumped down with a flourish and they ran for the door.

They heard voices coming from near the main door and upstairs leaving them no choice but to run quietly downstairs. They ran down flights of cold, dark, stone stairs until they reached the dungeons, or what looked like an armoury.

There was a series of dark tunnels illuminated by one torch flame near the doorway. Slowly they walked down towards the dark hallway looking for a way out or a hiding place. Preferably a way out. Behind them they heard someone's throat clear and they quickly turned to find Zazzi.

She was holding a gun in her hands, dressed up in all black with red lipstick smeared on her lips. Her long, dark hair loose over her shoulders.

"Now where are you off to?" she drawled.

"Zazzi please…" Lucas said slowly inching towards her. Zach smiled cockily. Zazzi raised an eyebrow and smirked at Zach who strolled over to her. He put his arm around her casually and smiled.

"Now now, there's no need to be such a malicious bitch about it. Just let us go." Zach said lightly and Clara gasped out a laugh.

Zazzi drew back from him.

"Asshole." She spat and he shrugged.

"Tell me something I don't know." He replied and she glared at him, even angrier than before. He sighed dramatically.

"Ok so that wasn't the right approach." He looked around thinking and he reached Zazzi kissing her on the lips distracting her completely. Clara acted quickly kicking the gun out of her hand whilst Zazzi pulled away in shock from Zach who had red lipstick smeared all over his face.

Lucas came behind her closing his hand over her mouth and pulling her behind a wall followed by the other as they heard footsteps. They stayed there silent and they heard what sounded like two people making out. Zach put his arm around Alana and she slapped it off.

Zazzi instantly stopped moving and her eyes widened. Lucas released her when she stopped fighting against him. They all peeked behind the wall to see who was having a make-out session. Clara suppressed a gasp and Alana went into shaking fits off laughter, Mason tried to calm her down but ended up laughing too. Zazzi's dark almond-shaped eyes widened at the scene in front of her. Her boyfriend, Antonio pressed up against a petite blonde girl kissed each other audibly. Her perfect blonde hair was mussed and her manicured nails in Antonio's hair. Her pencil skirt had ridden up. Zazzi drew away from the sight and the others silently watched and she buried her head into her hands and slipped off a diamond ring off her finger. An engagement ring, given to her two months ago by Antonio. Once she regained composure she looked into Clara's eyes, dejected, and shrugged, giving her a nod as a go-ahead.

The security guards clattered down the stairs and Antonio flew away from the blonde speedily as they hurriedly tried to compose themselves.

"Where did they go?!" One of them shouted at a bewildered Antonio. Zazzi then ran out from behind the screen out of breath. The others held their breath ready to be outed.

"Izabella..." Antonio started.

"They're not here, they must've gone upstairs." She said breathlessly. The others looked at each other in shock and let out multiple sighs of relief when they heard the guards leave along with Antonio and the blonde. They all stepped out slowly and looked at Zazzi. None of them said anything for a while.

"The only way out now is through below the dungeons, you'll have to go through the tunnel that leads to the lake. I'm sorry, and good luck." She finished curtly holding her hands out in front of her. Alana nodded her gratitude grudgingly.

"You're the good guys; I only hope you can forgive me someday." She said solemnly. Clara looked at her and nodded as they all ran to where Zazzi pointed out. It was a narrow tunnel, darker than the one they had just been in. Their footsteps echoed menacingly in the tight space. Zach stepped in and drew back when he stepped into water.

"Look's like we're going to have to swim." He said.

"So swim." Alana said and pushed Zach in forcefully. Clara burst out laughing whilst Lucas and Mason snickered.

"What was that for?" He exclaimed. She ignored him and dived into the water. When she popped up for air she replied "Zazzi." before diving under again swimming in the dark.

Clara walked past Zach raising her eyebrows and smiling slightly before going in along with Lucas and Mason. They walked in the water, the water slowly going from waist height to neck. Then they began treading water, the water below them was several metres deep. The ceiling of the tunnel was getting lower and lower until they had to stop.

"What now?!" Lucas gasped as the water lapped at his chin.

"Alana, you go check out what's there, try find a way out." Clara shouted over to Alana. Alana shouted back in reply and took a deep breath preparing to go in. She breathed in deeply and pushed herself deep into the depths kicking her legs as she propelled herself down. She opened her eyes in the murky, near-freezing water but could only see the darkness. She reached in her back pocket for a lighter and switched on the LED light as a few bubbles escaped her mouth. The beam landed on what looked like a grating in the ground. She swam over to it as bubbles escaped and she felt herself getting lightheaded. She went to the grating and tried to pull it up.

The last of her air went to she tried pulling it harder but it barely budged. She looked around for something to help her but found nothing so she tried again, this time getting a good grip on the bars and pushing with her feet. Finally it lifted up and she pushed up to get back to the surface but halted when she felt her leg caught on a stray wire. Her lungs burnt and she felt herself blacking out. She tugged at her leg once more panicking and felt the wire cut into her skin before releasing her, she tried to kick up, and ignoring the pain of her bleeding leg as she desperately swam to the surface six metres above her. When she reached the top she gulped in the sweet refreshing air feeling her lungs relax as Zach checked if she was alright.

"I'm fine I'm fine." She told him and he kissed her fully on the lips, taking her breath away again. Her heart hammered against her chest.

"There's a grating open just below us, we need to go through, it may lead us to the lake." She said. Alana and Clara went first; they squeezed through the hole and saw the light through the mass of water above them, shining through the weeds and plants. They swam up to the surface to see the sun shining on them, their teeth chattering from the icy depths. They breathed in the fresh air and stepped out of the lake to the awaiting Jeep.

"Hello girls."

"Hello Beck." Clara and Alana replied simultaneously.

"Get in the car." He said with a knowing smile the girls reciprocated. The boys joined them as they all climbed into the car as Beck sped off.

"Did you call them?" Clara asked Beck. He flashed a smile at her.

"Well of course."

Beck made two stops. One for dry clothing and food for the famished teens and one stop because Clara saw a pair of shoes she liked and demanded Beck stop so she could buy them.

When the car stopped for the third time they prepared themselves for what they were about to face.

"It's deal time team. Let's go save the good Doctor." Clara said.

They spotted Vanessa before she spotted them and they ran for cover. It was a perfect place to hold the deal. A warehouse, just behind a carnival with screaming children, loud music and bright lights. The team watched as Mr Blake dragged her through the crowds and said something to her the girls couldn't make out.

"Let's split up." Beck said grabbing Alana's hand as they disappeared into the mess of the carnival. Mason and Lucas went their own way and Zach held his arm out to Clara. To any outsider they looked like a group of teenagers out for the carnival. The smell of hotdogs wafted past Alana and Beck and they looked at each other and grinned.

"We mustn't…" Beck said already knowing he lost the battle.

"We must." Alana grinned and they bought two hotdogs. They walked hand in hand at a leisurely pace, laughing and talking, watching the festivities and following Vanessa closely behind. Suddenly two painted white faces loomed over them and shocked Beck and Alana. Two stilt walkers. They removed their masks and Alana and Beck burst out laughing. It was Clara and Zach, unaccustomed to walking on stilts.

"Being a vigilante agent has its perks." Clara called out while Zach laughed. They continued walking, practically over Vanessa who remained oblivious that she was surrounded by her best friends. Zach wobbled over to Clara who was now on the floor and in a laughing fit.

"I don't see why you're laughing, I'm awesome at this." He said carefully watching his step.

"Perhaps, but you look ridiculous." She walked over to one of his wooden legs and started shaking it making Zach wobble even more.

"No. Clara, stop. Please." he said trying to find his balance again, "CLARA! Don't make me come down there!" Zach shouted.

"Alright, alright pretty boy, I'll stop." Clara said recovering from her laughing fit.

Beck lead Alana down a nearby alley way.

"The boys and Clara are going for a ground attack, you and I will be going for a different approach. Got that A?"

Before they left Zach pulled Alana aside, now in his normal clothes. Beck went off giving them some privacy.

"What are you doing? I said I'll see you later." She whispered. He pressed her up against the wall and kissed her, softly, lingering.

"Just in case there is no later." He winked and disappeared. Alana followed Beck dazedly up a fire escape which led to the terrace of a low building, one which was not too difficult to jump off. The building was just opposite the warehouse and looked like some old abandoned offices leaving a clearing between the two buildings where the deal was going to take place. Beck handed Alana three throwing knives which she tucked into her boot and a smoke bomb. He loaded his gun and handed Alana one.

They were ready.

Clara and Zach hid out around the dark corners of the building as they waited for Vanessa and Mr Blake along with four other men and a tall, snake-like woman. Clara walked around trying to find a good place to stay hidden when she felt two strong hand pull her by the waist.

"Did I tell you you're the hottest spy I know?" Lucas murmured below her ear. She felt his hot breath on her neck and turned around to face Lucas. She smiled up at him, the adrenaline of the mission coursing through the both of them.

She smiled demurely and lifted his head to kiss him sweetly.
  "If only we weren't in the middle of a kickass plan."

He smirked but responded to her touch regardless.

"Just try not to get killed please." She whispered seriously this time. Lucas kissed her one more time passionately and grinned.

"Bring it on."

The sun had set but the carnival was still ablaze with neon lights and sounds of laughter, screaming and music. A Mercedes SUV drew up nearby and 5 men came out and walked towards the centre of the clearing. DeRico's. They all stood there, hyper-alert of every sound. Both Zach's and Lucas and Mason's fathers were there, looking like older versions of their sons. Zach tensed and Lucas glared at them. Clara looked around; Mason was nowhere to be seen. A van parked dangerously close to the SUV and six members of the Triad stepped out. They all stood in front of the DeRico's, the same icy look on all their faces. They nodded to each other in greeting,

"DeRico." A bearded man said, voice silky. He
 "Mr Yang" Lucas and Mason's father replied, adjusting a gold ring on his thumb.

"I believe you have something for us." DeRico said and Zach rolled his eyes. Mr Yang smiled a toothy grin and nodded.

"I must make sure it's going into safe hands, our faction in California is small and this is the only thing we have against the Vipers." He said, drawing out his words.

"I know the risk. I tell you it will be safe." DeRico said impatiently. He had the same colouring as his sons, brown hair and Lucas' serious jawline but instead of his sons' dark blue eyes he had coal black ones.

"Very well." Yang said and he reached into his inside pocket for a set of keys.

"He is in the van. Our men have received the payment from our partners in North Korea." He said as he held out the keys but before he dropped them into his hand a bullet slammed into his chest and he crumpled to the floor.
 Everyone instantly drew their guns when Mr Blake stepped out from the darkness with his men shortly behind him and Vanessa being dragged along. She looked around her anxiously. Blake walked over to Yang's body and picked up the keys.

"God, what is it with lousy dads." Zach scoffed. Lucas and Clara who nodded slowly.

"I'll be taking these." Mr Blake said lightly as his entourage surrounded the DeRicos, heavily armed.

"Don't touch that van Blake or you'll be sorry." DeRico spat, fuming.

Blake raised an eyebrow.

"Oh I'll be sorry? Any more words from you DeRico and I will kill your sons and the Rufus boy sooner than I planned." He replied with nonchalance. He strolled over to the large truck and headed towards the back of it.

"You have my sons?" DeRico shouted, furious at Blake who ignored him, pulled off the open padlock and opened the doors to see Mason.

"Surprise." He growled and sent a kick straight to Blake's shocked face. At that moment Alana threw a smoke\ bomb from the roof causing everything down below to become smoky and nearly impossible to see holding off any shootings. There were shouts of commotion and Beck and Alana jumped down on top of two criminals flooring them and rendering them unconscious. Clara, Zach and Lucas quickly moved through the smoke and Mason took Vanessa away gently by the arm leading her to the others.

"You ready?" Lucas asked the others, they all nodded and began to move through the smoke.

5 Vipers including Blake, 5 Triad members remaining and 5 DeRicos.

"You can save you and your men a lot of pain Blake, just give us the keys or we'll be forced to attack." Beck said loudly and coolly through the smoke and Blake appeared before them. He wiped the blood from his nose, a crazed look in his eyes as he shouted at them.

"Never."

"Zachary, what the hell are you doing?! You're working with them?" Zach's father hissed at him. DeRico looked at his sons, fuming.

"Kill them all." He told his men.

Everyone immediately jumped into action. The smoke had begun to clear. A DeRico member ran towards Beck and he grabbed his head, smashing it into his knee. He took a punch to the face and roundhouse kicked his attacker in the chest.

Vanessa snuck behind Mason's father whilst he was fighting with Alana and slammed the side of her hand into a pressure point below his ear, hard enough to knock him out. The boy's father slumped to the floor and she grinned at Alana happy to see her friend once more. Vanessa ran over to the van where a terrified Brian Dallow was huddled in the corner, tied up and gagged. Vanessa quickly unbound him, talking to him gently.

"Dr Dallow my name is Vanessa, you're safe now. As soon as I let you go I need you to run to the closest safe space you can and call the police." She said as she removed the last of his bindings. He was such a small man she found it difficult to imagine his brain held such explosive information.

Alana found herself facing Zach's father. Not the ideal way to meet your boyfriend's parent she thought. They circled one another until Alana dropped to the ground hooking her leg around his knocking him flat on his back. She ran over to knock him out but he kicked her hard so she flew into an empty wooden crate. All the breath was knocked out of her as Mr Rufus dragged her up by her throat, lifting her small frame three inches off the floor. She desperately clawed at his hands feeling spots dance before he eyes. She reached for her boot where her knives were, grabbed one and dug it in his shoulder. He released her, bellowing in pain. She took a deep breath and jumped up to punch him under the chin causing him to lose consciousness.

"Game over." She muttered.

A Triad member ran over to Vanessa, picked her up and threw her on the ground, he was about to step on her however she rolled to the right and slid on the ground and kicked his leg, making him topple.
    Clara looked around. The boys looked beaten up and bloody, Alana and Vanessa were holding their own. Suddenly she felt an arm go around her neck to strangle her. She looked up to meet her father's blue eyes.

"You ruined everything! I should have killed you when you were born." He spat and squeezed tighter. Clara tried to pry his arm off and started gagging feeling as if she was slipping from consciousness.

"Pl-please…" She croaked out. Alana ran over to help Clara and kicked Blake in
    the back. He released Clara but kept trying to advance on her.

"Please, I don't want to hurt you." Clara said as her chest got tight and she felt her eyes swimming with tears. She was reluctant to hurt the man she knew as her father. He lunged at her knocking her to the ground. She pushed him off and punched him in the face.

"You're holding back daughter. If you're going to screw things up at least do it right."
    He said as he got his gun out and hit her with the butt of his gun so she rolled off him. They both jumped up. Clara bit her

lip and kicked his hand to get the gun out of the way but he held on tightly.

"Too slow Clara." He said, Alana looked over, they all did, and Blake took his shot at Alana.

"NO!" Clara screamed out.

Alana squeezed her eyes shut but felt nothing. No searing pain, no black out. Nothing. Clara stood there, mouth open in shock, forgetting how to breathe, her blue eyes shining with tears.

"Son of a bitch." Clara shouted at him her emotions out of control. She threw a punch which connected with his nose causing it to bleed.

"That's much better." He said humouring his daughter. "Show me more."

Alana opened her eyes to face a pair of cat-like green eyes. Zach. He suddenly slumped against her and squeezed his eyes shut in pain. Alana's eyes were wide with shock and her lip quivered when Zach fell to the floor, blood soaking the back of his white t-shirt. She was shocked back into reality.

"No, no, no, Zach, no, no." She stuttered shaking him gently. Tears started spilling from her eyes. Zach opened his eyes and winced.

"Couldn't.. Let you take.. All the bullets now.. Could I?" He gasped out. She smiled through her tears holding his head in her lap. She stroked his hair and whispered to him soothingly. Her hands were shaking as she stroked his brow.
    Blake looked furious.

"I missed, let's see if I'm lucky the second time round." He raised the gun again and this time Clara pounced knocking his arm backwards. The gunshot had triggered ferocity in her. She felt like she could snap a man's neck with a finger. She kicked her father squarely in the chest with all her energy causing him to stagger back. She ran forward kicking him once more so he fell flat on his back. She cracked her knuckles and advanced.

Lucas and Mason ran after two men trying to escape the fight. The two men ran through the carnival but didn't get very far as Mason and Lucas soon outran them. Mason grabbed the shorter man and kicked him in the stomach causing him to double over in pain on the floor. The taller, bigger man swung for Lucas' face but missed, Lucas elbowed him in the face and pushed him, he stumbled back into a candy floss stall. Lucas grabbed his head and smacked it against the counter.

Mason and Lucas ran back to Zach and managed to get him to sit up. Alana was holding his hand tightly, both their hands blood stained. She was holding back the tears.

"It's okay it's just my shoulder." Zach said weakly laughing, then wincing at the pain. She nodded, and kissed his cheek softly. He seemed to breathe in relief when he felt Alana's soft lips on his cheek. The others were still fighting, Vanessa had a deep cut in her arm but managed to battle through, ignoring the biting pain in her arm. Her hair was a mess and the thought that nagged the back of her mind was that one of her nails had broken. She'd fix that later. She jammed her almost perfect nails into one guy's eyes and pushed him into the brick wall. She dodged a punch and saw Clara and her father. Her eyes met Alana's.

George Blake was on the floor but Clara kept punching. She hit Blake, again and again. She could feel the hands shaking her shoulders, she could hear the voices calling her name but they were drowned out by the roaring of rage. The fury masking the pain of her blistered fists. She looked down at his bruised and bleeding face and felt only bitterness, still punching. Tears of hatred and hurt were running down her face.

"Clara!" She heard Vanessa's voice and Alana shaking her shoulders roughly.

"He's not worth it C, get up." Alana said quietly and calmly and Clara stopped hitting him as the words set in. Tentatively she got up, astonished at how she lost control. She never lost control. Immediately Vanessa and Alana enveloped her into a hug as she broke into sobs. Vanessa stroked her hair. Clara broke away and turned to Blake who struggled to lift himself up. She brought out her gun from her waistband.

"I could kill you Blake." She said. She held him at gunpoint for a long time while everyone else stood still in a deafening silence. Lucas began stepping closer to her, calling out her name but she blocked him out.

She paused before throwing the gun on the floor.

"But I'm so much better than you." She said coldly with a smirk as the place began filling up with CIA agents.

"CIA, everybody put down your weapons." A man in a grey suit shouted and the girls sighed in relief. Beck brought out his credentials and went up to the man in the grey suit.

"Thank you for coming. You're just in time." Beck said breathlessly. The CIA men walked up to the girls whilst the paramedics dealt with Zach and Lucas who had a large gash on his forehead.

"Thank you girls, we'll take it from here." He said in a deep voice.

"I trust you'll have everything under control. Meaning we won't have to be fugitives anymore." Alana said almost sarcastically. He nodded.

"Of course Miss Hilford. Everything will be resolved I promise." He smiled in an attempt at friendliness, but no one was warm and fuzzy from the CIA. He left them to check on some other matters. Lucas hugged Clara again and she calmed as she breathed in his scent. Beck was deep in discussion with another CIA operative. He looked over to the girls with pride as he spoke.

"Can you bring them in for a debrief on Monday?" The operative said and Beck nodded.

"Thanks for this, tell Manuel I said hi." Beck said giving him a nod and walked over to the girls bringing them all in for a group hug.

"We love you Beck." They chimed clinging to him. He kissed them all on the forehead.

"Love you too girls. You totally rocked this mission. I don't know if anyone else could've handled it the way you guys did. I'm so proud." He said and they hugged him once more.

When they broke apart they headed over to Zach who was dramatising his shooting to the young paramedic woman who was tutting in sympathy.

"Dude you're such a diva." Mason said with a snort.
   "Does the night in shining armour get a kiss?" Zach said weakly, gazing up at Alana.
   Lucas leaned in and Zach slapped him away.

"Not you!" Zach said frowning The criminals were all being cuffed and arrested. Clara's dad was dragged past them giving Clara and the girls an angry look.

Alana said slapped Clara on the back comfortingly. Clara smiled but was distracted by a thought.

"Hey what happened to the Triad member who got shot, I didn't see them get him in." she said softly and Alana shrugged.

"They probably did him first. Who cares anyway, we stopped what could've been World War Three." Alana grinned. Clara and Alana turned to look at the boys sadly. They had one more job to do.

"You look like you just witnessed a duckling being slaughtered." Mason noted to Alana as she stood there looking glum.

"Vanessa we have to go..." Alana said hesitantly Vanessa got up slowly. They boys looked at each other confused but before they could say anything the CIA operative walked over to the boys.

"Gentlemen; Agent Spinner told me about your work on the case and we were wondering if you had ever considered joining us." He looked at the boys who stared at him, speechless.

The agent handed them all a card.

"Think about it" He gave them a tight smile and turned heel.

"I'm Agent Laurence, let me see the girls now." Said a beautiful, tall, auburn-haired woman in an authoritative tone.

"Aunt Jenny!" Vanessa squealed as they ran over.

"Girls I'm so sorry, I came as soon as I found out it was a set up." She said hugging the girls tightly. They stayed with Aunt Jenny for a while, giving her the basic outline of what happened before they finally went to the boys who had watched the scene clear out.

"Thank you for your help." Clara said, smiling genuinely.

"And thank you for saving me…" Alana said to Zach and he smiled coldly in return, her heart panged with sadness.

"Zach…" she started.

"So that's it isn't it. Polite thank you, and goodbye and you're gone?" He interrupted bitterly. The girls looked at each other.

"We'll really miss you." Vanessa said in a small voice and Zach softened.

"Come here little one." He smiled and opened his arms for a hug. Vanessa hugged him warmly careful not to hurt his wound.

Alana hugged the others while Clara stood silently looking at the ground. Lucas walked over to Clara and lifted her chin up gently. She shook her head avoiding his glare.

"Clara look at me." Lucas said his blue eyes carrying so many emotions. She looked into his eyes and lay her head on his chest for a while before walking away.

"So this is it? You're just going to walk off, without saying goodbye." Lucas spoke out as she slowly walked away. Clara stopped but didn't turn back, with her back to him tears rolled down her soft cheeks.

She carried on walking again and Lucas sighed and began to walk back to Zach and Mason head down. Clara suddenly stopped again took a big breath and turned around. She ran towards Lucas, he turned around and she jumped into his arms and their lips met as they kissed for the last time. Her hands wrapped around his neck as he held her close. He finally let go unwillingly and looked into her eyes.

"Goodbye Clara Blake." She nodded and ran her hand through his hair one last time.

"Goodbye Lucas DeRico." She said still staring into his eyes.

Vanessa kissed Mason and he pulled her close to him.

"I love you." He murmured against her hair and she smiled.

"Me too." She forced herself to smile- she would save the tears for later. He pulled her towards him and hugged her one last time reluctant to let go.

Alana looked at Zach, a million unsaid words in her expression. He was propped up in his stretcher, even that was too painful.

"Come here." He grinned pulling her in and hugging her tightly. She gazed into his green eyes.

"What you did today; I owe you my life for it." She said softly and he played with her hair.

"Don't go." He said seriously, a hint of sadness in his eyes.

Alana smiled slightly, leaning down for one last kiss.

"Goodbye Zach." She said quietly.

The girls walked off and waved at the boys leaning on the CIA van. Zach smiled back, Lucas nodded and Mason waved back saddened by the bittersweet goodbyes. They watched as the girls who had shaken up their lives walked away, without a glance behind them. Professionals, they thought.

Clara walked over to her two best-friends once more, exhaustion rolling through her body.

"We did it…" She said with a small smile.

"As we always do." Alana replied. A moment of silence followed.

"So what now?" Vanessa asked as they linked arms and walked towards Beck's car.

"Why, we get back to work of course." Clara replied mischievously.

Once the girls had gone, Lucas leaned back against the wall sighing. He felt something in the pocket of his jeans crinkle and he pulled out a piece of paper. Zach and Mason checked their pockets too, they all had one. They opened it up and read the note.

'Sorry for crashing the party,

-V,A,C'

Three Months Later

The school bell rang and the girls were the first out of the door. They turned to walk home together, arm in arm.

"Man, physics class was a pain." Alana groaned and Clara nudged her giving her a pointed look.

"Okay, I was a pain in physics." Alana corrected herself and the girls laughed.

"Jenny's out tonight, what shall it be; Pizza or Chinese?" Vanessa asked knowing the answer.

"Both!" Alana and Clara replied at the same time. The girls' phones then rang simultaneously, a series of songs, beeps and vibrations. They answered.

"Hey Beck." "Becky!" "Hello Beck."

Beck smiled on the other line.

"Hello girls, I need you to come into the office, we've got a new one for you. You'll want to bring your umbrellas for this."

Acknowledgements

       This story started out on Wattpad in 2012 and has introduced me to the fans that have made Party Crashers possible today. I am forever indebted to the Wattpad fanbase that encouraged me to go on writing not only Party Crashers, but two sequels.

   A huge thank you to everyone who spread the word about Party Crashers coming out- It has been so amazing knowing that Party Crashers was still remembered and loved 7 years later!

   Big thanks also to my wonderful friends without whom I would have never finished writing this book.

   Finally, thank you to my brilliant mother who was the one who encouraged me to publish Party Crashers.

Printed in Great Britain
by Amazon